FIRETIDE COAST

CLAIRE McKENNA is a speculative fiction writer from Melbourne, Australia. She is a longtime writer of short fiction with a background in environmental sciences. Book one in the Deepwater Trilogy, *Monstrous Heart*, was Claire's debut novel.

ALSO BY CLAIRE MCKENNA

The Deepwater Trilogy
Monstrous Heart
Deepwater King

FIRETIDE
COAST

BOOK THREE OF THE DEEPWATER TRILOGY

CLAIRE McKENNA

HARPER
Voyager

Harper*Voyager*
An imprint of
HarperCollins*Publishers* Ltd
1 London Bridge Street
London SE1 9GF

www.harpercollins.co.uk

HarperCollins*Publishers*
Macken House
39/40 Mayor Street Upper
Dublin 1
D01 C9W8
Ireland

First published by HarperCollins*Publishers* 2022
This paperback edition 2023
1

A catalogue record for this book is available from the British Library

ISBN: 978-0-00-833726-1

Set in Sabon LT Std by Palimpsest Book Production Ltd,
Falkirk, Stirlingshire

Printed and bound in the UK using 100% renewable electricity by CPI Group (UK) Ltd

For Dad

Book One: The Shore

1

Blood on the ebbing tide

Blood on the ebbing tide, like an old regret remembered during a long night. The embers breathed in the fireplace of the Coastmaster's Lodge as a squall pulled a shingle from the lodge roof, set it back down with a desultory clatter.

Harry Tanbark, seventy winters of memory casked in rawhide and hoarfrost, sat at a table of shipwreck timber he had built with his own hands. He stirred chicory root powder into his blue enamel cup and sensed the trouble massing against the walls. After forty years as Coastmaster he knew the Firetide Coast better than the hidden corners of his own head, and something in the fallen evening set the air off-kilter. A whiff of malfeasance on the breeze, the way a rotting carcass on shore will invoke bad magic and ill omens.

The living scent crawled beneath the eaves, settled into the corners of the lodge.

At Tanbark's feet a russet hound whimpered, causing its owner to bend and pat the rough coat with his rope-callused hands. A wet nose pushed into his palm, rooted and snuffled.

'Will be enough of that, Musket. We will stay in tonight as the storm passes us by.'

Had his wife been here he would have discussed the

strangeness of the night with her. A Coastmaster's job was by necessity articulated in facts and figures. Managing the southern navigation stations and sea-roads meant keeping up to date the shipping ledgers for the great administrative city of Clay Capital a thousand miles north, an endless ritual of tide times and barometric readings. But life on the coast was more than just a list of numbers. There was a spirituality here too, a superstition interwoven with stories of giant beasts that lived under the water, and of the mysterious, storm-brewed cathedrals of the air. He had often found comfort in his wife's shorefolk pragmatism. Six years gone was Maud, however, having walked into the red tide waters on such a night. A dangerous season. Longings peaked like mountains in the weeks after midwinter, and a heart became full of doubts and sadness. So much for marrying a local girl twenty-five years his junior in the expectation she might provide comfort in his old age.

Maybe in Clay Capital the isolation would not have tormented her so badly. The city provided multitudinous diversions to keep a person occupied within those hot, bustling streets. Not so much in South Lyonne, where the time between seeing another human face could be weeks or months, and where the spirits of the sea whispered their love songs. Maud had had too much time to dwell on her loneliness. And Tanbark had never been diversion enough for her, being a man suited to solitude, and not much of a conversationalist.

Not long after their marriage she'd begun to change. Day after day he'd watched Maud burn inside out from a disease of dark yearnings, then, in the superstitious manner of the shore-people, she had gone into the ocean rather than waste away on land. The Constable called to verify her death had murmured his sympathies but remained circumspect about the manner of her leaving. One of those seasonal afflictions of the local folks, he said. A cluster of them that season. Cannot be helped. *The Firetide gets into their heads, sometimes.*

Musket whimpered again, turned a circle. His claws clicked agitatedly on the flagstone floor. Sensing Harry Tanbark's grief in those long weeks following Maud's loss, the deacon of a nearby village had gifted him the runt of an unexpected litter. Musket was a true shore-mutt, from a long line of harbour-keeper's companions, animals bred to find half-drowned sailors and bloated corpses alike.

Tonight, those old rescuing instincts made the animal fret.

'We mustn't go out. Listen to that wind, dog.'

Not yet discouraged, Musket trotted to the door, scratched the old wood. Tanbark stood up with a grunt of exertion and decided to let Musket out, certain that he would only venture far enough to do his business before returning to the warmth of the hearth. As far as harbour dogs went, Musket had inherited a lazy streak that caused him to seek comfort over duty.

Instead the dog was out the door in a flash of red fur, baying as he ran. Fat drops of rain fell on Tanbark's face as he leaned out to yell after the mutt, the first salvos of an impending deluge. The sun had already dipped below the eastern mountains. It would be full dark within the hour.

'Dog, I won't have you back in if you're wet!'

Musket paid no attention, for he was in the twilight, barking and barking.

Hissing through a missing tooth, Tanbark took up his portable lantern and ignited the wick. Again the dark yearning feeling, old as stone in him. This was the Firetide shore in the low violet stormlight, when the woven fabric between known and unknown kinked and frayed. The ocean monsters most often came to the shore in such weather, in that hour when the daylight still held but night was fast approaching. Things attracted not by food but the wielding of powers and sympathetic magic.

Magic was always strongest in the transitions, and what was stronger than day into night, sea into shore, calm into tempest?

Tanbark took his long-arm down from the wall, a walnut-stocked rifle of questionable antiquity, shut the warped ash-wood door behind him and followed his dog out into the bluster of the dunes. The breaking waves had taken on a low crimson glow. The Firetide Coast – the region that held the name – supported the smallest of the southern cryptids, a species of plankton with a scarlet bioluminescence. In midwinter they shone so vividly that the sea appeared to smoulder like hot coals. Firetide season, the locals called it. For the rest of the year the plankton glowed an agreeable and common shade of blue.

A brisk wind laid the sedge-grass flat. A smell of smoke reached Tanbark, and not just ordinary woodsmoke. Given his Coastmaster experience in things marine and exotic, he recognized it at once: the unmistakable smell of salt and kraken oil.

'Musket,' he shouted, worried now. 'Musket.'

Tanbark crested the nearest dune and saw what sunset had disguised from him. A huge paddlewheel ship run aground upon the beach with such ferocity it had left gouges in the sand and a valley exposed by the retreating tide.

'My God . . .'

A deepwater hunting craft, easily fifty-foot long.

The flames engulfing the vessel licked upwards, and the heavy, oily smoke roiled low across the tideline. His dog bayed again. Tanbark squinted. The years had made his once-sharp sight milky and hazed. He realized Musket had spotted people milling down where the shoreline ended and the sea began. Perhaps a half-dozen figures encircling a seventh, who wore . . .

. . . a woman's dress . . .

. . . and who cradled a broken oar like a staff in her arms, swinging wildly at the figures as they scurried around her. They encroached on her unprotected sides, only to retreat as she lashed out with the oar.

The spell of surprise broke and Tanbark shouted, a harsh caterwauling yelp, before tipping his long-arm into the air. He pulled the trigger. The rifle kicked into his shoulder and let out an almighty crack, followed by a bloom of blue smoke.

Startled from their attack, the aggressors stopped to look at him up on the sandy ridge.

'Begone with you!' he shouted raggedly, for the kick of the

rifle had quite stolen his breath. He shuffled down the dune face, moving towards the huddled figures. 'Begone!'

As soon as Tanbark stumbled down to the tideline, his arthritic knees shooting pain each step of the way, he confirmed what manner of creatures these were. Not men but *Usagie* – merfolk – finned and slimed, as gaunt as skeletons.

He raised his long-arm once more and pulled back the hammer.

'Get back to Hell, devils!'

One scrawny monster bared its teeth, exposing a row of glassy spines in its piscine mouth. Tanbark was not afraid. Every glass tooth would break upon Tanbark's skin were the creature fool enough to take a bite. Theirs was a diet of sponge and snail, soft innards, whale-falls. Starvation had pushed them close to land, but their prey tonight was tough and inedible.

'I won't say it again!' he shouted, and pulled the trigger. The rifle kicked, a chorus of hissing, and the merfolk scattered back into the shallows before submerging into the ocean. He knew better than to think them gone. They would wait and then take a chance on whatever he might leave behind.

Through the smoke the woman gazed at him with blank disinterest. The fight had not been his to stumble upon, and he caught a great wave of annoyance at his presence. Her task of staying alive had been complicated – rather than helped – by another human being.

'Hoy there, woman! Come away from the water's edge lest they try to drag you in again.'

The setting sun and smoke pouring from the great burning vessel had made a shadow of her face, so that all he could see was the outline of fire-glow on her cheek. He could tell she was young, perhaps thirty years old, and even in the low light it was evident she did not have the thin, aged look of the Southern folk, nor their cold sea-foam complexion.

Yet she had come in their boat, and wore their clothes. A long deepwater krakenskin coat almost completely covered her shin-length dockworker's dress. The unmistakable bronze coat-panels were crusted in blue spots freckling down to the sleeve-hems, small circles glowing as bright as the plankton in the water. It caught the setting sunlight, seemed almost on fire itself.

Tanbark came closer. 'Madam?' he inquired, softer. 'Are you all right? Are you alone?'

She brandished the oar. 'Are you man or monster?'

He held up his arm apologetically. 'Man!'

She dropped her weapon. The setting sunlight behind him outlined her face properly for a brief shining moment, and to his surprise he saw a high-born Lyonnian face, cast in despair. 'I cannot tell which is which any more.'

'Then come inside and think about it no more.' He shrugged out of his coat and draped it over her shoulders. She flinched at first, but then begrudgingly accepted the goat-wool weight of it – she was too woebegone to put up much more of a fight. Despite the chill of her skin she was surprisingly warm, and Tanbark would go so far as to say she smelled a bit *singed*.

'Take my arm,' he said, and the woman did so, holding him tight as if he were driftwood in a storm.

Together they stumbled along the sedge-grass track that led back to the Coastmaster's lodge with Musket circling them anxiously, his instincts wanting to offer assistance but his body a shaggy obstacle.

2

The quiet warmth

The quiet warmth of the lodge lay upon them like a great blanket. The woman visibly relaxed. The lodge was decorated in the old pennants and heraldry of the Lyonnian Seamaster's and Coastmaster's guilds and now they were out of the weather it was easy to see she was a Lyonnian guildswoman. She was an edge taller than the average height for a South Lyonnian, and her complexion was that bright-penny Old Lyonnian so common in the capital. Her dark hair was in the sensible braid of someone who might work around machinery and dock equipment, so she was not some lost waif.

'I prayed that I would reach the Firctide Guild Lodge,' she said, her voice quavering with relief. 'I thought it so remote that its location was only a rumour.'

'No, it's quite a real guildperson's sanctuary, and I am the Coastmaster for South Lyonne. I maintain the climatological records for this part of the country on behalf of Clay Capital.' He took his coat and the krakenskin from her shoulders. Apart from her wet stockings and boots, her dress was dry underneath. Krakenskin had an *aura*, a radiance that kept everything it touched dry. It was why the material was so prized among those who worked the cold oceans. And why it was so odd *she* would be wearing it.

When she turned about to extricate her arm, Tanbark drew a breath. A tattoo. A chevron. So fresh as to be not more than a month old.

Deepwater marriage.

Well then, he thought. You have indeed been around, if you've secured yourself a southern ocean husband.

'Most official cartographers tend to ignore our humble station and leave it off their maps. Who would come here voluntarily?'

He spoke casually, but even his distracted guest would have been able to work out the pointed question beneath.

'It's almost too much to explain,' she continued. 'But Brother Coastmaster, can I impress upon you a most urgent request: I need a boat.'

He scratched his head, startled by her request. She'd practically been shipwrecked already.

'Please,' she repeated. 'There's hardly time—'

'There are others, apart from you?'

'Yes!'

The wind clattered the roof-shingles, as if to remind Tanbark exactly where he was and the impossibility of what she was asking. As gently as possible he said, 'I can keep the lodge beacons on, for them to find us if they made their way to shore. But if they were lost to the water, I cannot help. I do not have a boat.'

The Lyonnian woman stared at him, dismayed. 'You do not? How can you live out here without a boat?'

'It's not necessary. If I need transport, I walk around to the fishing encampment on the other side of the harbour. We certainly cannot do that tonight. I'm sorry. Your companions – well, their fate is in the lap of the gods now.'

He braced himself for grief but she became still and frowned, as if working out a problem in her head.

Then she nodded. 'There's still time, they could make it through the night. Tomorrow you may take me to this fishing encampment on the other side of the harbour, and we shall obtain a boat.'

Tanbark had a sudden feeling that he was being press-ganged into doing more for this woman than giving her shelter and passing her on. Such a note of command in her voice. And quite from instinct his attention fell to her hands.

One hand was covered in fingerless gloves and the other— *Devilment, how did I not see it earlier?*

She'd balled the other hand into a fist and tried to hide it among the folds of her skirt, but there was no mistaking the mottling of her skin, the flash of silver.

'You're sanguis!' he exclaimed. 'Goodness gracious!'

The hand went into her pocket. 'And if I am?'

'Sister Guildswoman, I have no desire to quarrel with the Lyonne Order over their property. If you are sanguinem, then I must report you to the Coastal Magistrate.'

The woman glared at him. *She's a sanguinem*, he thought again, despairingly. They were people whose body and blood were aligned to incredible physical manifestations and powers. They could do things even machines could not do. Their blood-assisted labour was worth a hundred men. Magic work, almost. The Lyonne Order and Nomenclatures, that society of Parliamentary edicts and enforcement, would not have allowed so valuable a person to waltz around the southern shores alone.

If she were here, then she could only be here illegally.

If he did not report her at once, he would be aiding and abetting a crime.

The woman saw his conflict and tipped up her chin in defiance. 'I am nobody's property, sir. I am a free agent.'

'Well might you say that, but the coins in your hands say otherwise.' He pointed at the visible bloodletting grommet she could not quite hide. 'And I'll be in a tremendous amount of trouble if I'm seen to be disobeying the Lyonne Order. They're not called the *Lions* for nothing.'

'My bloodletting coins will be coming out soon. I have not yet had the opportunity to rid myself of them.'

Of course she hadn't. Only a Clay Capital phlebotomist could do such a risky surgery, and the Lions controlled every one of them.

Tanbark let out a sigh. 'All right, I will surrender to your legal assessments.' He hung up both their coats by the door. 'But let us see out the storm and leave our decisions until morning. You say these companions of yours are safe for a while longer?'

She nodded. 'They have found a temporary shelter.' Her expression became both evasive and as defiant as her earlier temper. 'An island in the ocean.'

'An island? I did not think that the Firetide Coast had any such islands.'

'Nor did I.' Her jaw was fixed in such a way, such bubbling rage under her seemingly controlled surface, Tanbark knew he should not press any further. If she said her companions had found shelter on an uncharted rock, then so they had. Let the morning bring better truth.

'Since we have no choice but to endure each other's company this evening, then official introductions are in order.' He straightened himself up. 'I am Harry Tanbark, Coastmaster of South Lyonne and the Firetide Coast,' he said. 'I keep the tide charts and the weather readings, and am a conduit between the local people of the shore and the odd Lyonnian official who may require residence in the South.'

She did not offer her name in reply. *Suit yourself, madam*, he thought. I know when someone is trying to hide something.

Tanbark relit the stove and made to boil the kettle again, only to fumble the lid at the woman's sudden question.

'How far from Harbinger Bay am I?'

Harbinger Bay. Even the name had made his body react convulsively. Tanbark fetched the lid from the floor, replaced it on the kettle. The prison's name should have been familiar enough to him he'd become desensitized to it, and yet here he was, shaking like a leaf.

'Ah, well, the prison is far enough away for us not to be afraid of it. Dozens of monster-infested miles before we get to the prison outskirts. Devilment, sister, tell me how does a woman from Clay Capital know of the Bay?'

'I am from Clay Portside,' she corrected him. 'And what sanguinem does not know of the country's infamous prison? Much of that dire place is expressly built to house our kind.'

A crack in her voice made Tanbark realize she was not talking of a remote and unexperienced happening. 'Someone you love is there.'

'Once, but thankfully no longer. He was released.'

'Ah, fortunate for him. Very few make it out.'

She touched the marriage tattoo on the back of her neck as if it were a wound. 'But someone very unbeloved may be there soon.' She put her hand down with an unmistakable deliberation. 'Coastmaster Tanbark, I was not alone on that boat. I had an unwanted passenger, a deepwater man. He may be here on this coast. He may be on his way to Harbinger Bay.'

'To the region?'

'To the *prison*,' the woman said. 'What are his chances of getting there on foot?'

The idea of someone voluntarily trying to go to that citadel of torture was so ridiculous he almost wanted to laugh, and had she not looked so serious he might have laughed anyway. 'Goodness gracious, without a guide, next to impossible.'

'I hope you're right.'

The thought of humour ebbed away, and now Tanbark felt that loom of worry. 'Should I be reporting a possible trespasser?'

'If you report him, you'll have to report me, and I cannot endanger my friends. No, your priority is rescue, and getting me a boat.'

He wanted to interrogate her further, desperately curious now. Not that she would answer, of course. She was right to be cautious about him. As a member of the Seamaster's Guild he was still kin to the Lyonne Order and Nomenclatures. He'd already blurted an intent to give her up to the local magistrate, information that would lead her directly to the Lions.

The rain pelted the lodge's stone walls as she pulled off her boots and wet stockings to set them by the fireplace. Her hands were not dextrous; either she was carrying an injury or the bloodletting coins were well past their replacement date. The phlebotomists installed the coins by strange biomechanical means. Though officially the discs of metal were to protect a bloodworker who might have to draw several times a day, the resulting surgical injury required constant attention. A sanguinem sent out for remote work would need to return to Clay within the year—with a ticking clock in their hands there would be no chance of them abandoning their posts, or their masters.

She had clearly achieved both.

Tanbark handed Arden Beacon a cup of hot tea. She sipped it gratefully and nibbled on some flax-seed biscuits he had left over from the vicar's visit a few days before. The biscuits were not tasty. Even in her hunger she would be circumspect in eating too many. He turned away to put the plates in the great enamelled sink, and fetch the map from the rolls above the dish-cupboard, but when he turned back he saw that she was curled up on his lumpy couch, fast asleep.

'Ah, poor girl,' he said, and fetched a blanket from the chest by the fireplace. He laid it over her. He picked up her boots to move to the boiler closet. They were showing wear, but would last for many more years, such was their uncommon craftsmanship. Inside one a name label, sewn into the tongue: *Arden Beacon*.

Beacon, he thought. A true sanguis family name. So then, she trammelled flame, or some kind of light. With her dockworker's dress and her air of wildness, the Seamaster's Guild had clearly sent her somewhere far distant.

He went to his bookcase of ledgers and thumbed through the spines. Found the volume he was looking for. A journal of navigation stations, and the *ignis sanguinem* who husbanded each one.

The Beacons mostly clustered around Clay Portside and its great river, except one dwelt in Fiction, that country to the south. A Jorgen Beacon, who maintained the lighthouse in Vigil.

Through his name a line in red ink. *Deceased.*

3

At daybreak

At daybreak Tanbark and Musket went down to the sandbar where the woman's ship had burned. The sun was rising above the horizon, louring and orange behind the slate-blue clouds. No sign of light in the water, the Firetide had faded with the coming day.

Tanbark had a feeling – even before he reached the boundary dunes – that the boat would be gone. His suspicions proved correct. As he crested the last dune there was only the long, weed-tumbled length of sand where the water kissed the shore. A low-tide wreck was always in danger of getting dragged out once the tides turned, and sure enough, the storm swell had been enough to float the remains out to sea.

He raised his long-arm upon seeing a dozen dark shapes lounging by the water's edge. Because his concerns were so fixated on merfolk he at first thought her attackers had returned. On further inspection Tanbark relaxed, lowered the rifle. Compared to merfolk, these beings were fat and sleek. Either seals or selkies. Either way, they were harmless if you left them alone.

'Fear not, ladies,' he called as he approached, although if they *were* seals he was only making a fool of himself by talking to the animals like a woebegone hermit. 'I am only looking for the boat that was beached on last night's tide.'

They looked at him suspiciously. A few of the closer seals humped back into the waves, but the others resumed their lounging, unbothered by his presence.

Musket pawed at a patch of disturbed sand near the highest water mark. Ah, Tanbark thought, the woman's weapon. The unmistakable blade of a dinghy oar protruded from the damp grains.

Then a flash of colour caught his eye. The other fingerless glove, half-buried. He shook the sand from it and put it in his pocket.

'That's all we'll recover today,' Harry said. 'Come, Musket, let's move on.'

He returned to find Arden Beacon awake and agitatedly pacing the long hall of the lodge in her bare feet. Musket found this game interesting and wound himself about the fabric of her dress, compelling the woman to stop moving.

'Mx Beacon?'

She rescued herself from Musket's joyous attention and frowned up at Tanbark.

'Where are my stockings and my boots?'

'They are drying in the boiler closet,' he said. 'Better than beside the fire. Sit down, Mx Beacon, you are exhausted and you'll bring on a fever.'

She stopped pacing. 'How do you speak my name?'

'Whomever made that fine footwear also had cause to sew your credentials inside. Unless you are not Arden Beacon, in which case we may have a greater problem.'

She gave an exhale of exasperation. 'I am her, but I'll admit to nothing else.'

'Don't fret, sister, I've given up on the idea of involving the local laws. They would take a week to come out here anyway, and evidence of your wrecking has all but gone from the shore.' He held out the sandy glove that he had picked up on his walk.

She took the glove with a sullen murmur of gratitude.

'And I also suspect you are somehow connected to Jorgen Beacon, whose lighthouse in Vigil was recently vacated due to his passing.'

'I am his niece,' she confirmed with equal sullenness, not pleased at having all her secrets revealed at once. 'I took care of the Vigil navigation station up until last month. But right now I need a boat—'

He nodded. 'The weather is mild. In an hour the tide will begin to recede, and we can walk around the spit to the Glasfolk fishing encampment.'

Tanbark said this, for he knew that was what she wanted to hear. But of course the Glasfolk shore clan would give her the truth in a much more unvarnished fashion. That truth Tanbark could not tell Arden Beacon. Guide or no, there was not a hope of Arden ever getting back out past coastal waters during the Firetide. Not with merfolk and monsters around. If she had abandoned her companions out on those waters, secret island or none, there was no getting them back.

When the ocean began to recede in the silky noon light, Tanbark, Musket and Arden loaded up their satchels and set off across the intertidal zone. Tanbark had procured iron picket-stakes as walking sticks and showed Arden how to dig her stick into the sand in each of the places she intended to step.

At first such caution made her impatient – she was hardly an old lady and she did not want to dally – but an ill-timed surly jab at a clear patch of sand turned into a near disaster as a corrugation of snapping shell as big as a steamer trunk jumped out of the sand, closing down on the stake with such force it whipped out of Arden's hands.

'Goodness!' she cried, jumping back. Muddy sand splattered down the front of her dress.

'Stay where you are!' Tanbark shouted over Musket's excited barking.

'I'm not moving!'

'Ah, *megacardium robustum*,' Tanbark said, collecting the

stake from several paces away. 'Big cockle. I knew this old lady would be lurking around here somewhere. You surprised her by jabbing this toothpick into her mouth. Now, open up, dear, let us see what you have been eating.'

The giant cockle had jumped so far out of its hiding place and with such force it had fallen on its side, a great ridged, spiky pillow of a thing. Tanbark poked the hinge ligament until it opened up wide enough to see inside. Between the leathery siphon tube and the purple gills lay an iridescent, lumpy, blue-green pearl the size of his forearm.

Tanbark flicked the pearl out of the cockle before the hinge shut again. 'Go and get that for me, Arden. But . . . step carefully.'

She rolled her eyes but accepted the return of the stake and went to fetch the pearl. The weight of it and a kink in the middle made it hard to handle. Whatever irritant had entered the cockle had been so big the nacreous layers had barely covered the surface.

'It's heavy.'

He took the pearl from Arden's arms. Its shape reminded him of something, and he tried hard to conceal his grin when it slowly revealed what it might be. 'Well, well!'

'Well what?'

He dropped the pearl to the ground and held it lengthwise along his shin.

'It's a foot.'

The rest of the journey was uneventful, save for a crab the width of a dining table that stood up and scuttled off irritably when poked with the sounding stick. Most of the other creatures of the intertidal sands kept to a regular size, like the armoured trilobites that scattered every which way as they rounded the spit, or octopus-like crinoids splashing in rock-pools far too small for them.

Tanbark thought of the last time he had trilobite chowder, for the arthropod flesh had a creamy sulphurous sharpness somewhere between century eggs and cryptid kidneys. His mouth watered, but the chowder had been Maud's dish, and it never tasted quite the same made with his hand and not hers. He called back Musket, who had clearly had much the same – albeit more urgent – idea about eating.

'You'll get yourself nipped on the nose, dog.'

'How does he get to run about,' Arden asked, 'and we walk so carefully?'

'A shore-mutt has instincts. If he didn't know how to avoid getting swallowed by a giant anemone, well, he'd not be of much use here.'

'Pity your dog can't stick to a path we could follow.'

'That is why he's *my* dog. It's not like the shorefolk would gift a Lyonnian guildsman the best of the litter.'

They rounded the spit at the tide's lowest mark and came upon a rockier bay, and there was the Glasfolk encampment, a semi-permanent cluster of huts upon the water's edge, perched upon a natural shelf of scoria-stone. The loose rusty-black rock seemed barely held together by drab outgrowths of lichen, and the huts had the look of boat sheds about them, functional structures on stilts with sloping rooves, but not very homely. Three flat-bottomed boats – none of them meant to venture far beyond the coast – moored at the stone pier. A fourth jostled at the breakwaters on its way in towards land. Several seals basked on the rocks. They were used to people and did not slide away as Tanbark and Arden walked past.

Musket bounded on ahead and was greeted by more than one set of barking, a rambunctious chorus of *hoof, hoof*. Arden gave a small anxious murmur as two shaggy behemoths bounded up to them with enough careless excitement to knock a body over. They were as red and shaggy as Musket was, though the good Lord had seen them grow half a dog larger again.

'Don't fret,' said Tanbark to Arden. 'These are Musket's brothers.'

'Hoy, Coastmaster,' a cry sounded from across the rocks. A shadow dressed in an oilcoat and rubber boots strode out across the rocky shelf. The man had come in the fourth boat, having just secured it to the natural pier. 'My dogs smelled your arrival even before I did.'

'Handsell, my friend,' Tanbark said.

In the deepening afternoon Handsell looked just as Tanbark remembered him from several seasons ago, a man perpetually haunted by a hang-dog expression, bags of skin drooping beneath his eyes and from his jowls, his nose crooked, broken and reset a dozen times from struggles with the threshing sharks he'd pulled upon his boat. He carried in one hand a bucket filled with fresh-caught eels.

'You'd not have come were it not important.' He looked at Arden with open curiosity. 'And escorting a guest too.'

'I've come to ask a favour from Cadmus, if he be in a mood to hear it.'

'What kind of assistance?'

'We're in need of a boat.'

Handsell gestured towards his own, to which Tanbark shook his head regretfully. 'An ocean vessel. To pick up some stranded . . .' he glanced at Arden for help.

'Friends,' she finished. 'They are on an outcrop out past the shore boundary, half a day west.'

Handsell let out a short cough. 'Too far.'

'Cadmus goes further. His boat can cover it.'

The shoreman tipped the eel bucket into the shallows, sending the seals squirming for the sudden feast. Then he gave Tanbark the kind of look one gives a child when it requires humouring. 'I cannot vouch for his mood. Mr Cadmus leads the ceremonies this evening,' Handsell said. 'The prayers to the Suitor of Tides for the return of our women. Afterwards he might listen, though it would be a first. Come to the lodge, the fire is lit.'

When Handsell had moved on some distance ahead Arden leaned to him and said, 'What does he mean, the *return* of the women?'

'A funeral rite. A memorial. These years have not been kind to the shore.' He didn't want to say too much, because in his heart he knew Cadmus might not allow the use of his boat, not to an illegally existing sanguinem, and not for so vague a rescue. If she were given a hint that things might turn out badly, this sanguis woman might prepare for a long argument.

They came upon the main lodge, the largest of the huts. The building was raised four feet off the ground on concrete stilts. Some dried mussels clung to the stumps, almost to floor level.

Arden was quiet all through Tanbark's greetings with the other Glasfolk as they filed out of the lodge. Despite their isolation, the people of the shore were not suspicious of strangers. They tended to extroversion and gregariousness. The woman's krakenskin coat drew murmurs of appreciation from them, and Arden answered their questions politely, saying only that she had purchased it in Vigil upon the death of its previous owner.

As it was, they had arrived a shade too late to catch the man who owned the only ocean boat for miles. 'He's already on the beach,' said the final Glasman to leave the lodge. 'Mr Tanbark, I know it's Cadmus you're looking for. No need to ask.'

'Is he in a good mood, perchance?'

'Never. But give him some of that Clay-distilled whiskey and he might loosen up.'

Tanbark could feel Arden bristling with impatience as they walked across the lichen-dressed stone to the beach, which was really an outwash of sand from a braided river.

'All this talk. Every minute puts my friends in danger,' she said. 'After two days they may die of exposure.'

'Mx Beacon, you were fortunate enough to have made it this far; if your friends survive then that is a boon on top of a miracle. Don't court trouble by asking for more.'

'What if I deserve it?' she grumbled. 'After what I have been through.'

'Then I wish I had an ounce of your self-belief. Now, assume a position of respect, sister. It's the evening rituals.'

Sometimes city-folk used to praying their one ritual a week were ill at ease upon seeing people who prayed as many times of the day as there were hours, but Arden Beacon looked upon the gathered group with an intense familiarity. You have seen such things, Tanbark wanted to say, as they watched a dozen men gather on the shore and shout entreaties at the waves. They tore off their coats and shirts, beat their chests, shouted at the ocean. The waves rolled in, red as blood, the tide bright with fire.

Then she spoke.

'I thought he meant only a *few*. But he meant all.'

'All, what?'

'All the women.'

Tanbark sighed. 'Three winters ago. The doctors of Clay Capital would call it a *cluster sickness*, a shared madness. 'Twas a Deepwater Night when the Suitor of Tides called the first of the women. Over the space of a month they all walked into the water. Every last one. Even Maud – my wife.'

'I'm so sorry.'

'The shore knows these tragedies. Especially here. There's a living to be made on the edge of these dreaming tides, but a dying, too.' Tanbark gestured across the bay. By now the light had faded enough that even his face was in shadow, and the red ripples bloomed wherever a Glasman walked. 'Sailors and landfolk alike call the Firetide the boundary between our world and the world of spirits and magic . . . and if you are of a superstitious nature perhaps that is true.' He tapped her knuckles with his own. 'Your kind. The ones who share the mysterious symmetries of blood and physics, they perhaps have more experience with these boundaries than anyone else.'

'But I've only walked the shore of both worlds,' Arden said. 'There are some who've waded deep and I'm afraid of what they will bring back if they are left too long unsupervised.' She turned to him and searched out his face in the darkness. 'I must find my friends, guide or not, Tanbark. Don't make me do something rash.'

He was about to ask what could she do, being a woman alone in a country she barely knew, then held his tongue. In her expression he could see that she'd used that fire of hers to get something she'd wanted dearly, and had the motivation to do it again.

Whatever the Glasmen meant to achieve by the howling, it was not altogether in service of a memory. They did not come away from their coastal entreaty empty-handed. For not more than half an hour later a dozen men waded out of the wash supporting the terrible length of a large, dead eel in their arms. The creature trailed slime like a silver veil. Exposed gills fronded about its dished face.

Not an eel. Tanbark corrected himself, a *bucca*, a somewhat lesser thing, an antediluvian cousin to the merfolk. It had a face like an ugly man, but only when one got closer would you see the eyes were mucus-pits, and the lips were a bony shelf concealing a venomous jaw. The *bucca*'s true eyes were set back on its high forehead. Hideous to look at, but the non-edible parts were useful either as fish bait or a cryptid repellent, depending on what one required.

'It's the biggest they've caught yet,' Tanbark commented. 'I thought there were no larger *bucca* left in the sea.'

'I've seen larger,' Arden said quietly. 'I saw the deepwater people bring a sea serpent up, on the Deepwater Night. It was a creature as long as . . . oh, the longest train, and its head large as one of those huts over there. Was my *husband* who brought it ashore.'

As Tanbark made to respond, a voice from behind them said, 'Well then. A *Maris Anguis* is formidable enough, but this husband of yours would meet his match if he came upon the Harbinger Wyrm.'

Tanbark and Arden turned about, but not before Tanbark caught a grimace in her expression.

'Smart as a man, those things,' the interrupter continued, tilting his chin towards the dead *bucca*. The man might have been considered handsome, save for a broad, thin mouth better suited for sitting on a lily pad and catching dragonflies. 'Mr Handsell says you had a cause to meet me. Muttered something about a rescue, which I did not quite catch, for who would be so foolish as to ask for a boat beyond the coast during the Firetide?'

'We—' Tanbark started, but Mr Cadmus turned on his heel and set off in the direction of the longhouses. He jerked a thumb at Arden as they hurried to follow him. 'This is the madness that has you coming out here round the spit?' he said to Tanbark.

Tanbark threw an apologetic glance at her. 'Would have taken her myself, if I had a boat that could navigate those waters.'

Mr Cadmus made a noise in his throat and spit phlegm. 'You would never have reached such grandmasterly years if you were allowed a boat, Harry.'

In the bright hiss of the rockblood lantern, Cadmus' lodge was cosier than the main lodge, and the walls of the building insulated by a layer of dried felt-weed stuffed behind stretched nets punctuated with small, milky windows. It had that air of impermanence about it, with its stretcher-cots and blankets, and a strong odour of sweat, for the Glasfolk cared not to wash during their winter sojourns to the Coast, only rubbed *bucca*-fat on their bodies to obscure their human scent.

A woman worked before an iron stove, stirring a pot of food with a smell that would have been a stretch to call delicious. She was younger than Cadmus, pale and thin. Tanbark caught Arden's expression of disbelief, and then saw what she saw – the chain running across the bare wooden floor and ending under the skirt, where it was wound around the Glaswoman's ankle.

'I'll be done soon,' she said in harassed friendliness.

'Thank you, wife,' Cadmus said, kissing her on the cheek. 'It smells delicious as always.'

More men came in, and they sat at the long salvagewood table. Mrs Cadmus ladled out food for them, her chain scraping on the floor-slats as she walked. Had Arden Beacon been an animal, Tanbark thought, her hackles would have raised.

Thin-lipped Cadmus was not oblivious to Arden's disapproval. He had already seen the stranger's eyes upon his wife. He spoke gruffly. 'Better you'd have done the same to Maud, Harry Tanbark.'

'She'd not have forgiven me if I'd tied her up,' Harry said.

'Forgiveness is worthless if they're dead, friend.'

Cadmus turned to Arden, his lips stretched tight around his teeth. 'This is Lise, my bride and love, who I will protect until our deaths part us.'

Lise nodded. 'It is a good thing that I am kept so safe. My husband caught me before I went into the water. The Suitor of Tides was strong, but my husband was stronger. Please sit and eat, allow me to honour our guests.'

Arden slid into the offered bench-space, and accepted the bowl of stew, her eyes never straying far from Lise, even as she spoke. 'About my request for a boat, it's already been two days since my companions were—' she began.

'I offer you food and lodging for the night,' Cadmus interrupted, 'because this is the graciousness of the coast when the Firetide is up. But neither I nor any of the others can take you further from the coast than you already are right now.' He stamped his foot, placing his boundary. 'You should never have been out there in the first place. It is forbidden.'

'Perhaps you should interrogate why things are forbidden,' Tanbark said. He reached into his satchel, still slung about his chest, and took out the giant, lumpy pearl. Dropped it onto the bench. 'I found your foot, Cadmus. An unfortunate stroll that must have been in a place completely allowed.'

The other fishermen had been minding their own business, but the appearance of the odd pearl made them stop pretending their disinterest.

In the hissing lamplight the Glasman's rough features grew stormy before he let out a laugh. Cadmus stuck out his wooden foot, hidden beneath trousers and gumboots, and measured it up.

'Been twenty years since I lost it. A fine coat of nacre on my boot. But once again, I cannot help you.'

Arden at last spoke up. 'If you say my friends are dead and you cannot help, then take me to Harbinger Bay.'

Cadmus blinked. Her request had come completely out of

the blue. 'The prison? Exchanging one mad request for another? What is this nonsense?'

Sensing trouble, Tanbark had to jump in. 'Cadmus, when Mx Beacon's boat ran aground last night, there may have been a man aboard.' He exchanged a glance with Arden. 'A deepwater man. We think he might have gone that way.'

'Why would a deepwater man want to go to a landlocked prison?'

'He's not there for the prison,' Arden said. 'He's there for the *Wyrm*—'

'Enough!' Cadmus slammed his hand upon the table and the plates clattered. 'The deepwater things know the abyss and the cold, cold dark and the great lonely immensity, but there are things in the shallows that crawl close and hot and *intimate*.'

He pulled up the sleeve of his linen shirt. A poorly etched tattoo of a *bucca* lay almost like a scar upon his skin.

'See this? The Harbinger Wyrm lies coiled in that estuarine country and will not suffer the clumsy incursions of your so-called deepwater fellow. Go there or stay here, it makes no difference, but do not drag my people into your folly.'

Arden took a breath to say more, and Tanbark urgently pressed his knee against hers. The breath of obsession was in her, but he willed her to silence.

Yet even Tanbark's warning would not turn her away. 'So the Harbinger Wyrm is real? There really is an inland water monster?'

'Yes.'

'And what is its purpose to the prison? A guardian?'

'Oh, much more than that,' Cadmus said with a bitter, knowing chuckle.

Arden's eyes were wide, and her breath came short. 'This man comes from a family of big cryptid hunters. His people are *sanguis monstrum*, and I've seen what they can do to the giants of the deepwater. You say that the shallows breed the monsters more powerfully? That means more power for him, then, and soon, if not already.'

'Rubbish,' said one of the fishermen.

Cadmus held up his hand.

'Everyone out. I need to speak with our guest.'

Peeved, they muttered angrily among themselves, for some had not finished eating, but he was the leader here and so the fishermen left, some still holding their plates. Lise, sensing perhaps the change in the air, had retreated to her stove. Cadmus wiped his face on the back of his sleeve.

'*Sanguis monstrum*. And how do you, a rich Lyonnian, come to know of the existence of such a man?'

'I know two, in fact.' She pulled down her collar and turned her head so he might see the marriage chevron on her neck. 'One I was forced to marry in Equus, the Sainted Isles. He may already be within the prison territory. The other . . . Well, I don't know where he is.'

Tanbark found himself frowning at the emotion in her voice. She was lying. Did Cadmus also catch the crack in Arden's speech as she revealed the existence of a second monster-aligned man? What trials had she endured? For a moment he regretted having brought her complications to these simple folk.

The Glasman's eyes narrowed. 'We sit in the south of Lyonne, a part of the country nobody takes much notice of to visit unless they have a *reason*. It's not by chance that strangers come to the Firetide Coast, not when the current runs so swift and strong between Clay City and Morningvale. But they are fools to think we do not harbour the same kinds of dangers as cold Fiction or cruel Clay Capital. You say this man who speaks to monsters is dangerous? Look inwards, sanguis woman, perhaps it is not just him of whom we need to take warning.'

'You're right. I'm not here by chance,' she said bitterly. 'Less than a week ago I was going home. I'd survived a deepwater marriage in Equus, I'd survived brutality. All I wanted was to go home.'

'And what got in the way?'

Her smile did not reach her eyes. 'We paused to do some fishing.'

Book Two: The Coast

(ONE WEEK EARLIER)

4

Hold it

'Hold it, Fred!' the pilgrim shouted. 'Hot-water cryptid, a *big* one!'

'I see it, Orphen!'

From her position on the side-deck, Arden watched the two pilgrims snag a jenny-ray on the line. The young Clay men had become much more seaworthy in the month since they'd first collided paths with Arden and her crew. It was hard to reconcile this salty pair with the miserable flotilla of religious travellers crusading off to the island of Equus with little more than prayers and soggy scriptures. Now they looked somewhat likely to get through the journey without the risk of sudden death.

Despite the wickedly curved hook in its gills, the ray fought the hook, quicksilver skin catching the late afternoon sun. Arden couldn't help but laugh good-naturedly at their combined efforts, and had to call out, 'Lads, that's the *smallest* I've seen!'

The effort of keeping his grip made Fred cry out. He had never fished in anything deeper than a puddle in his life, and wrestling up a thing as big as he was took a great deal of effort. Still, a jenny-ray was hardly a giant sea dragon *Maris Anguis*. The fish-creature was mostly shark, and some monkey, and weighed about as much as a petite woman.

Still, it put up a great muscular effort to break free.

'I can't hang on! I can't! It's too heavy!'

And then Jonah Riven was there, securing the rod-head, slinging the filament between his elbow and his hand. The pilgrim boys had remained strong and well-fed looking even after a month of hardship, yet next to them Jonah looked far bigger and stronger – a woven mass of pale, scrimshawed tendons left to bleach in the sun.

The jenny-ray wasn't about to let go of life gracefully. Jonah grunted, braced himself against the railing of his grandfather's boat, and began to drag the dead weight up the side of the hull. The grotesque thing sensed its coming execution and began to writhe upon the hook in earnest.

Jonah held firm, unconcerned by its struggle.

He motioned that the young men should help. It was not his catch to claim.

The wire sang and gouged splinters out of the transom as the ray lashed. Jonah let the young men labour unsuccessfully for half a minute before re-joining the haul in a charitable act of assistance.

Together they brought the ray – the size of an adult – over the side.

The pilgrim lads cheered, slapped their hands, and knocked their ankles. One danced a jig Arden had seen drunkards do down by the banks of the Clay River when they'd won a gambling bet. The jenny-ray flopped pitifully. It was a miserable death, made worse by its vaguely human-shaped features above its mouth, the cold, black eyes, accusing.

It would make for good eating though.

'I didn't think they came so far north,' Orphen said, breathless.

'Must be a current in the water. A warm current, the one that keeps the Sainted Islands from becoming ice in the winter,' replied Fred, who, despite being younger, seemed to be more knowledgeable about the geography of Lyonne.

'God is good in his ways.'

'God is good. I say, Orphen, you must not nick the intestines. Cut neck to hole. It's how they slaughter the lambs back in the Clay uplands.'

'I know that, Fred, wasn't it me who took you to see the slaughtering?'

'But you would not touch a knife!'

Not more than ten paces away Arden Beacon tipped back on her seat – one of several rigid trilobite net-frames stacked up against the wheelhouse and forever in danger of toppling – to watch the young men gloat over their catch. Jonah knelt and finished the jenny-ray off with a pair of cuts across its gills.

He was physically bigger than he'd been when first they'd met in Vigil three seasons ago, Arden noted. The pale tattooed skin had gained a scuff of abrasions and scars, many of them just healing. More changes to the memory of the lonely, suffering fisherman she'd come to love so briefly in the ending days of summer. Another layer of separation between them.

'She certainly worked him hard,' Chalice Quarry said, as she unexpectedly joined Arden in spectating the catch. 'Queen Bellis, I mean, when she had him prisoner all those months. Shove over.'

Arden shuffled across her net-seat to let the other woman sit on the trilobite cage with her. Chalice Quarry had taken off her male pilgrim disguise for an equally grubby pair of dungarees, and had pulled her unruly red hair into a topknot with a twist of wire that was forever threatening to break.

'You aren't in the wheelhouse,' Arden said with a note of reproach. 'Who's watching our course?'

'Mrs Cordwain volunteered to take over; wanted some skipper experience on top of her pilgrimming.'

'Really? And didn't bleat that assuming the *authority of a man* was a sin?'

'Probably a lesser sin than watching her boys bringing up from the water every antediluvian abomination under God. Of course, all her moral absolutism goes out the window when the sinful thing is cooked and delicious on a plate, darling.'

'Huh.'

Chalice then nodded towards Jonah, wiping the bloody knife on his ragged canvas strides. 'How is he?'

Arden wanted to scold Chalice and say that Jonah was *fine* and to *not ask questions*. But there was only so much she could hide from Chalice. Her friend was a *Lion*, a Lyonne Order and Nomenclatures agent. In the few days they'd been on the journey back home to Clay, Madame Spy would not have missed the strangeness of Jonah Riven, the absence in his eyes, and the fact that since their reunion he had not spoken one word.

'He hasn't gotten worse,' Arden said hopelessly. 'It's not as if he's jumped overboard and swum away. So that's a start.'

'And you still believe there are people in Clay City that can help him with his odd condition?'

'There must be,' Arden said. She touched her gloves, felt the numb portion of her hands, the snag of the bloodletting coins. 'There are *sanguis mesmerii* practitioners who can cauterize bad memories, open minds, and return a person from the most awful despair. One of them must be able to diagnose Jonah's condition.'

'My dearest girl. Those are conditions of the *psyche*. Have you considered that he spent so much time underwater that the very matter of his brain was damaged?'

'He wasn't under that long. He's a deepwater man. He can return from that.'

'Nearly an hour you said, at your cousin Stefan's funeral. There may not be anything to return from.'

Arden twitched. She was in no mood to be smothered with harsh realities, especially concerning Jonah. After all they'd endured, this denouement just wasn't fair. There must be a cure.

'If you aren't driving the boat, Chalice, then shouldn't you be fixing the motor? We could row *Sonder* faster.'

'Excuse me? At least we are moving.'

'Five knots an hour is hardly moving! We won't get to Clay until next winter at this rate!'

The Lion folded her arms over her denim bosom and smacked

her lips. 'First of all, darling, this is an electrically powered boat. If I put too much salt into *Sonder*'s motor your delicate sanguinem senses are going to be itching as if I'd released a swarm of bees under your dress. Secondly, some of the capacitors on that bedevilled regulator panel are as old as Adam. Why, they must have been powering the pumps in the Garden of Eden before this old tug.'

'*Sonder* belonged to Jonah's grandfather,' Arden said defensively. 'Of course it's not going to be modern.'

'And I'm doing my best. Anyway, the boys wanted to fish. We'll give the generator as much of a kick as you can handle when they're done.'

'Well, I'm glad it's under control.'

'It's always under control with me, darling. In case it's escaped anyone's notice, *Sonder* has those old sodium batteries, and that is an element very near and dear to my heart.'

Then Chalice stopped talking, and the weight of the unspoken request hung between them. *Sodium*. That one element that Chalice would likely have been associated with, if she were officially sanguis like Arden. The line between sanguis and commoner had blurred over time, and no matter how the Eugenics Society might try to isolate the breeding lines, the old talents still spilled into the general population, and so Chalice had certain . . . abilities that were unique.

'Speak it, Chalice.'

'I came to ask for a little jump-start, that is all. I don't quite have the––' She made a pumping-handle gesture as she screwed up her face. 'A little bit of *evalescendi* would really allow me to restore the sodium electrolyte, get the most power out of the pile. Please don't be upset that I'm asking this. I know it's hard to use a shadow talent.'

Arden looked down at her fingerless gloves, pressed her thumb into an inflamed coin until it hurt. Her shadow talent lurked under her regular Beacon endowment of *ignis*. The one she kept secret, the one kept secret from her. *Evalescendi*. The power to increase, to expand, to escalate. She would combine her blood with Chalice's, smear it in the place that Chalice wanted to affect. Almost barbaric, when one thought about it, like the deepwater folk who would injure themselves to attract the giant sea serpent.

'My hands are really bad, Chalice. My coins won't take another cut.'

'We'll use another place. Just a nick. Just a little bit of blood so the sodium pile gives me more power.'

Arden knew she could refuse. She also knew that *Sonder*'s propeller screw turned thanks to the stored energy of fifty-two salty piles of copper dunked in a sodium solution, and Chalice did not have enough affinity with sodium to eke more than a few more watts out of the already depleted batteries. If only the engines could have run on rockblood or kraken oil! The other two Riven-owned boats, *Sehnsucht* and *Saudade*, had been big, noisy, fuel-driven hunting boats. Old *Sonder* was made to be slow and stealthy, the electrical motor so quiet she could sneak up on the catch. She'd never been meant to go far, or fast.

In surrender, Arden pulled up her skirt and tugged down one stocking. 'Cut me on the leg.'

The thing about the Lyonne Order agents was that they knew how to use knives. The spies and covert skulkers of that shadowy organization were skilled in the arts of disfigurement and assassination. It meant Chalice was quick. A snick of her blade, and before Arden felt the pain, Chalice was already wiping the bloody knife on to a slice of broken mirror.

'See? The day after tomorrow and we will be sailing through the Clay Mouth. Just let me know if the electrical field is too much, and I can throttle back, all right?'

'Chalice, I'd suffer anything to get home faster at this point.'

They turned back to the drama on the forecastle deck. In the dying light the jenny-ray's black blood stained Jonah's hands, and the twilight turned his pale, southern-latitude skin deathly luminous.

He looked up then, meeting Arden's gaze.

Who is in there, she wanted to ask. Speak your real name, spirit, and leave.

But the strange, pale absence in his eyes struck her into stillness, as she once again realized how much his recovery had cost her. Cost them both. Had they ever even shared intimacies? One could imagine that she'd dreamt them.

It was too much to hold that strange gaze, and she turned away. As she did so, Arden's sharp Beacon-born eyesight spotted a curl of smoke staining the yellow-tinged horizon.

Her hands bore down hard on the transom, her fingers dug into the golden wood.

A boat. A boat burning heavy oil – and coming towards them at speed.

5

Look

'Look, Chalice!'

Arden's visual acuity across long distances and through low light was so much better than Chalice Quarry's that Chalice had at first not believed her. It had taken her fetching the spyglass and tilting her head in just the right direction before Madam Lion finally saw their pursuer clearly enough to make her assessment.

'Oh. Oh my. She's coming from Fiction,' Chalice breathed. 'Lyonnian ships don't burn fuel rockblood like that.'

Arden quickly calculated what that meant. The south country of Fiction was now several days behind them. The navigational charts had put *Sonder* almost halfway up the coast of Lyonne now. They were not more than two days from Clay Capital.

'If it's a Fiction boat, why have they waited so long to appear? It could have caught us before entering Lyonnian waters.'

'I cannot say, darling. But it's headed right for us.'

Arden suffered the crush of worry at once. Her first thought when she had seen the spot of smoke on the horizon had been *Saudade* following them. The boat her *husband* now controlled.

At once the marriage tattoo on the back of Arden's neck itched, and she could have sworn her copper wedding ring burned.

Then she put the fear aside. It wasn't *Saudade*. Miah couldn't have followed and plotted Arden's route back to Lyonne even if he could still see. Two weeks had passed since he'd stumbled away, blinded, collected into the arms of his relieved deepwater clansmen.

Besides, kraken oil had a very specific blue-sparkling tinge. The emissions from the distant ship were pure black rockblood. So Chalice's identification of a Fiction vessel was most likely correct . . . only who was the captain?

The pilgrim Mrs Cordwain joined them on deck, squinting her disapproval of all the fuss.

'All this yelling over a boat? Are we not on a shipping road?' Mrs Cordwain said. 'My anxieties will not do well if I'm shouted out of my meditations every few seconds.'

'Meditations? Mrs Cordwain, I thought you had your hands on the wheel.' Arden might have addressed Mrs Cordwain, but she glared at Chalice.

'Oh,' Chalice said, '*Sonder* doesn't need a skipper when the panel is discharging. The wheel is actually disengaged.'

Mrs Cordwain spluttered. 'Mendacious trollop! You explicitly said I could have experience skippering the boat!'

Arden held up her hand to stop the brewing argument between the Lion and the pilgrim. 'Mrs Cordwain, with all due respect if it took you till now to work out the boat was not responding to your control then perhaps it is a skill that requires some work.' She turned to Chalice. 'And I agree: *someone* is being a mendacious trollop. *Someone* who may know who is following us.'

Chalice wrung the spyglass between her hands. 'We've been going so slowly. They were bound to catch up.'

'Catch up? Give me that!' Mrs Cordwain screeched, and snatched the spyglass from Chalice. She didn't need it though. The boat was visible to the naked eye now.

'I see no country flags. Are they following us? Are they pirates? I won't have my journey home interrupted by criminality!'

'Um,' Chalice started, 'I can assure you we have put all our dealings behind us and closed the book upon our adventures. Perhaps they are just passing. Unless we hail them, they will likely continue on, taking no notice.'

Chalice's response didn't smooth things over with the religious woman. She directed her ire towards Arden instead.

'You best not have invited evil upon this ship, *sanguinem*,' Mrs Cordwain hissed. 'If they are murderous pirates, there will be demons with pitchforks waiting for you in Hell after your head gets lopped from your shoulders!'

The first time Arden had met the sour-faced pastor's wife had been nearly a month before, a few days before Deepwater Night. The woman and her fellow pilgrims – nearly fifty of them – had rescued Arden and *Saudade* from wallowing adrift on the Darkling Sea. Back then Arden had been in love with a dead man, intent on carrying out a rite of honour, and Mrs Cordwain had been slightly sympathetic to Arden's predicament.

Now she was a delinquent bride in an odd, emotional arrangement with a silent man with Sainted Islander ink, and heading back home the long way around on a slow boat. Even an open-minded person would do well to be cautious, and Arden admittedly could not begrudge Mrs Cordwain her irritation.

'Mrs Cordwain, I understand completely,' Arden said with all the charity she could muster when all she wanted to do was scream in frustration. 'Perhaps now would be a good time to see if we can get more *power* to the *motor*,' Arden said, once again glaring at Chalice with such a look she could feel her eyes ache. 'It would make us appear less vulnerable. Chalice?'

Chalice adjusted her jacket. 'Right then, I'll see what I can do.' She headed for the wheelhouse. Jonah tilted his head from where he was still butchering the jenny-ray and looked up at Arden. The pilgrim boys had forgotten their fish. Arden could hear Chalice yell for Fred, the older and more water-experienced of the two, to come up into the wheelhouse and take over so she might go down below.

Electrical motors made no noise, but a minute later the water frothed and foamed underneath *Sonder*'s hull.

It made little difference though, for their top speed of five knots could not have been increased beyond a solid six.

'We're not going home, are we?' Orphen said to Arden.

'I cannot say.'

'We *are* going home,' Chalice snapped as she emerged from the hull's trapdoor onto the deck. She sidestepped the remains of the jenny-ray and lit one of the two lanterns at *Sonder*'s bow. Arden noticed how badly her normally unflappable friend's hands shook. It would not be out of fear but the high, singing kick of adrenaline. 'It's just that my dear brother Lion would not have sailed on back to Clay empty-handed.'

'Your brother?' Arden repeated faintly. 'So you *are* familiar with that craft, Chalice?'

'Do you not recognize it too, darling? Well, you were in a state . . . and it was stormy that night.'

At Mrs Cordwain's gesture for her to elaborate, Chalice added, 'That vessel over yonder was last under the charter of Mr Absalom, my Order colleague.'

A sudden sparking pain pricked just above Arden's left eye. Her alarm came from her own reaction. *I should be relieved it's not* Saudade, *but I can't shake this bad feeling.*

Even though she'd excised her forced-wedded husband Miah Anguis from her life, the black mangrove boat he now owned had lurked in her anxieties like a shadow she could never completely rid herself of. She might have disabled Miah well and truly, but there was no real guarantee that he had forgotten her.

Sonder didn't have a wireless telegraph, so they were made to wait until the iron ship drew close enough for the passengers of *Sonder* to make out the twin smokestacks and its churning wake. A light appeared on the bow, flashing a code Arden did not recognize. To Arden's dismayed sense of betrayal, Chalice popped the previously bloodied bit of mirror – meant for the battery – into *Sonder*'s lantern. Even in dusk the coldfire beamed as bright as a full moon across the fading water.

'That blood was meant for the motor,' Arden protested.

'And the sodium batteries. Not a secret conversation among Lions.'

'I have to find out what Mr Absalom's business is before we go further,' Chalice replied. 'He is a dangerous man to ignore.'

'I know far more dangerous men.' Arden scratched the marriage tattoo on the back of her neck as it suddenly itched her most dreadfully, and for a moment she was back in the lodge of the deepwater folk, having her identity stripped from her in preparation to become the bride of the Deepwater King.

After flashing some obscure code in return to the iron ship's query, Chalice climbed off the bow and slipped her arm around Arden's waist.

'This Order man may outrank me, but he is not my enemy. In his own way, Brother Ozymandias Absalom did keep Jonah alive while he was a guest of Queen Bellis Harrow.' Chalice indicated the south direction that they had come. 'We all wanted you safely back in Clay, darling. Brother Absalom had different methods, but our end goal was the same.'

Among them, only Jonah was bored. The spirit behind his vacant eyes had no care for iron boats or secret messages. He took up filleting the discarded jenny-ray, losing himself in his preoccupations.

In a state and with nothing to do until the iron boat caught up with them, Arden slipped below decks, wanting a few moments alone to prepare.

Unlike Jonah's beautiful, dark *Saudade*, nobody had ever kitted the brown, waxwood, hunting ship *Sonder* for comfort. Because her aged batteries and vintage motor took up such a lot of space beneath the waterline, the below decks were as cramped and gloomy as a condemned church. And if not for the kraken oil soaked into the timber, *Sonder*'s hull would have long ago surrendered its hardiness to the barnacles and saltwater borers. However, there were things in here that *Saudade* did not possess.

Arden opened the map drawer, a middle-country pistol scraping the bottom as it slid out. It was black iron, with a grip made of ivory. The metal was shiny with a layer of oil. Next to the pistol was a revolving barrel with seven soft-tipped bullets.

Prepare for the worst.

Arden slipped the pistol into her coat pocket and took a deep breath, willed her thundering heart to steady. She realized then that she was not alone down here and with a gasp turned about.

Jonah was standing behind her, having materialized as silently as a ghost.

'Oh, Jonah! I thought you were still on the deck.'

He watched her with his stranger's eyes. Had he seen her take the pistol? Did he guess what it meant?

The ship rocked suddenly as the soft bump of the other ship's pontoons collided with the hull of *Sonder*. Arden grabbed Jonah's wrist, then let it go as he startled.

'Don't come up,' she said. 'He'll try to manipulate you . . . or something. The Lions can't help themselves. Not even Chalice can stop herself from trying and she's my best friend.'

Did Jonah nod? Was that a nod of acknowledgement and not simply his head rocking with the boat?

She carefully reached out and touched his angular face, found it clammy. He did not lean into her hand, but she did not expect him to do so. At least his stowaway spirit was friendly towards her. How awful it would be, she thought, if it were not.

By the time Arden returned to the deck, the sky had turned to dark rust and the iron boat bobbed alongside them. Darkness fell quickly in these warmer latitudes, though not as quick as in Clay City, where twilight might last for no more than ten minutes before night came.

Lanterns swayed on both ships and the waters stayed calm enough so that the boats kissed and released gently. The wind made a mournful howl in the guy-lines.

Arden noticed excommunicated Captain Mx Greenwing in the iron boat's wheelhouse first, a tall, slim woman with short hair and a gaunt, sinewy face. Then she saw another man she recognized from the wharf in Burden, low forehead, grey complexion of a Fiction native. He wore a little deepwater ink upon his neck and chest.

The others stood aside as Mr Absalom joined them with his gold-toothed smile. The druzy ring on his finger flashed gold in the lamplight, as did the threads in his waistcoat and shawl. He smoothed down the velvet faluche upon his head. There was a businessman's air about him, a sense of urgency and purpose.

The pilgrims stood back at a wary distance, so it was up to Chalice Quarry to step forward and greet Mr Absalom as a peer.

'Ozymandias Absalom.'

'My dear Chalice. How long has it been? Three weeks? Four? Time has quite sped up.'

'Am I of the understanding you are here to give the Widow's Son some help?' Chalice asked tartly.

'That would depend on who the Widow's Son is, right now.' Mr Absalom stroked the hat on his head once more. 'The Widow's Son could be all of us.'

Arden had heard the phrase often enough. *Widow's Son*. The Lion's secret code, the words by which fraternity bound them to assist one another in times of dire need.

If all of them were Widow's Sons, then he had not come bearing good news.

'It's odd that you should be in such a hurry,' said Chalice. 'At the rate your boat is running, you'll be on rockblood fumes by the time it reaches the Clay Mouth.'

Behind her, Arden heard the door open and shut. She winced. For all her warnings, Jonah had joined them on deck.

Mr Absalom pulled a pocket-watch from his waistcoat, flipped it open. Its movement was complex, with a moon-phase, a date and tide. 'It's true, Sister Quarry, we do not have the luxury of time. Please, let us talk out of the wind.'

He pointed towards the below decks, but to Arden's relief Chalice wasn't having it.

'First tell me what is so important that we must meet like this, Ozzy.'

Out-argued and too polite to pull rank, Mr Absalom nodded at Arden. 'Early this month after Mx Beacon took her leave of us in Burden—'

'Escaped you,' Arden corrected.

'Made her apologies and departed,' Mr Absalom said with a respectful bow, 'I was quite at a loss. Had I returned to Clay without our *sanguis evalescendi*, my colleagues would have been quite aggrieved.

'Yet I had my suspicions as to where a woman with no friends might go in Equus. Mx Greenwing is a sanguis finder as well as a stormcaller. She sensed you among the Equus survivors on the northern shore,' Mr Absalom said, tilting his chin towards the iron boat's captain.

Arden frowned as she pieced that distressing episode together. After she had fled Mr Absalom's kidnapping attempt she'd walked for nearly three days, only to fall into the arms of a monster . . . and nearly lose her life.

'Mr Absalom, you were nearby all that time? With the ability to rescue me off that damned shore and take me to my poor cousin Stefan . . . and Jonah! You let me be . . .' She sucked in a breath, trying to find the word that would most encompass the corrosive anger inside her. 'Violated!'

'Or Mr Anguis was violated by you,' Mr Absalom replied. 'You blinded him with your *ignis* powers.'

Arden stood taller, a quiver of righteous anger making her shake. She forgot all about the possibility of seeking an alliance with Mr Absalom. 'Oh no, Mr Absalom. I will *not* take the blame for that brute.'

'Mx Beacon, not blame, but praise! Had I collected you earlier, we would be in a position of weakness, and now we are in a position of strength!'

'Strength? Sir, I will only be strong when I am home in Clay Portside; not a minute before.'

'My dear, listen to me. Brother Lindsay would still have made his way to the deepwater clan regardless of your presence there or not. He always suspected a *sanguis mandatum* – a powerful metal wielder – was on the island. One half of the legendary powers of the Unnamed Saint! Lindsay would have exercised every ounce of charm, and Miah Anguis would still have left with him afterwards.'

'Wait, there was a *mandatum* wielder on Equus?' Chalice interrupted. 'And now Brother Lindsay has him? Arden, you never told me this!'

Arden took Chalice's hand and squeezed as hard as she could with her numb fingers, stopping her friend in her rant.

'Yes,' Mr Absalom concluded dolefully. 'My colleague has brought Miah to meet Bellis. *Orientis* and *mandatum* are together at last. All the legendary powers of the Unnamed Saint are now within Mr Lindsay's authority. He intends to do something with them both. Something awful and wicked, and we do not know what it is, only that it could destroy everything we know and love.

'And you, Mx Beacon, are the only one who can stop him.'

6

Arden allowed

Arden allowed him below decks. He'd invoked something in her, a Lion trick, and yet she knew she needed to hear him out.

But as they sat around the table, she drew her line. 'Ozymandias Absalom, from the bottom of my heart I must say that I absolutely do not trust you.'

The Lion put his hand on his chest, and the druzy ring caught the light in the same way a cluster of insect eggs might, horrible and gaudy at once. 'I'm telling truth. Brother Lindsay encouraged Mr Anguis to join him, and put aside the feud with Bellis Harrow.'

'Where are they now?' Chalice asked, frowning. She would have been content to stay up top, but Arden had not wanted to be on deck while Jonah was there. He had not yet come down below.

'They are forty miles west of our position. Brother Lindsay has taken sanctuary in his father's agarwood plantation on the Firetide Coast.' He dipped his head closer. 'Arden, now that he has two powerful sanguinem at his beck he thinks himself undefeatable, but his success – or otherwise – solely depends on you. I come bearing bad tidings, but tidings of help, too.'

'Did you assure Bellis Harrow of the same assistance when you were her trusted adviser, Mr Absalom?'

Mr Absalom briefly smiled at her barbed words before turning to his officer. 'Mr Berry, as a neutral observer who is knowledgeable about the Equus deepwater clans, can you confirm what I have told Mx Beacon?'

Arden peered at Mr Berry with suspicion. She could tell by just his appearance that the crewman was not pure deepwater aligned. Mr Berry had a Vigil mainlander look about him and his florid pigment-ink tattoos were only there to tell a local that he was sympathetic to their ways so they might trust him and talk freely. Whatever he knew about the deepwater people was tempered by his allegiance to the land, and that land was controlled by the Lyonne Order.

'Brother Absalom does not lie about Mr Lindsay, lady,' Mr Berry said. 'I spoke to the tradesmen who work the ghost-ship river. Apparently, Miah Anguis was in a state when he returned to the clan on the north shore – blinded and spitting angry, like a shark denied a meal. The little Order fellow gave him his sight back. Something about a potion he had, in a vial.'

Arden groaned and covered her eyes. 'Devilment! I hoped to keep him out of our hair for longer than a week.'

'Well, that cure fits,' Chalice said. 'Lindsay is a Lyonne Order officer. He'll have an antidote to any sanguis affliction.'

'Guess that unholy medicine was enough for Anguis to kiss his damn feet over it,' Mr Berry finished with a disapproving sniff. He was clearly familiar with the fiendish chemicals in the Lyonne Order's arsenal. 'Man followed him around like a hog with a ring through its snout. The Lions use that immoral poison for other things—'

'Which we need not go into,' Mr Absalom said quickly. 'What we need to concentrate on is that my brother has lured Anguis away to join Harrow. We need to find out what exactly he intends to do.'

Mr Berry folded his arms in a sulky huff.

'The boys – David Modhi and Sean Ironcup,' Arden asked Mr Berry. 'Are they well? Miah didn't take his anger out on them, did he?'

'My riverboat companion says they are doing fine among the deepwater clan.' Mr Berry flicked a look at Arden before returning to a neutral position of staring at his feet over his folded arms. 'Mr Anguis was mostly upset at you.'

Arden was in a bind. She wanted more than anything to tell Mr Absalom and his crew to get off her boat. She was not responsible for Lion politics, and did not care what a rogue Lion planned. But Mr Absalom had come so urgently, when they could have easily met in a Clay Portside tavern two days from now. Some of the wharves were Seamaster's Guild controlled, so tightly loyal that even the Lyonne Order struggled to find co-conspirators there, and Mr Absalom knew this.

Everything in her signaller's instincts told her not to ignore a sense of trouble. And a banking, looming disturbance was gathering in *Sonder*'s hull. It smelled of bad air and blood. Why would a Lion like Mr Lindsay – a sworn protector of Clay City – do something so reckless as to bring Miah and Bellis, *orientis* and *mandatum*, together?

Arden thought of the minuscule way she could combine her sanguis talents with others. There was a tremendous, vertigo-inducing difference between what Arden could do and what Bellis could do.

And bringing someone as vindictive as Miah Anguis into the mix—

'If you had to indulge me for a moment, what would *you* say Mr Lindsay's goal is, Mr Absalom?'

'I do not wish to invoke in my mind what horrors I believe my brother is capable of. On the surface I could explain this business of mixing sanguis talents a capricious experiment. Brother Lindsay has long been known for his impish malice. He's the type to put a scorpion and a spider in a bottle to see which one will kill the other. He does it with people too.'

'Oh,' Chalice tutted, 'that little devil. In his heart of hearts, he probably hopes they'll mate and create a brood of something much more nefarious.'

'Fortunately, Bellis isn't the breeding kind,' Arden replied.

'I'm sure *that* plan would give us twenty years of grace before we have to worry.'

'So his end is something else,' Mr Absalom said. 'He has always been loyal to the Order. Until now.'

Arden shoved her hands into her dress pockets. The pistol knocked against her knuckles. The time was coming when it would be beyond a waved gun to solve her problems.

Chalice tapped the surface of *Sonder*'s lone table, where a map had been at one time glued, though it was now little more than a few scraps of discoloured paper. 'Honestly, I can't see what Brother Lindsay can do from his plantation. Look, say he did get those two to manifest the godlike powers of the Unnamed Saint – what end would it serve? South Lyonne is practically unpopulated, Ozzy. Not enough people to make an army. And it would be impossible for Mr Lindsay to walk both Bellis and Miah into Clay Capital with a view to enslaving them. The watchtowers are constantly in operation, the city has powerful sanguinem guards that can kill a threat from fifty miles away – they will know of such a menace.'

'Yes, they will know. And this concerns me. My brother Lion may be capricious, but he does not act without first securing an advantage for himself. I feel he has a plan. This whole folly is not just conjecture on his part. Brother Lindsay has figured how to get past the Clay Capital sentries with his two horrors. If that is so, we are looking at a catastrophe in the making. His only weak link is Anguis.'

Arden was about to launch into a torrent of invective about how Miah was so much worse than Bellis Harrow, then stopped before the first word passed her lips. Yes, Miah had been impulsive and overbearing, and yet . . . he had never harboured ambitions beyond his small, north-island clan. Even when he'd threatened Arden with harm, it was in service of protecting his people from Equus' living machines. He had never mentally chained four thousand innocents to his will on Maris Island, the way Bellis had. He'd never decimated entire island populations, threatened children, marched people to their deaths. It was the Riven side of him, she decided. As Jonah's first cousin, Miah was not entirely sunk into malevolence.

Absalom saw her hesitation.

'It becomes clear, yes? Bellis would push for absolute worship until nothing is left and she commands only bones. The bones of your family, Arden, of everyone in Clay you have ever loved. Miah Anguis is another matter entirely. Arden Beacon, you still have some influence over him.'

She was drowning in a primordial soup of duty and fear. The last time she had seen the man who had forced marriage upon her, he'd been cursing her very bones, invoking her death.

'How am I to influence him when I nearly killed him?'

Mr Absalom gave a great shrug. 'The same way it has always been done through the centuries. The maiden throws herself before the monster and begs his forgiveness.'

Sonder creaked as the ship rolled and yawed. The lanterns threw their arabesques from side to side, drowning the gathered group in turn with gold and shadow. The bilge-water sloshed in the deeper hull below the battery floor, breaking the silence of the passengers.

Arden felt her hands shake. Everyone's eyes were upon her. Mrs Cordwain and her pilgrims had not moved from where they had been standing upon Mr Absalom's arrival down below, and the pastor's wife had her fingers laced together so tightly it almost seemed her knuckles would split open. Mr Absalom was speaking of a great sin that the religious woman could barely comprehend – the sin of purposeful destruction through the misuse of power. Mrs Cordwain was attuned like a lightning rod to trespasses and prohibitions. She could sense the deeper meanings of what the man had asked of Arden.

Chalice murmured a word, but it was not exactly a *no*.

Arden plucked at Mr Absalom's sleeve, motioning that he should follow her back up into the new-dark upper deck for a private conversation, and shook her head at Chalice when she moved to follow them.

*

Once alone, she turned on Mr Absalom.

'You intend for me to be a spy.'

'Yes. We can arrange a delivery. Brother Lindsay still believes I am under his thumb.'

'I cannot. Find someone else. Look at my hands, Ozymandias, I have barely a week or two before the sepsis of my coins sets in. And you saw Jonah . . . every day he slips away from me. The rogue spirit in his mind is too strong. Any day now he will stop fighting. I cannot help; I'm stretched too thin.'

Mr Absalom reached out and took her hands. She wanted to jerk back. Even numb, she could feel his insistent pressing.

'You've been to Equus, seen how despoiled it is, desolated by the lingering influence of the Saint of the Islands. Think of an entire city cursed that way. Think of your own family, Arden, think of your friends,' Mr Absalom said. 'The little beggar children on the docks, the traders in the marketplace. You must have courage from this moment on.'

'It's nothing to do with courage. I've already been to Hell and back! I couldn't stop those three going to Clay,' Arden raged. 'It's because Mr Anguis will *kill* me if he sees me, sir. I blinded him! He'll want revenge, if not on me, then on Jonah. He has never forgiven his cousin.'

'But if you survive the reunion – and there is a great chance you will – you can find out how Brother Lindsay intends to get them past all the Order's defences.'

'Devilment—'

'And in return, your charges of vagrancy will be dropped, your hands restored, and the best psychiatrists in Clay will help your man.'

Arden chewed her cheek, tasted blood. 'And if I don't do this?'

'Then we are *done*. Go home. See how far you get with only the help of Chalice Quarry and a father who stepped on toes when he allowed his *malorum* daughter to hold a signaller's position in the first place. I will intervene no further.'

Done. She knew what he meant. This was no favour after

all. This was not him imploring her to help. This was blackmail, and an order.

As if he saw the capitulation, Mr Absalom released Arden's hands and took out a gold coin from his pocket. The Lyonne Order coin of instruction. The imprint on the coin face had been smeared into nothing more than crenulated ridges by all the fingers that had, sweating and trembling, taken it. Now it was Arden who took the coin in her numb hands.

Mr Absalom breathed in. He gave the instruction.

7

Mx Greenwing

Mx Greenwing wore an astrolabe – a complicated compass rose – about her neck, and she spun it in her fingers. A sanguinem often kept something on their person as a token of her talent. Arden had once held a flint necklace for being *sanguis ignis*, a bloodworker who trammelled fire, but only the gods of storm and sea knew where that was now. She wondered where she might have lost it. Maybe in one of her many dunkings, or in the deepwater clan's encampment upon the north shore of Equus Island when she'd spent those torrid days as prospective bride for Miah Anguis. Besides, it wasn't entirely correct that she should hold such a token. She trammelled more than just coldflame.

An astrolabe token meant that Mx Greenwing primarily expressed talents of being a *finder*. Among the Lions such people were often made to bring runaway sanguinem to heel, so Arden could not help but be dreadfully uncomfortable around Mx Greenwing, with her pale, yellow hair razored so short and severe, and the sharp, angular cut of her ray-leather coat.

'Like Brother Absalom says, Brother Lindsay and his pair have taken sanctuary not far from here,' Mx Greenwing said. 'An old agarwood plantation on the Firetide Coast that was once owned by Brother Lindsay's father.'

She put the rose pendant upon the silk map she had rolled out for the purpose of tracking their quarry. The south coast of Lyonne was marked with a jagged coastline and mountains behind. It was a tumultuous country, and Arden knew from her finishing school studies that the local people were scattered now. Only a few plantations and abandoned fishing factories dotted the coast. It was a strange place to hide, for the old plantation families had loved their luxuries, meaning there was a functional network of roads too. Unannounced visitors could come from land or sea.

Without the privacy afforded by walls, Mrs Cordwain and her pilgrims were obliged to sit stubbornly in the furthest corner and distract themselves from the sinful discussions with a prayer circle. Every once in a while Arden would see the woman's eyes flicker meanly in her direction, no doubt wishing for all the devils and bad luck to befall her.

Even deeper in the darkness, another shadow lurked. Jonah, almost unbreathing, waiting.

'Oh, so we are going to knock on their door then?' Chalice said with her now permanent tartness. 'Hello, gentlemen, please accept our friend Arden Beacon, who is certainly not going to be spying on you on behalf of the Lyonne Order and Nomenclatures?'

Arden sat back and folded her arms so as not to show how badly the anxiety was knotting in her belly. 'If you are so certain Mr Lindsay has worked out his scheme, what is Mr Lindsay lazing around at his plantation for?'

'Transport,' said Mx Greenwing.

'They have *Saudade*, and probably a fleet of agarwood boats.'

'Yes, they do. But the Lyonne Order's whisper network said he was after a different kind of vessel.'

The finder's face remained as still as a pool of water, but one eye twitched. Mx Greenwing reached into her pocket and dropped an irregular-sized bulb of metal and teakwood on the table, before continuing.

'It appears Brother Lindsay contacted a shipwright of our

mutual acquaintance to organize the delivery of a very particular boat of a most ancient construction. *Velleity* it was named – an antique vessel owned by a merchant in Garfish Point.'

'A boat from Fiction?'

'Yes,' said Mx Greenwing. 'An old tub from Fiction, when he owns so many new ones. It made me prick my ears.'

Chalice picked up the bulb Mx Greenwing had discarded. Arden caught the word *Velleity* inscribed in silver inlay.

'Why,' Chalice exclaimed, 'this is a starter handle for an electric motor!'

The tic almost closed Mx Greenwing's eye this time. '*Velleity* had an accident five days ago,' she said. 'A weak hull. Such a shame. There were only a few of her vintage ever made.'

Chalice stared at the other woman. 'Did this weak hull happen before or after you became aware of this odd request?'

'Accidents happen.'

'I'm sure.' She sucked her teeth. 'A shame, such a sudden sinking after she'd run for two hundred years.'

Mr Absalom nodded, and added, 'It was unfortunate, yes. Brother Lindsay still wants an electric boat from the era of the Saint, though.'

Mx Greenwing continued. 'The good ship *Velleity* had a motor that was built back in the days of the Saint of the Islands. It was powered by piles of copper, zinc and sodium. She had been launched in the same era as the un-piloted ghost ships that bring the rockblood from the Sainted Isles to the Fiction and South Lyonnian shores. There is one other craft like this.'

She tapped on one rib of *Sonder*'s old hull.

'*Sonder*, and Arden together,' Chalice spoke quietly. 'An irresistible gift. And what will you receive in return, Brother Absalom, if you were to offer these tasty morsels to Brother Lindsay? He will see this gift as suspicious.'

'I have a coin of instruction. My freedom from him writ upon it. I give these things to Brother Lindsay, and then he will absolve me of my debts to the Order.'

What happened next happened so quickly it caught Arden

completely by surprise. Chalice kicked Arden off her chair and had jumped over the table before she even hit the ground. Mr Absalom grunted and jumped to his feet, but not before Chalice had slipped behind him, wrapped a garrotte of wire about his neck and tightened until he cried out.

Mx Greenwing flung her astrolabe an instant later, and it whizzed past Chalice's ear, sticking a full half-inch into the pitch of *Sonder*'s exposed ribs.

'What in heaven's name is going on?' screamed Mrs Cordwain, prayers forgotten.

Struggling to keep up, Arden dug about in her dress for the pistol, ready to point it at Mx Greenwing, who now flourished a pair of extremely sharp blades.

The tic in the finder's face had stopped. 'Let him go, Quarry.'

'Drop the knives first,' Arden retorted, but it came out with a croak, and she was shaking so hard it was unlikely she could have aimed true anyway. Besides, the hammer wasn't even back. Mx Greenwing could throw her knives and kill Chalice before she could fire.

Mx Greenwing looked at Mr Absalom, who nodded almost imperceptibly. She placed her blades – weighted throwing knives, Arden realized – on the table. Mrs Cordwain's protests had subsided somewhat as Orphen and Fred struggled to keep her calm.

The clattering brought Mr Berry down from the wheelhouse. He looked at them all, grunted in exasperation, and then wisely retreated.

Arden got to her feet, still holding the quivering pistol. *Sonder*'s rocking wasn't helping; her outstretched arm bounced like a pendulum.

'I admit this could have come out better,' Mr Absalom rasped. 'But it has to look real.'

'Real?' Chalice snarled, her fingers still tight on the garrotte. 'Why make it anything else?'

Mr Absalom twisted his head as much as he could. 'Sister Quarry, in what world do I only hold *one* coin? When I make

my great catch that absolves me of all the debts I have in life'
– he paused to take a breath, grimacing in pain before continuing
– 'it will be for bigger fry than Brother Lindsay, I can assure you.'

Chalice didn't budge, but there was something in the way
Mx Greenwing held herself, a kind of surrender, that made up
Arden's mind. Mr Absalom was telling the truth.

'It's all right, Chalice.'

'Arden?'

'If he'd wanted us delivered in exchange for coin, it would
have been all too easy to do. That iron boat out there could
hold ten men, but he only came with two.' She put the pistol
away, wincing, for the thoughtless activity had caused her hands
to ache.

Cautiously and reluctantly, Chalice let Mr Absalom go. To
his credit he did not gloat or say anything provocative, only
rubbed his neck and nodded at Arden.

'Well. I think tea is in order after such activity,' he said.

Orphen and Fred nudged each other, but it ended up being
Orphen doing the work, clattering the kettle on the hob so
much Arden debated whether she should tell him to sit down
and let Chalice do it. If she hadn't mistrusted her hands so
much, she might have even made the tea herself.

'Right then,' Mx Greenwing said, not showing the slightest
sign of being flustered. She went to the wall and plucked her
astrolabe pendant out of the pitch and sat herself down again.
'We have two lifeboats aboard my vessel, both with motors
and enough rockblood fuel to reach the coast. Miss Quarry,
you and your pilgrim guests will take one.'

'But—' Chalice started to say.

'Miss Quarry, seek shelter along the coast until we are done.
There is a military fort due north by ten miles.'

'What about Arden?'

'Arden Beacon will take the other with Mr Berry, in order
for us to deliver her to Mr Lindsay's plantation shore.'

Chalice shook her head. 'I cannot possibly leave Arden alone.
Not after almost losing her the first time.'

'Don't worry, Chalice. We will be around.' Mx Greenwing winked at her, and even in her righteousness Chalice blushed, for Mx Greenwing was especially handsome, and the lady Lion was not entirely made of stone.

Mr Absalom rubbed his thumb along the silk map. 'Five days. This is all the time I will allow Mr Lindsay of your company Mx Beacon. On the sixth I will come for you.'

Arden thought about arguing, but by then the cornered despair of her inevitable situation had quite sucked the fight out of her. 'What will be the manner of your rescue? I cannot help thinking that I'll practically be a prisoner by then, if not dead.'

'I shall not go into detail, but you will know of my rescue when it happens. Hopefully you'll have many a tale to tell about my brother's plans. Get him talking, Arden. He does love to gloat.'

Arden sighed. 'All this plotting is very nice, but have you for a moment considered that Bellis Harrow might just get in my head and have me blubber out my real intentions?'

'Which is why I shall not reveal all my methods.' He leaned forward conspiratorially. 'Besides, I understand you have a certain invulnerability to Bellis' wiles.'

Chalice's face was still flushing with protest. 'I must fully oppose this, Ozzy. It's irresponsible, sending an untrained agent into that nest of vipers.'

'There is no training we could give someone for this particular task. It is something Mx Beacon needs to do on her own. We won't abandon you, Arden Beacon, you have my word. When you return after the exchange, I will have both a letter and the coin of instruction for you to use. These tokens will grant you freedom, forever. All doors will open to your life, your career, and to your healing. No Lyonnian official will refuse any request you may make of them.'

Had Mr Absalom been so sincere when he'd made similar promises to Bellis? He'd been with her a long time, and the Island Queen had not suspected him, not once. Arden sank deeper into her despairing pit.

'What about Jonah?' she asked.

Chalice put her arm about Arden's waist. 'We'll keep him safe with us until you return.'

The kettle whistled. Mr Absalom smiled. 'Now that's settled, I suggest that after tea and supper we all get our sleep. Tomorrow at first light we will find our position. Sister Quarry and our esteemed guests will take the first lifeboat to the shore five miles north of the plantation, and we will deliver the second, bearing you, Arden Beacon, to my ambitious Lion brother.'

8

Arden woke

Arden woke suddenly in the deep nighttime. All it took was a noise, a wrinkle in her awareness, and her Lightkeeper senses would not allow her to sleep.

One week. Seven days. She could be dead at the end of it – would be, most likely.

Someone coughed nearby, one of the young pilgrims from the sound of it. Her hammock creaked as it moved with the gentle yaw of the ship. The blanket strung up across the ribs of the hull around her hammock afforded her little privacy, for *Sonder* had been fitted out more like a cargo vessel with a cavernous hull, unlike the rooms found below decks on *Saudade*.

A faint crimson glow showed through the porthole. Crimson, as if something was on fire . . .

The plankton, she reminded herself. They were in the southern reaches of her home country now, the Firetide Coast. Alone out of all the luminescent creatures of the water, the plankton shoals of the Firetide Coast could glow red rather than blue-green, and sailors reported the ocean alight like banked coals for a few scant days each year. For them it was a warning to keep clear. The merfolk, on the other hand, loved such waters, for the leviathans swam north during the wintertime to calve, and the plankton was the food of large things, though other predators followed, like the small kraken and the giant sturgeon.

The blanket-wall trembled as a body moved on the other side.

'I'm awake,' she said softly.

A hand moved the blanket away. Jonah stood there in the lantern light, watching her. Seawater droplets gleamed off his bare shoulders like pearls. There was a silver gleam in his eyes as the whites reflected the half-light. He was naked, pale as a fish, his earliest tattoos – swirled layers of chevrons like sea-serpent scales – darkening his hips and sliding up his flanks. In the cold lamplight the images appeared to move, like gills fronding in the coldwater current.

Why do you stay, spirit?

She did not speak the words, but Arden suspected he heard it in his new, strange way. On first reuniting on her cousin's island, she had known far too well what a delicate condition Jonah was in. He had suffered a full season of torture under Bellis Harrow, but at least then he was still a man with his own mind. A hurt mind, nonetheless, wracked with guilt over what he'd needed to do in order to escape his monstrous wife.

But still him. Still Jonah.

And then he followed her cousin Stefan's funeral boat into the sea.

Arden had thought he'd drowned. She'd made her peace with it during the dark hour on the islet beach that she waited for his return. Had been relieved when he'd finally risen from the waves.

But what came out of the water was not him. Oh, he wore Jonah's face, but the passenger was altogether a different creature. A half-man, voiceless and changed. Even his features seemed smeared, like a face glimpsed briefly behind porthole glass.

'Sometimes I think it's worse that you brought his body back,' she said. 'It hurts me more to see him like this.'

He slunk next to her hammock, put one hand on the eyelet

hook. Slight remnants of humanity clung to Jonah – the way he cut short the gingering hair on his face and head and cast the remnant brown locks from his scalp into the water in the deepwater way, but he had done so clumsily, so there were nicks upon his scalp and cheek, clumps of dark red hair left behind. He'd groomed himself the way a thing unused to air mimicked breathing. Pretending to be human but useless at it.

It was his indifferent imitation that frightened Arden the most.

His face darted close, not to kiss but like some half-living thing remembering human scent, sniffing her out.

'Have you a name, even?' she asked, and tried to touch him, but he darted back. The spirit that enlivened him was not interested in human contact.

He bent to kiss her then, a sliding kiss, even his tongue tasting of salt. His lips were so cold. She reached up and clung to him, trying to bring warmth back into his body, but it was as if she were on a thermocline precipice, a great welling fall of warmth diving into ice.

I will break this enchantment. His eyes will become clear, and he will return to himself and remember that he loved me.

Jonah removed himself and rocked back on his haunches, watching her with an ancient, inhuman expression. Then he was gone, leaving only the curtain shuddering in his wake.

'Wait!'

She twisted herself out of the hammock, grabbed her coat and followed him out onto the deck in her bare feet.

A wind had kicked up, the squally remains of a storm further out to sea. All about her the water eddied in scarlet stripes where the waves peaked, the disturbed carpet of luminous plankton flashing bright in the almost complete darkness. A tiny sliver of moon was not enough to quash their brilliance. The iron boat had lashed itself to *Sonder*. It sat lower in the water than *Sonder* and the biggest waves washed straight over the iron decks.

Jonah sat naked on the prow of his grandfather's ship like

a wraith, haunted and beautiful in the lamplight. He was utterly and incomprehensibly different to all that she held familiar, from the slight crookedness of his features to his deep-set eyes.

He watched her approach with no more than a limpid patience.

'I can only imagine what keeps you around, Jonah,' she said. 'If you have been listening, then you know I have been instructed to find out where Mr Lindsay intends to take Bellis and Miah.'

If he understood or not, he showed no sign. His jaw worked as if he was going to speak, but no sound came out.

Finally her resolve broke.

'Oh, damn it, Jonah! Are you in there? Show me a sign!'

His face rimmed in sympathy and his hand reached out, stroking her face with the gentleness of something very old touching something very young. Or the spirit did, the lich that had taken over his body. Arden pressed her cheek against his palm.

A soft footstep fell behind her. 'So the sea takes back her own.'

She turned about, and found that Mr Absalom had joined them on the deck.

'Bellis told me once,' Mr Absalom went on, 'of her fiancé, Vernon Justinian, who kept a specimen jar in his library, the pickled remains of a curiosity – a monster born from a twin birth. The other child was normal. That living child was Jonah Riven.'

'For goodness' sakes,' Arden snapped. 'I was having a private moment.'

'Would be better off if you left him,' Mr Absalom said. 'Clay City is no place for curiosities.'

Huffing at the rudeness of him, Arden cast a last hopeless glance at Jonah before taking Mr Absalom's elbow and leading him to the other side of the boat.

Once they were alone she spoke in a low voice: 'I don't care to play this game of yours. You are aware the problem of Bellis can be solved with a bullet between her eyes? Give one to Mr Lindsay too, if there's another left in the barrel.'

'Would be kinder to give the bullet to your fish out of water with his broken mind.'

'I'm not giving up on him, Mr Absalom. I can find a doctor in Clay, someone who understands trauma. There are sanguis psychologists who can—'

'—Who can tell you what I will tell you. Jonah Riven has given away too much of himself to the water. It is a deepwater injury, the kind so common in this place where they worship the ocean. Our physicians cannot heal it.'

'*Common*blood physicians may not be able to heal him, but a sanguis could.'

Mr Absalom sighed. 'Do you know the legends of this place? Surely the signallers collect such superstitions when working on the Portside docks. Late winter is Firetide Season for south Lyonne, when the Suitor of Tides might yet allow a dead man to return from his watery grave.'

'I have heard versions of that tale, yes,' she replied sullenly, remembering Chalice's words back on Equus, of the shorefolk and their own superstitions about the water. At any other time she'd have accused Mr Absalom of being facetious, but they'd both seen miracles in this past season.

He turned his face outwards, an air of nostalgia softening his remote, noble features. 'These brief, cold days have even the stoutest seafarer asking for a boon under his breath. They imagine the veils of our world and the lands of abyssal magic are thin tonight, especially among those who wield their bodies and blood as payment.' He gestured at her gloved hands. 'Make a wish, bloodworker.'

'Well then, I wish not to be dead tomorrow, Ozymandias. Or dead next week. That's all.'

'Then don't stay up too long. Such a wish will be demanding, and you will need all your strength to see it through to the end.'

9

By nautical morning

By nautical morning Mx Greenwing made the pilgrim lads turn the anchor winch, and once *Sonder* was free, she instructed Mr Berry to take over the wheelhouse so he might follow her as she steered the iron boat. They tacked a course west, towards the coast. Even before the sun rose in the east, the air began to exhibit a peculiar, almost buttery warmth.

Under her navy broadcloth dress, Arden sweated. She toyed with taking off her krakenskin coat, but a wave of superstition made her keep it on. The coat had seen her through any number of calamities. Within it she felt protected, embraced almost. Without it . . . well, any number of misfortunes could befall her. Five days was almost an eternity when it was in the company of people who despised her.

So onwards they travelled, into the ballooning, almost effervescent heat. The part of South Lyonne they called the Firetide Coast was well known for its strange, almost tropical atmosphere. The cold, wet currents from the south met with the milder climes of the north, but for a few hundred miles the dry winds from the arid eastern uplands came over the region and made that narrow part of the country a climatological island of heat and moisture.

The water tended to be rougher on the boundaries, too, and though the coast was not in view, both ships kicked and rolled. Mr Berry kept a few lengths behind the iron boat, a feat not too difficult, for slow *Sonder* was not powered to go more than strolling pace.

A hot, slimy fog-wall bore down upon them as the sun fully rose.

'We might not see it, but we'll be within a stone's throw of land soon,' Mx Greenwing called over on the shortwave. 'Time to evacuate all unnecessary players.'

'Don't tongue-lash me darling, because no, I don't like it either,' Chalice said, joining Arden on the deck. She stomped her feet out of habit to get them moving in the morning air, even though this air was as sticky as warm blood. Dark circles smudged under her eyes.

'I'm glad I'm not the only one to not sleep well.'

'By the Devil's Rear End, I should have agreed with Mrs Cordwain to sell this tug at the first opportunity. Should have tried to take a land route. Lyonne has rail and roads, we needn't have stuck to the ocean like marine savages.'

'They would still have caught up with us.'

'Yes, all the while exhorting that you should throw yourself like a diseased corpse over the walls of Mr Lindsay's little operation,' Chalice grumped.

'Will you promise me something?'

'Anything.'

'Look after Jonah,' Arden said. 'If I should not make it out, you must take him to Clay. Find him help. Don't let him live like . . . like he is now.'

'Darling, you will be doing that come next Maunday, I don't have to make such a promise.'

After they'd spent the morning transferring a week's worth of supplies to the little lifeboat that sufficed for a tender, *Sonder* was ready to become the peace offering. Mr Lindsay would only pay close attention to the iron boat and his prized electrical gift from Mr Absalom. The hot, heavy mist would help Chalice and the others slip away unnoticed.

Arden knew she would feel better once the lifeboat was gone. Her own survival was one thing to negotiate, but the worry of others was something completely different. It weighed on her like a stone, and she thought that this was what it must be like to have a child: that constant alertness and concern, forever.

Oh, she thought, thank all the gods that I am not beset with such a condition.

With people, supplies and a rockblood motor perched at the rear, the lifeboat was smaller than Arden had expected it to be. The craft wallowed low in the water. She braced herself for protests from the Hillsiders, but to her surprise Mrs Cordwain did not have to be encouraged to get in. The pilgrim boys followed along with the submissiveness of converted souls.

'You'll have to do the rowing, boys,' Chalice instructed them from the stern, her elbow slung as casually over the tiller it was as if they were going for a Hewsday punt along the Clay Mouth in their church-day finest. 'We can't use the motor until the exchange happens, if at all.'

Arden looked around anxiously for Jonah, only to find him surfacing in the water nearby. He bobbed up onto the bow, much to Chalice's displeasure, and it was with both relief and love that Arden heard Chalice scolding Jonah for his tardiness.

'Stay safe,' Arden cried.

'The same to you!' Chalice returned, then barked, 'Pull away, boys! We have a day on the ocean before we reach land.'

Arden watched the lifeboat buck away with her heart in her mouth. Stay safe, she murmured to herself. Stay safe until I return.

Mr Berry climbed back into *Sonder*'s wheelhouse. The motor churned up the water as he called from the open window. 'Fog looks like it's letting up ahead, we'll be in view of the coast soon.'

Mx Greenwing winched down the last lifeboat from the iron

ship, this one an old dinghy with an engine in its central bilge well. She had perhaps one good year left in her before the borers and barnacles replaced the wood entirely.

At once Arden saw it was a craft to be discarded. At least Chalice and Jonah were making their way on the better boat.

'Will it stay afloat?' she wondered aloud.

Mr Absalom said, 'It only needs to make it to the coast. When I come for you, it will not be by water.'

He had drawn up next to her while she had been preoccupied. So, finally he was giving up some of his rescue plan. 'I don't care if you fly me out, Ozymandias, as long as it's on time. Us Clay Portside signallers don't care for tardiness.'

'I never forget I'm dealing with a Seamaster's Guild member,' he replied with a wink, before opening up the canvas bag he'd been holding. 'May I?'

The bag contained a length of rope, a slippery rockblood fibre that was easy to untie, even when wet. 'Part of the disguise.'

Arden exhaled and pushed out her wrists. 'I'm ready.'

'I'll keep it loose. When we get close, pull on the running end, here. It creates a tight pair of loops you can get out of, like this—'

He displayed the rope restraint upon himself and let her practise a couple of times to make sure she had it before he tightened the rope on her for good.

'There, that looks—'

He did not have time to finish as a great crash skipped *Sonder*'s entire deck sideways, throwing Arden and Mr Absalom back into the trilobite pots.

Mr Berry screamed—

—and from the corner of her eye Arden watched the man be thrown out of the wheelhouse in a shower of broken glass. The front end of the ship swung high into the air and Arden saw for one terrifying second the bow vertical against the sky . . .

. . . before the deck dropped out from beneath them and she was underwater.

A long, desperate silence.

Water filled her ears, and her body jolted from the cold shock of water everywhere, including under the coat she'd not tied properly.

There was not even time to panic. Something moved past her with such a displacement of water and with such force she felt she had swallowed half the ocean. She would have drowned had she not kicked up towards the light. Salt streamed into her eyes, blinding and disorienting her . . .

. . . only at the last second did her senses tell her to surface not into open water but into an air cavity afforded by the bilge well of the rotted old lifeboat.

She took several petralactose-stinking breaths before her head cleared and she could properly understand what had happened. They'd been struck by something huge. Had they been moving she'd have put it down to a collision with debris, a pylon or a wreck below the waterline.

They had not been moving.

A delicate light from her krakenskin coat filtered up through the darkness. Seconds later, another face emerged next to her. Mr Absalom's lieutenant, Mr Berry. He stared at her with wide eyes, pale as a ghoul. Blood leaked from a cut in his head.

'What hit us?' he spluttered.

'I don't know. Did you see anyone out there? Mr Riven? Mr Absalom? Is anyone alive?'

'I didn't see,' he said. 'One second we were cresting a wave' – he spat salty water – 'and the next . . . something hit the boat!'

Yes, something had struck them. She needed to collect herself. Not panic. It could be just a rogue leviathan. They were in Firetide waters, the monsters were everywhere. And Jonah . . .

No, Jonah would be of no help here. Through blinks she saw Mr Berry huff with horror in the low light.

'What's wrong, sir?'

'Something. Something's in the water!' He began to kick and shriek. 'In the water! In the water!'

'Mr Berry, calm down!'

'In the water! In the water!' He continued to kick wildly, spinning little circles in the bilge well, splashing Arden and blinding her.

'Mr Berry! Your panic isn't helping,' she shouted. 'Stop it!'

Then, as abruptly as he'd started, he stopped.

'Let's get out from under here and find the others,' she said, relieved and shaking at the same time. His terror had been infectious, and she tasted her fear like metal in her mouth. 'Sea-things don't normally like the flesh of men.' She spat out more water. 'A bite is usually accidental.'

'I think something bit me.'

'Where?'

'I don't know,' he said. 'I can't feel it.'

'Then it is your imagination.'

He opened his mouth and blood welled over his bottom lip. 'Something bit me. I can't feel it!'

'Mr Berry—'

He grabbed her collar, and she pushed him away with a yelp of alarm.

'*I CAN'T FEEL IT!*' he screamed.

'Mr Berry, I—!'

But there was next to nothing in his grip. His eyes looked towards an unseen, faraway place and she saw him tilt and said his name once more before he inverted completely . . . to expose a torso bitten completely in half.

The nubs of his spine showed white against the pink meat of his flesh and the blue clot of his liver. His torn organs fronded in the water like ragged lace.

Arden opened her mouth in wordless disgust before a slop of water sent Mr Berry sinking down and out of sight. His fingers grazed her hip and she felt them flexing abortively at her hem as he sank, trying to live, pleading silently for her to help him . . .

Then he was gone. She was alone under the boat.

The smell of spilt petralactose filled the cavity, and the chill that she'd ignored for the past few minutes came thudding back so hard she feared she'd vomit from cold. Great shakes wracked her body. She could barely hold her head above water.

It was still very early in the morning. Sunlight had not yet been able to penetrate the black water, and now the craft's empty weight seemed to crush her towards the icy depths. Her legs dangled into black nothingness. She needed to get out from underneath the upturned boat and out of the water, but she couldn't bear putting her head underneath again.

Arden felt something knock against one flailing boot. Something that slid like sandpaper alongside her calf, with a great slinking weight behind it.

She tugged her knees up as high as she could, but it returned, stronger. That same vast expanse of displacement accompanied by a forced pressure, belying a great mass, and bulk. The tiny space locked her in like a tomb. She could not bear the prison of the bilge well any more than she could bear the threat from below.

A flash caught her attention. Something was down in the depths, a massive sinuous thing festooned in bioluminescence and electric arcs. *Jonah*, she thought with a ferocious hope. *I need you now.*

But she knew better than to depend on wishes.

With every ounce of fortitude she had, she took a deep breath and dived underneath the capsized boat, flailed through the grey water and emerged gasping into the dull morning light. From her position she could see no other craft, only patches of sunrise-bruised sky and the fog giving way to rainclouds.

The rain came in stinging sheets upon Arden's face. Frozen, she clung to the wooden cleats in the side, willing the boat to turn about so she might catch a view of *Sonder*. The waves obliged, lifting her up until she saw it – the plume of smoke rising from it, the iron boat already half submerged and sinking.

'What's happening?' The words fell from her lips. 'Mr Absalom, where are you?'

The upturned boat juddered, and she realized at once that

another craft had knocked into it. She pulled her entire body down as far as it would go beneath the waterline, but her krakenskin coat would not allow her to sink.

A figure stepped onto the flat surface of the lifeboat's hull then. She saw bare feet, ankles laced in deepwater tattoos, a belt of rope and leggings of stingray-skin, half cured and as rough as sandpaper, and the naked torso of a man, striped with blood.

Standing above her, his bruised eyes filled with rage, was Miah Anguis.

Her deepwater husband.

10

He didn't touch her

He didn't touch her. Not at first, though there was a moment when she expected him to drag her up and onto the hull. A rockblood-motored longboat pulled up alongside them, and there was Mr Lindsay. The Lion was a small, slight man with a beautiful and ageless face, yet a soul so cavernous with malice and ambition that Arden wondered how she had not noticed the true horror of him before this moment. Two Clay-born men sat in the longboat with him, along with a South Lyonnian wearing a necklace of polished wood chips.

Arden tried to edge out of Mr Lindsay's sight.

'Mr Anguis,' the Lion said, 'what of your cousin, Jonah Riven?'

Miah sucked in a breath, irritated by their arrival. 'Hasn't surfaced. My serpent took him deep and made a meal of him.'

Arden pressed her cheek to the overturned boat. *They don't know where Jonah is.* His disappearance could mean anything. She had seen Jonah survive almost an hour beneath the water. Granted, he had not been the same when he came out, but she comforted herself with the knowledge that there was little more damage that the water could do at this point.

Surreptitiously she looked about. The iron boat had disappeared, but *Sonder* was still floating where Arden had been tossed from the deck, now with one broken window in the wheelhouse.

'Inform me when you have proof of death, and then bring in our replacement boat,' Mr Lindsay said.

Miah grunted in response, not a yes or no. Belatedly, Arden remembered what Mr Absalom had told her. Mr Lindsay had healed him of the sight-injury Arden had caused. The deepwater man was beholden to the Lion now.

'And could you kindly bring your wife on board. She might not think I've noticed her, hiding back there, but I have.'

Miah glared down at Arden, and even submerged in water with the waves slapping her face she could smell the hatred coming off of him in great buffets. Despite his bruised eyes he had not changed in the weeks since she'd seen him last. He was still powerfully built compared to Jonah, his features ragged and merciless, giving him the sort of expression cliffs might obtain when the weather eroded the stone to look like a human face. She wanted to protest weakly that their disagreement was now based on nothing more than a memory. Had Mr Lindsay not healed him? They had no argument now, right?

He slid into the water.

'Turn around. Get on your back.'

A brusque command. No sooner had she turned before he slid his arms around her torso and began towing her as he swam in a powerful sideways crawl.

His skin burned hot. In fact, everything about him burned furnace-bright, as if his very bones were molten. By the time they reached Mr Lindsay's craft she was certain he'd left scorch marks across her chest. At her release, a pair of tattooed arms dragged her out of the churning salt and into the boat.

There she flopped in the bilge, exhausted, like the jenny-ray the pilgrims had caught the day before.

Mr Lindsay looked down at Arden with a tranquil curiosity. 'Are you very cold, dear? Your coat seems warm enough but even krakenskin can't keep out the water. A flame-trammelled woman might survive long in this chilly slop, but even fire meets its match somewhere.'

'May God curse you,' she said, but it came out in a whisper, and mostly despairing.

'Curse me indeed, if He has not done so already. But at least He gave me the forethought to investigate exactly who had control over *Sonder*.'

Saudade's longboat – as she now recognized it to be – cut through the fog, and soon it scraped the sandy shore. The other men jumped out to secure it, waiting for them to get out so they might drag the craft further up onto the beach.

A stiff breeze was up, one with an acrid undertow to it – not fresh but stale, like air that had never seen sunlight.

'Come.' Mr Lindsay held out his hand to Arden in an offer of assistance. Arden slapped him away. She tried to stand up herself. But the chill had wrecked her to her bones and she found she could only wallow in the bottom of the longboat. When she tried to hoist herself over the side, she fell ignominiously back into the water. The foamy wash of the tide covered her head, and she would have been content to stay there, had not those same arms from before scooped her out.

'I'm too hot,' she said, trying to fight Miah off then finding herself too weary to do so.

'You're freezing.'

He carried her over the last few paces until the sand became dry, then propped her upright. She saw him in double vision. Miah Anguis, her nightmare.

A flush of crimson spread across his bare, squid-inked chest. 'You left me blinded.'

Arden pulled the krakenskin tight about her. 'You were going to kill Jonah . . . and me!'

He let his hand fall on hers, and for an awful moment she thought he might tear open the coat on the beach before divesting her of the rest of her decency, but instead he rubbed his thumb over the sharp edge of the copper ring on her finger. In their time apart she'd tried to remove the ring; no doubt he could feel the abrasions where she'd failed to budge it . . .

'My deepwater bride.'

She froze as his hand moved slowly to her shoulder, before taking her neck in a caress. The grip turned hard when the fingers wrenched her hair. His newly sighted eyes had an animal glimmer within them.

'My fucking deepwater wife,' he said. 'Stand up.'

He yanked her upright. She made herself meet him eye to eye. Don't show submission, she thought wildly. He will hate you even more for that.

'I never consented to marry you,' she hissed. It came out in a chatter when it should have been defiance. Her very bones ached.

'No?' He bent his head to catch her in a crushing kiss. She'd have bitten his tongue had Miah not released her at once. Arden reeled back, her nape smarting.

'That kiss was for our marriage,' he said. 'This is for my fucking eyes.'

Arden had only a second's grace to see it coming. The back of his hand, the wallop of bright light at its contact with the side of her face, and the sand rising up to meet her.

11

There was a halfway memory

There was a halfway memory – mostly because she had been flat on her back preparing for another blow – of two figures jumping at Miah and dragging him back while he grinned madly. 'You're still my fucking *wife*! He wouldn't touch you after, would he? Huh? My ring on your fucking finger means you will always belong to me!'

He wrestled free of the guards but kept his distance.

Mr Lindsay approached Arden as she sat in a petrified silence on the white sand. In all his threats and bluster, Miah had never once been this violent towards her. She had entered darker territory and she wasn't prepared.

With a disconnect born from fright she heard Mr Lindsay's curt voice telling Miah that it was far too dangerous for him to be in the presence of the sanguis who had blinded him in the first place. Miah would have to wait until he'd calmed down. Mr Lindsay could later assess what kind of control she had over him.

Over him? Oh, of course. There had been a brief moment where Miah had fallen in love with Arden – or some other silly word that described the conflagration that had ignited between them.

Laughter bubbled out of her like hysterical sobs. So much for her saving Clay and all its citizens now! Mr Absalom and Mx Greenwing were most likely dead. Chalice and her rowboat could not have covered enough water to have made it clear of Miah's leviathan. Right now they too were either in their Heaven or taking their places in the Court of the Deepwater King.

'Oh, my dear,' Mr Lindsay said after he'd finished his scolding of Miah. 'A brute of a thing to do, hitting a woman. I'll make sure he understands what line he has crossed.'

Arden heeled the tears of pain from her eyes with her hands and with all her effort stood up. Her ankle throbbed horridly in her boot. Mr Lindsay knelt to re-tie the damp laces. 'Is it broken?'

'Just twisted, I think,' she said mulishly, and wondered if the joy of kicking him in the head would match the punishment and pain that would likely follow.

'Best we go to shelter,' Mr Lindsay said as he stood and brushed the sand from his knees. 'When the rain stops, you'll not believe the change. The heat is horrendous. Like a steam bath.'

Mr Lindsay clicked his fingers, summoning the men over so they might fetch a chair, which he guided her into, making her sit on a cushion of damp, lumpy velvet. He put a blanket over her shoulders, rough but dry, and though she wanted nothing more than to throw all his little briberies back in his face, she clung to it for warmth.

'Where am I going?'

'To my house.' He pointed towards the cliff.

The forests that grew on the cliffside along the Firetide Coast were almost impenetrable, great tangling battlements of ancient cycads, tree-ferns, aloe-wood and ginkgo. Arden could make out the giant epiphyte fronds on the larger trees, dripping down off the trunks like paintings left out in the rain. She remembered from her childhood bestiary studies that there were fauna in these forests that the zoologists had struggled to catalogue, for the growth was too thick and any explorer venturing too far within the verdant tangle never found a way out.

A rough track wended along the cliffs, a northern route that looked too perilous for anything bigger than a small automobile and an iron constitution.

And then she saw the plantation house through the trees.

However impossibly, settlers from generations ago had managed to fight their way into the forest and clear enough space for a collection of buildings. Placed precariously on the cliffside, the estate was not quite a village but could definitely be considered a compound. Creepers wreathed every balcony and structural pillar, as if the forest was in the process of devouring the large central house. Walls once painted white had faded to yellow, or else they were fronded in lichen the colour of sulphur. The entire compound seemed constructed out of the very treetops.

So this was Mr Lindsay's estate: an oudwood plantation. The estate seemed at odds with the man who owned it. Mr Lindsay was the sort of person who seemed to wander agelessly through the earth like the fey stories of old, and Arden would have more believed that he lived in a barrow rather than a house.

The men hauled her upright in her dining-chair litter and began an arduous trek up the hewn side of a fog-wreathed cliff. The men's feet sometimes slid on the leaf-litter, making her cling perilously to the carved and gilded chair arms. This was not the low, scrubby saltbush of Fiction, or the pine-timbered arcadia of Stefan's island. This place had a rotting fecundity, a thick, organic miasma of hidden, secret things.

Odd lights and glows filled the darkness.

At the top of their trek, the men put Arden's chair down to catch their breath. The thick, fern-topped trees seemed to lean in, damp and smothering. She reached out and touched a stone outcrop furred with green, and her handprint remained, the depression filling with water.

At last they reached the creeper-wreathed main house.

'This is the mansion I was born in,' Mr Lindsay said, in

between breaths. He mopped his brow with a handkerchief. 'My father was a man of some standing, my brothers ready to inherit a fortune. They are dead now.'

At one frowsy balcony overhead a shadow moved and Arden spotted tatty lace, pale hair, and a face washed out into vulpine thinness.

Bellis Harrow.

'She will not hurt you,' Mr Lindsay said, noticing where Arden's attention lay. 'She has been asked to behave herself while we prepare her for her next evolution. The geological phenomena of this place will help keep her talents under control, more manageable.'

'How can a place do that?' she said, and straight away regretted asking. With Mr Absalom gone, there was no need to gather information.

Mr Lindsay stroked the rose-and-thorn brooch at his scarf. 'Someone was here before her, a long time ago. Moved things around a bit. Under the soil. The rocks are rich in metals and the calcium in the plankton adds an odd quality to the sand. They used to make glass here. Telescope lenses, delicate instruments. All the geology combines into a chemical stupor, puts a lid on our Queen's worst impulses.'

Two servants carried the litter into the house's dim foyer and placed Arden's chair onto the floor. Arden looked around cautiously at the small room lined in whitewashed salvagewood. Faded photographs in thick, wooden frames crowded upon the peeling-paper walls, along with odd curios that belonged in a carnival museum. Dusty taxidermies of unknown animals, mounted skulls, hunting trophies. A map of a land she could not recognize, the paper gone yellow with age.

Arden slid out of the litter. Her ankle still smarted, but it held some weight. As she tested her balance, a crackling of footsteps on the woven floor-mats alerted Arden to the woman approaching behind her. Even before Arden turned around, she smelled the sweat and spices – almost medicinal, as if covering a wound that had never quite healed.

The woman's drawn face averted from Arden's gaze in a way both servile and hostile.

'I am here to give you assistance. I am Mrs Valley. Come with me, please.'

As Mr Lindsay had disappeared with most of the men, she nodded. 'All right, Mrs Valley, I will come with you.'

Arden followed Mrs Valley at a limp up the stairs of the split-level structure and into a shabby, wicker-filled guest room that smelled of damp and the same decayed wood that permeated the forest. A suspicious mould grew in between the plaster ceiling cornices.

'This is where you will stay,' Mrs Valley said, curling her upper lip. 'With your husband.'

'He's not—' Arden started to say, then gave up. As if the servant cared any more than she did.

The posts of the four-poster bed had swelled and peeled in the years it had been in this climate. The varnish on the wood cracked like a dried lake in high summer. Gauzy curtains surrounding the bed moved in the hot breeze from an open window.

'Undress,' said the servant woman.

'Excuse me?'

Mrs Valley thrust what looked like a dressing gown towards Arden, the thin, cotton wrap printed with carnivorous flowers. 'Your dress, please. I will have it cleaned. There will be more clothes in the wardrobe, some of which may fit.'

'Oh, of course.'

Feeling shy in front of a person who clearly hated her, Arden ducked behind a wicker divider and pulled the damp broadcloth uniform dress off her. The cotton wrap dress wound about her twice, and she tied it off with two bows. The sleeves were loose and long, hanging over her knuckles, but she had to admit that it probably better suited the sweltering heat.

Arden returned with her broadcloth dress folded and quickly took back the krakenskin coat.

'I'll keep this.'

'You will not need a coat here.'

'I do . . . uh . . . for sentimental reasons,' Arden said, trying to smile and hold tight at once. A sense of déjà vu hit her then, for less than a year ago she had held this coat to her chest while a man had tried to take it off her, as Mrs Valley attempted now.

Vernon Justinian, the Baron of the small coastal town of Vigil, seemed a world away from this estate, this place. Imagine, she thought. She had once thought him the worst kind of man, when he'd merely been an irritation.

Mrs Valley gave a sharp inhale of disapproval, then left without further complaint.

Once the guest door closed, Arden sat on the end of the bed, sore, exhausted and adrift. *What now?* she thought. *Where do I go from here? Escape?* She was days, weeks away from anywhere on foot, even with the semi-passable roads. Leaving the estate with all the guards was impossible, but fleeing down a singular road alone?

A motor vehicle then. If this place even had one that she could drive – and she had never driven a car.

A boat, if the boats weren't as guarded as the house.

Why did she even think of impossibilities. She was a prisoner. She had slammed up against a cage of her own stupidity. Oh, if only she'd told Mr Absalom to get off *Sonder*, and taken her chance with Clay Portside herself!

She crawled onto the top of the coverlet as a wave of exhaustion came over her, a tiredness so absolute that all she could do was sleep.

The scrape of furniture across the wood of the balcony made her startle.

She opened her eyes and a pair of yellow ones stared back at her.

'Devilment!' she shouted and fell off the bed in an effort to put as much distance between the creature and herself as possible.

A snake-thing hung pendulous from the poster bed cross-beam and opened its mouth to hiss, before a pair of wings flapped from its body. The creature would have been beautiful – a dragonet encrusted with coloured jewels – if not for the venom that dripped from its mouth to fall sizzling onto the broderie of the coverlet. Small, smoky embers burned like a deadly constellation under the dragonet's chin.

The scraping from the balcony grew more insistent, but there was a venomous beast between her and the wicker shutters. The sun had moved from where it had hung earlier in the morning, and the westerly light pinholed through the pattern.

'Ugh, get out. Get out!'

A full glass of water beside the bed caught a stray beam of light and Arden snatched it, throwing the water at the smouldering coverlet. The dragonet hissed and darted at her. A stream of venom splattered across the floor, and where it touched the flax mat, began to burn.

Arden grabbed a towel off the room divider and smothered the scorch.

'Oh, have you met one of my babies?'

She looked up from her work of not getting burned alive. The light moved over tatty, pale lace, and a peplum of feathers so denuded of their down that only the shafts and barbs remained.

Bellis' tiny body was topped by the crown of wire and sea-things that rested on her head. Mouth permanently twisted, her pale skin was slightly furred and Arden could have sworn volcanic ash still covered her.

Bellis Harrow, the Queen of the Islands.

Bellis reached up and took hold of the little winged snake about its waist, and it rewarded her with a great bite to her arm, a hundred needle-sharp teeth digging in.

'Devilment,' Arden said again in disgust.

'My dear Mr Lindsay had an antidote for the venom,' Bellis said calmly, almost oblivious to the blood welling up around the creature's mouth. 'I'm sure he gave you some. Or didn't.

Oh look, my pet realizes his mistake. That's right, my love,' she cooed to the snake. 'Don't bite now.'

It released Bellis' arm and flopped into an intoxicated stupor. Bellis let it fall to the floor like a discarded shoe and inspected her bite casually. 'Yes, it does sting a bit.'

Arden felt the scratch on the inside of her skull. Bellis was poking around. Had the woman not been restrained by the landscape, there might have been more to Bellis' probing than this static buzz, and had Arden not been immune to Bellis' talent, she'd have fallen quickly under the Queen's spell.

As much as Arden hated to give Mr Lindsay his due, he'd put the Queen of the Islands in a secure hold. Bellis' unbridled powers of *orientis* could turn people into slaves, mechanically following her every command. Unbridled powers, of course. Here she just chafed at the bit.

'What do you want, Harrow?'

'*Riven*,' Bellis hissed, just like her pet. 'Adulterer, I never divorced my husband.' She touched the four-poster bed frame and flicked at a peeling leaf of paint. 'Soon my friend Mr Lindsay is going to drain you of your sanguis blood and give it to me, and I shall bathe in it and become stronger than the Saint ever was.'

The death-threat should have landed hard, but Arden was actually curious. 'That's an odd promise for someone to make. How did Mr Lindsay even know I was coming?'

'Bellis!' In the doorway Mr Lindsay looked just the same as every other time Arden had seen him, dapper even when slightly sweaty and dishevelled. 'Leave our guest alone, dear. And please, if you must bring pets indoors, can you ensure they do not make a mess?'

Arden experienced the *flex* in her mind again, only this time it twisted towards Mr Lindsay. The Lion shook his head.

'Bellis, I will require all my facilities intact if we are to get to Clay in a manner that does not require creeping through the sewers and making intimate friends with the shit-worms.'

'And when is that supposed to happen, huh?' Bellis flounced

towards him. 'We've been here for days. She's *here* now. We could have been on our way already. Fucking bleed the bitch and be done with it!'

'As I have previously stated, it is delicate, and political. I will explain in time.'

'*Political*,' Bellis repeated mockingly, then uttered a Fictish curse-word that was untranslatable but the meaning of which was clear. She turned back to Arden, who stood as motionless as a statue, not wanting to chance either of these fiends turning their hostility towards her. 'Keep both eyes on this one, slattern,' Bellis said to her. 'He cannot be trusted.'

Mr Lindsay gave a fatherly, disappointed sigh as Bellis swept past him, then smiled apologetically at Arden.

'Once again, a meeting in less than ideal circumstances.'

He shut the guest-room door behind him, gave another sigh at the ruined towel and the venom-spotted coverlet.

'I am sorry for Bellis' rudeness. For everyone's rudeness, this morning.' He reached out for her face.

Arden would have stepped back if she could, but she was already pressed up against the bedpost. She grudgingly allowed him to inspect her, his hand cupping her chin to tilt this way and that as she silently cursed him for every moment of it.

'How is the bruise? Anguis did give you a bit of a wallop. I'm sorry again.'

'Not that sore.' Seeing that he had finished inspecting her, Arden shook his hand off and moved closer to the balcony. She sat on the edge of the bed, pretending to be casual, but her ankle had begun to throb again, and something in Bellis' words made her suspect that Mr Absalom had not been entirely truthful with her.

'Miah's backhand was an incorrigible act, and I despise thought-less violence. However, the man did have a legitimate grievance and it was best he get it out now rather than dwell on it.'

'Better for me or for you?'

'Indeed, Mx Beacon – or Mrs Anguis – you represent some-thing of a complication for me.'

'Not according to Bellis,' Arden said sulkily. 'Getting bled in service of her power. She's practically gleeful about it.'

'Oh, such world weariness! Have these few months jaded you so? I remember a young lady from Clay Portside who would have jumped at the chance to help the Lyonne Order.'

'I very much doubt the Order is behind whatever you are plotting.'

'You would be surprised. This reminds me: Mrs Valley found something while cleaning your dress.'

Arden blinked. With a sleight of hand, Mr Lindsay was suddenly holding the coin of instruction. *Her* coin. The one Mr Absalom had given her, worn down and unmistakable.

'You received this coin. What for?'

Arden swallowed a knot of anxiety. This moment was not supposed to have come, but here it was. She wondered about her wish, of surviving these few days. So much for that.

'Mr Absalom said I was to cooperate with him.'

'To what end?'

'To come to you.'

'And you agreed, knowing what waited for you here.'

'Jonah is sick,' she said vehemently. 'Mr Absalom said he could save him. My life for his!'

Miracle of miracles, she said nothing more and realized she had given enough for him to believe she was telling the truth. Mr Lindsay had promised her to Bellis. He truly believed Mr Absalom was bringing a gift, and that Arden was besotted enough to sacrifice herself for Jonah Riven.

'Strange thing to waste a coin on,' Mr Lindsay mused. 'Could easily have popped you in a sack and dragged you to my doorstep. Oh, well, you're here now, and cooperating.' He held out the coin. 'Don't lose it again, dear. This is the currency of your debt.'

Arden took the coin hesitantly as he sat next to her on the bed.

'On the matter of Bellis, it is true that your *evalescendi* talent, pitiful as it is, could help me immensely. However' – his hand fell upon hers – 'it has proven hard to entice Mr Anguis into following me with the same amount of enthusiasm. His motivations are simple, and his ambitions have never cast their net wider than his backwater island. I have struggled in finding what gift might bind him to me.'

He squeezed, and a line of pain shot up her arm. Arden tried to pull away but the agony of his grip only intensified.

'I would very much like Jeremiah Anguis kept happy,' Mr Lindsay said through the roaring pain. 'I prefer he not to be complicated with anything other than completing tasks I will set for him. If you hope to see your family again you will keep him happy.'

Only by sheer will did she hold herself together and not cry in front of him. When he let go, Mr Lindsay took a handkerchief out of his pocket and wiped the sweat from his hands, as if her agony had corrupted him somehow. Her heart was thundering. Oh, she could probably give him a wallop to remember, for she was taller than him and likely outweighed him by at least half a hundredweight, but her instincts for survival told her she needed to keep herself from making any mistakes. The more wretched she seemed, the more likely they would not expect too much from her if by sheer luck she might find a way to escape.

'And now you think of escape,' he said, as if reading her mind. 'Let me tell you of the monsters in the forests, the creatures that forever seek out blood and flesh. Go if you must; you will not get far. As for the cliff road, my guards patrol it every hour of the day, and they have orders to shoot on sight.

'Don't get to thinking about taking your own life, either. I assure you, dear, I have been known to take vengeance after the fact, and you still have family in Clay Portside.'

He nodded towards a mantel clock sitting on the dresser.

'Join us for dinner upon the hour,' he said. 'But first wash, and make yourself decent. Summon Mrs Valley if you need anything.'

She did not reply, because whatever came out of her mouth

would undoubtedly be outrageously offensive and make Mr Lindsay angry again. After waiting for a long minute, he fished inside his emerald-coloured waistcoat and pulled a small metal container from an internal pocket.

He placed the container upon the mantelpiece and tapped the top.

'An ointment. For the coins in your hands. It will ease the pain, bring some feeling back.'

Then he was gone. Arden crawled into the corner of the room as if his very presence had reduced her to a crawling thing, and with all her ferocious despair screamed into the pillow.

12

She did not fuss long

She did not fuss long. Her composure came like a cold, hard wave over her. Arden went to the mantelpiece, looked at the small silver container Mr Lindsay had left for her.

Every part of her screamed: *do not open this gift.* Had she not been a prisoner, had things gone to plan, she'd not have touched it, so it was with an anguished cry that she snatched the pot off the mantel and twisted it open, her numb fingers slipping on the silver.

Inside was a paste, like softened beeswax, only it smelled unpleasant and medicinal and was of a metallic black so deep not even the ocean could have replicated such a colour. When she brought the coin of one hand close, the black paste slopped sideways of its own accord, the way iron filings might yearn for the magnet.

'Did this cure your blindness, Miah?' she said resentfully to the mantelpiece, before sucking in a breath and rubbing the gross, living salve into her palms. The paste drained into her skin, and the most awful coldness filled her veins.

To her surprise, the numbness faded at once. The new feeling in her prickled slightly, but it was almost as if she were good as new.

Except ever so slightly corrupted.

For clothes she stuck with the cotton dress – the long sleeves were formal enough. Her leviathan-leather shoes had almost dried – she sent a begrudging thanks to the Fiction cobbler who had made her boots – so she slipped them on and walked out of the guest room.

The dining room was spread across an upper floor, in a ballroom-sized space with large windows that might have once looked out to sea but now opened to the forest in the late afternoon. Black mould grew in the corners and moss had already colonized the windowsill and a patch of rotted floor.

A man stood guard on the parapet, a blunderbuss slung over his arm – a shotgun meant to disperse a lot of small pellets quickly. Another stood in sweaty wariness one balcony over with a wide harpoon connected to a crossbow.

When Arden peered over the parapet to the overgrown courtyard below, she spotted two more similarly armed folk watching the forest. A rockblood electric generator thumped out a heavy tattoo from behind a row of trees and, as the lamplights glowed, Arden's palms itched.

'Night comes soon in this season,' Mr Lindsay said, coming up behind her. He nodded towards the men standing watch. 'The worst creatures live in the treetops. Malign things that carry men away and feast upon their innards. We have heard they do even worse to women.'

Arden retreated from the balcony. 'What is it that your family grows that necessitates living in such a wild place?'

'Agarwood. Have you not smelled it? It is the perfume of the infected trees – the *oud*. It is a perfume, both an incense and a medicine. We cure it in the furnaces a short distance over yonder.' He tilted his chin towards the forest. 'I was a younger sibling, so my fortune was not bound in the profits of this house's industry. Sadly, I am the only true heir now, and I have been called back.'

Mrs Valley came in bearing a tray of glass teacups, and a fragrant tea that gave off the same menthol smokiness of the agarwood curing furnaces. Arden might have declined to drink had Mr Lindsay not taken one glass for himself.

'I see my lotion has given some feeling back to your hands. There is more if you need it, and if you continue to keep up appearances.'

'So, did any of my shipmates make it to shore while I was asleep?'

Mr Lindsay paused mid-drink, then shook his head. 'None. I am sorry.'

He was telling the truth. When he lied, he always had a sneer, as if he were capitulating to weakness. Those in full possession of their power did not need to mollify others with lies. When Mr Lindsay told the truth, he was benevolent, bestowing the grace of honesty, but never without cost.

She sat upon her seat at the table diminished by grief, and did not even look up when the others came in. Mr Lindsay introduced them all – the foreman of his factory, the overseer, and both their wives, who gawked at the house as if they'd never seen the inside before. Bellis, who gave off flashes of sanguis power like a live wire, sat at the end of the table, practically sparking.

Last of all was Miah Anguis, sliding into position at the end of the table with two men she assumed were bodyguards of a sort, though whose body they guarded she could not quite work out. Even with ten adults, the table could have held three times that number and the empty spots made the table appear sparse and the former ballroom too huge and dim. The servants had dressed in waistcoats of the same emerald tweed Mr Lindsay always wore, golden buttons winking in the lamplight, and they brought out the meal with a slightly harassed flourish.

Arden was starving and though she ate she did not entirely register their supper – a bowl of soup, fresh tuber-bread, some delicate white meat, gourd-like vegetables, and a sweet sauce on the verge of fermentation. Everything was overlaid with the flavour of the oudwood furnaces. The wine was heady, and soon her head was spinning, but she took a second glass, and a third. She chased intoxication like an addict.

When she looked up, the others were still eating.

Though she swore she would not, she glanced towards Miah Anguis, but his large companions obscured him from her view as they stuffed uncounted helpings of white meat into their mouths like brutes.

When dinner wound down to third helpings, Mr Lindsay poured a dessert wine and sat back on one of his mismatching chairs. 'It has been a day.'

'A day stuck here,' Bellis said. 'A day when we should have been headed for Clay Capital like gods, but you won't fucking get on with it!'

One of the serving girls threw down a plate, shattering it. The girl let out a wail of horror and fell to her knees to pick up the shards, but her hands clenched reflexively in the broken pieces and Bellis, with her pale face a guileless mask, only raised an eyebrow.

The girl kept letting out choking sobs as she closed her hands so tight about the razor-sharp porcelain that blood welled through her fingers.

One of the serving women ran to the girl's side but did not try to pry the shards out of the girl's bleeding hands, only held her shoulders as if this act was a syncope that might pass, and murmured along with the girl's bleats of horror, the pieces of plate crimson from blood.

Arden could bear it no longer. She knew exactly who was causing this.

'Stop it,' Arden shouted. 'Stop it, Bellis!'

Bellis blinked as if wilfully not understanding Arden's protest. And Arden, distressed beyond measure, hefted her heavy crystal wine glass in Bellis' direction, sending a wave of sticky liquid spilling across the table.

Bellis jerked upright, her malign *orientis* powers surrounding her like a crackling aura.

The man in the balcony threw down his long-arm and ran for Arden, his mouth an O of pain . . . only to be tackled at once by Miah Anguis. Two hard blows to his ribs, one to his face, and the guardian slumped, unconscious, onto the thread-bare rug.

A sound of running came from the other room, but Miah only walked calmly to Bellis, and placed his hand heavy on her shoulder, a thumb where her blood pulsed through a vein. She was so tiny he could clearly throttle her with one hand.

'Call off your dogs, for I can wring that neck of yours and you'll be dead in seconds.'

She hissed at him. 'I smell your weakness, fool. It sits at this very table.'

The clatter of approaching footfalls stopped. Through the cane dividers the shadows of Bellis' other controlled men loitered in confusion, having forgotten why they ran so urgently towards the dining room.

The girl, however, kept screaming, the sound coming out in short sobs.

The air smelled like the dry crackling atmosphere before a lightning strike. Miah's voice was a low thunder. His command was so laden with *mandatum* threat; even the wedding ring he'd placed on Arden's finger back on Equus seemed to tighten.

'Sit. Down.'

Bellis sat down. Released, the servant girl ran from both the room and her forced self-harm. The elder woman – her mother, perhaps – began to pick up the bloodied shards of the broken plate and carefully pile them into her apron with a steely determination, as if willing herself not to faint from hysterics.

Miah looked at Arden, his gaze shot through with irritation, before returning to his seat and the rest of his food.

Mr Lindsay only gave a beatific smile. 'Now that we are finished with our little interpersonal dramas, then let us speak. You may also sit, Mrs Anguis.'

Arden hadn't realized she had remained standing, her heart hammering like a battle-tattoo. She sat.

'My dear Queen Bellis,' Mr Lindsay said. 'There are reasons why we have not made the grand entrance to our capital city and her Parliament. The citizens are not vulnerable in Clay, as it is not some scabrous little Sainted Island hovel. The Order employs sanguinem for security as well as labour; they will sense we are coming. Sanguis bloodworkers with talents even I cannot imagine, who could execute us at a distance before Your Majesty could work her talent for *orientis*.'

'Just let me try!'

There was a clatter of cutlery from Miah Anguis as he threw down his fork and half a chewed bird-wing.

'We aren't going anywhere. This fucking endeavour is all pigshit. If there's no way forward, then we should all go home and take the remains of our fucking honour with us.'

Bellis slammed her cutlery down on either side of her plate in return. 'No! Mr Lindsay promised!' She turned to the Lion. 'You fucking promised the city would belong to me, that we would sail in like gods! Avenging, conquering gods! You promised me an army!'

'Guests, Bellis. Guests,' Mr Lindsay soothed. 'We are not among friends.'

Even though the gold Lion coin of debt Arden held meant nothing, her attention was piqued by the word Bellis had uttered. *Army.* They had discussed the possibility back on *Sonder* the day before, and had dismissed it. There were not enough people in South Lyonne to form an army, and the effort to both collect people and keep them alive would have brought unwanted attention, spoiled the element of surprise.

You do not need to listen in to this, Arden, her good sense cautioned.

Yet still, why did Bellis use that word?

'Give me six hours, Mr Lindsay,' Bellis said. 'It will take me six hours and that slattern's blood. Then the entire city of Clay Capital will be mine.'

Mr Lindsay subtly rolled his eyes. 'Dear, there is more to overcoming the sentries than that. Let us discus it later.'

He shooed off his Foreman and Overseer, and they were well pleased to scuttle away, wives in tow. He then spun his finger thoughtfully on the crystal of his glass, making it sing. He turned to Miah.

'Mr Anguis, where did your father get that boat?'

Miah lifted his head from where it focused on his plate and wiped his mouth on the back of his sleeve. '*Sonder*? He always had it. Inherited it from his grandfather and a grandfather before him.'

'From the days of the Saint, am I right?'

Miah shrugged. 'The ballast is iron and copper. He used it to hide from the sea monsters—'

Mr Lindsay interrupted. 'I was meant to take possession of the electric vessel *Velleity*, also from the days of the Saint of the Islands. As soon as it' – he made a face – '*sank*, and *Sonder* was offered so suddenly in its place, I saw the outline of Brother Absalom's strategy as clear as day.'

When nobody asked any further questions, Mr Lindsay threw down his napkin and continued. 'We have a *spy* among us, listening. Your wife. She is here to collect information to pass on to my less-enlightened colleagues. But my Order brother was clumsy and did not cover his tracks, and now she is discarded here, and at my mercy.'

All Arden's hopes dashed. So Mr Lindsay knew why she was here after all.

Miah didn't look at her, but if Bellis stared at her any more pointedly she would be boring holes through Arden's skull. Mr Lindsay linked his fingers and leaned in Arden's direction. 'Do you wish to know why I wanted such an antique boat as *Sonder* or *Velleity*?'

Shaking, she drained her wine glass. 'Why did you wish for such a boat, Mr Lindsay?' she echoed without looking at him.

'I will not tell you, my dear spy. And you will remain among us in relative comfort until the day we sail away for our bright future and my Queen's ascension into the highest levels of authority.'

His words appeased Bellis somewhat. 'Just as long as it's happening,' she huffed.

'Oh it is. It certainly is.' He leaned forward again, closer to Arden. 'It is not for my Queen that I need your *evalescendi*. Tomorrow I will request it. But tonight we will take rest, and prepare ourselves. We have work ahead of us.'

He summoned one of the blunderbuss-holding guards who stood watch at the balcony. 'Glaucon, please take Mrs Anguis back to her room.'

Arden was entirely grateful to go. She wondered if Bellis would attempt some foolishness, then saw the look Miah gave her, full of warning.

As they walked down the stairs, a pair of similarly armed servants ran up the stairway beside them. More followed, bearing hissing lamps, ready to provide light in the fading day.

'So the night starts,' said Glaucon. He was a typical South Lyonnian, stocky and strong, his long hair braided in a single queue down his back and covered with a sheath of giant-ray leather.

Arden couldn't help herself. 'Why does the plantation need so much security?'

'Shadelings.'

'Shadelings?'

At the foot of the stairs Glaucon summoned her over to stand next to one of the candle-blackened picture frames, and then took it down from the wall. He looked at it thoughtfully, and then slid it in front of Arden.

'Shadelings. Take this for identification. Though if you see one, it will be the last thing you see.'

She didn't want to look, but looked anyway. The frame held a silver-print of two men in full colonial dress, shorts and long socks, white shoes, and suits with pockets.

Between them was a pole upon which they had ostensibly speared a third figure.

No, not a *figure*. A mass. A tangle. Like someone had looped a giant onion bulb with creepers and left it to rot for a month.

'It's not just the shadelings. The forest is home to a great many animals that God cursed before the Flood, abominations prohibited shelter upon the Ark of Noah.' Glaucon made the sign of the Redeemer upon his chest.

'Including flying snakes that spit fire?' she ventured.

'Many of those,' Glaucon said, nodding. 'The forest holds many secrets. If you are fortunate, you will only discover the least of them.'

13

When Glaucon escorted

When Glaucon escorted Arden back to her room, they took a detour past the guest-lodge library, which housed a meagre wall of books. He signalled that she take some, and Arden was so grateful for his little act of kindness, she had to remind herself sternly that nobody here was to be trusted, not a single soul. These men were Lindsay employees, and their ancestors had probably also been, going back generations.

She dumped the books upon the coverlet, changed in her absence. A scar of black on the mat was all that remained from the dragonct's venom.

The wind blew humid down the mountainside and a fan turned lazily above, charged by some primitive system of gears and pulleys. It was getting dark, even for her. To make things especially irritating, the lighting in this room was electrical. The wires inside the lantern by her bed glowed as she turned the switch dial and let out a hum of current. Her hands prickled. She rubbed more of Mr Lindsay's lotion into them.

The trees rustled.

From deep in the forest came a crack of guns, a shower of sparks. One of the window shutters flew open.

'Devilment!' she cried, thinking of the shadeling strung up

between the poles. As she went to close the shutter a body lunged from behind the balcony door and pulled her outside. They were so quick she did not even have time to yelp in surprise. The being pushed his head against her mouth, held a metal hook to his lips.

'*Shh.*'

The electric light through the slats illuminated a man's face. He was sweaty and quite grotesque in appearance; one could certainly never call him handsome. One eye socket had sunk into his face, the lid seamed shut. His skin and clothes smelled of distillate oil, and his clothes were grimy with agarwood sap, but after everything that she had already experienced today, she could only be grateful that he wasn't something worse.

'Don't scream. I bring news.'

She nodded to him that she was calm. When he slowly brought his hand away, all she could croak out was, 'Speak.'

'Your man. The one from the water. We have him.'

'Who? Mr Absalom?'

The visitor shook his head. 'The deepwater man.'

The information came so unexpectedly and joyfully it intoxicated her. Arden wavered where she stood. 'Jonah's alive? How is he? What about the others?'

The man put his hook to his lips again and shook his head.

'All I can say is that he is alive. As to his condition . . .' He shrugged. 'I am not a physician, I cannot say.'

'Surely you can make a guess enough to tell me?'

He shook his head again. 'I have some questions the others wanted to ask of you. They say . . . they say your blood can make the Vigil sea-witch more powerful than she already is?'

Ah. Judging by his rough linen shirt and his injuries, this man was a forest worker. They'd likely have had the same taste of Bellis' nastiness as the young girl in the kitchen that evening.

'Yes,' she admitted. 'My blood talent is called *evalescendi*. It brings out latent sanguis powers and increases current ones.' She could feel her own sour expression. 'My being here is not out of choice, believe me.'

'The others want to know if she is a friend of yours.'

'Devilment, no!' Then Arden stopped. 'Are you working for Mr Lindsay, sir? Is this a trick, because I can tell you, not even Mr Lindsay would believe me if I said Bellis Harrow held a fond place in my heart.'

The man suddenly stood back, his brow knitting.

'Someone comes. I cannot talk more. We will meet again soon.'

'What the—'

Before she could finish, the man had pushed her back into the room and slammed the shutters.

Behind her the door crashed open and Miah Anguis stumbled in, a bottle of wine almost empty in one hand, a pistol in the other.

'It is in here?' Miah shouted. 'The guards said they saw it on your balcony!'

The plantation worker, or whoever the one-eyed man was, had sensed Miah's arrival just in time. Had Miah seen him, he'd have killed him on sight. Arden, too, probably.

Her body ringing like a struck bell, she summoned a voice. 'I saw a shape, but it fled into the trees.'

Her joy at the one-eyed man's news helped the lie come easy. If Jonah had made it, then maybe the others had made it as well. Chalice, she thought. She would even be happy to see Mrs Cordwain!

Miah put the wine bottle on the table with the over-cautious deliberation of a man who knows he is drunk, and crossed the room to the shutters, finding them closed but not locked. 'Must have given you a great fright.'

'I've suffered worse.'

His expression inscrutable, he opened the panel and peered out into the gloom. Fragrant, smoky air gusted in. There was just enough of a sunset to give a red tinge to the sky. It was not entirely black beyond the shutters.

'It aggrieves me as much as anyone else does that we are here,' he said sulkily. 'My passions overwhelmed me earlier on the beach. I should not have struck you. Had I been in my right mind I would have stayed my hand. I, too, would much prefer to return home.'

'Then why not go home?'

'He won't permit it.'

'Strange, that Mr Lindsay could force a deepwater man to go where he did not want to go.'

His pistol remained by his side, and she could not help but look at it dangling at the end of his hand.

He turned to her, his expression dark with loathing. 'I *owe* him. You *blinded* me. I was mutilated.'

'Only temporarily. Your sight would likely have returned in time.' It came out insincerely, and she immediately wished she hadn't tried to defend herself.

'It was long enough for the clan to see me weak. The Lion forced me to take his help. I had no choice but to let him cure me.'

They always thought you weak, Miah Anguis. You were always a shorelander to them, a refugee from Vigil. You should have accepted what you were and not wished for more.

Maybe she didn't speak those words aloud, but they were loud enough in her own mind. He placed the pistol on the warped, pitted wood of the bedside table and she looked at it with despair. *Maybe I could pick it up. Maybe I could kill him. It would damn my immortal soul forever, but . . .*

He began to unbutton his sweat-dampened shirt, and with each button his grievances seemed to magnify. Beneath his black tattoos his skin bunched, and the keloid scars he carried gave him an otherworldly look. The twin prongs of a black squid beak emerged from the waistband of his strides, finishing just below his navel. He looked at her with an expression in between impassiveness and desire.

Arden sighed. 'So that is what it has to be.'

'Tell me *no*, then. Tell me to leave. If it's going to be awful, I can get it from one of the servant girls.'

'If I do that, then Mr Lindsay will punish me. I want to get out of this *alive*, Miah Anguis.'

With a terrible effort she untied her dress and pulled off her underclothes, lay upon the bed and looked up at the scant remains of the insect netting on the canopy. Like cobwebs, she thought. In a crypt.

He climbed onto the bed and kissed her, his mouth gnawing her shoulder, hungry, devouring. He pulled off his strides. A screech sounded somewhere in the shy crowns of the nighttime trees. A hubbub of things, the boiling busy-ness of their lives.

'Make it not awful.' She said it as if a stone was falling from her mouth.

Even in his enthusiasm he lingered upon the act, taking with impartiality the gift Mr Lindsay had given him. He embraced her and bit her other shoulder and murmured hungry words in Fictish as he covered her and thrust, jerky and clumsy in his eagerness. He had barely found a rhythm before he peaked and climaxed with a grunt of joy.

Then it was completed, and he rolled off with a murmur of satisfaction. 'I cannot say that I did not miss it.'

Arden turned off the light, for it was attracting moths and some of them were huge. Relieved not to deal with the constant itch in her palms for once, she lay in the dark and listened to the night, listened to the moths in the room, their soft bodies colliding with the walls, the whisper of their wings. Her thoughts were everywhere and nowhere, somewhere between hope and despair. Had someone watched them? She had no doubt Mr Lindsay would have his own methods of knowing if Arden had held up her side of the bargain or not.

'What did Bellis mean by an army?' she asked after a while.

'Really, you ask this question now?'

'I ask it because my survival is tied to the successful achievement of Bellis' wishes as much as they are tied to yours.'

She felt him shrug next to her. 'She can't walk into Clay. Can't sneak in. The Lion has promised Queen Bitch Bellis an army to protect her from all the sanguis guards that are supposedly there.'

'An army won't do anything,' Arden said. 'The chosen

protectors can explode a heart from a distance, crush a ribcage with barely a blink. And they are loyal to Clay City – will always be so. He's lying to her.'

A grunt came from the darkness. He did not disagree with her.

She propped herself on her elbow. 'Miah, I know there's bad experiences between us, but understand me when I say that man is not to be trusted. Whatever he has offered Bellis and you there's no truth to it, none at all.'

He paused for a while, and then she felt him roll over. 'Go to sleep, Beacon. He'll have use for you in the morning.'

14

At last

'At last, you're up,' Mr Lindsay said when he came in seconds after Arden had dressed. Miah had left before sunrise, not even taking the time to wake her up. She had opened her eyes to an empty bed. 'You left the dining table in such a state I was half-certain there would be barricades at the door come morning.'

She tied her shower-wet hair back into a braid. 'Regardless of your efforts to keep me in the dark, I am aware of my place in this scheme of yours. If I wish to stay alive, I have to cooperate. So, I will cooperate.'

'Cooperation is good. Have you applied the reverso paste this morning? It's quite the handy balm; you can use it for a lot of medicinal ailments. An old family recipe.'

She held up her stained hands to show him her application, and then slid on the fingerless gloves.

He held out a sun hat. 'Put this on. The sun can be wicked.'

Arden accepted the roughly woven hat reluctantly, not quite ready to follow his every command. 'Where are you taking me?'

'A small tour of our operations this morning. I've allowed you to sleep in as a token of gratitude. They've made quite a start.'

Start in what? she wanted to say but did not. Instead she followed Mr Lindsay out beyond the house to the forest boundary. It was a cleared staging area of tilting telegraph poles and nondescript sheds. The surrounding air was clotted with the thick smell of fresh sap and broken branches. Even breathing felt difficult, for the resin in the air stuck to every exposed surface, with a special affinity for throats and tongues.

Arden spotted Miah among the workmen crowded about a giant rolling mechanism lying between the blocks of huge iron plates. It was a manner of oversized pulley, six bobbins of steel wider than the reach of two men, a lonely, rusting monument set into the hillside upon a foundation of stone.

The remains of a braided steel cable looped about the winch sheaves before disappearing up from the clearing and into the riot of greenery. Arden recalled the complex snatch block arrangements of the Clay Portside stevedores. There would be an equally huge standing block somewhere in the forest.

'Cable's goddamn rusted right through,' one of the workers gruffed. 'The slightest tug could break it, leaving every soul within fifty feet without a damn head.'

A chorus of concern followed his warning, which died down to a sulky mutter as Mr Lindsay approached.

'What seems to be the problem?' Mr Lindsay asked.

The foreman pushed through the knot of men, and glared at the one who had complained.

'There's some issue about the integrity of the winch cables, Mr Lindsay.'

'Integrity? This is a perpetual motion mechanism. It is meant to run forever.'

'Maybe the machine lasts, but the parts aren't going to do squat. The cables need to pull the counterweight up the slope and withstand the shock of releasing the plumb weight into the pit. But, sir, these cables . . . they must be over a hundred years old. You can see the oxidation on the surface.' He rubbed his glove over one cable braid and it came away covered in red dust.

The foreman's words were familiar to a dockworker like Arden. *Counterweight. Plumb. Pit.* She found herself listening intently as Mr Lindsay turned to Miah.

'Mr Anguis?'

Despite his solid, deepwater-man bearing, Miah seemed diminished among the workers, too exotic, too much a stranger. His usual forthrightness harnessed, he gave only a non-committal grunt and licked his thumb where the rust had stained his skin. 'Like I was trying to tell them, I can test it,' he said wearily.

Mr Lindsay nodded at the foreman. 'Our guest is *sanguis ferrous.*' His lip curled slightly as if speaking with distaste. 'He knows the metal. Let Mr Anguis inspect and give his verdict.'

It was a lie of course, but *ferrous* and *mandatum* abilities overlapped when it came to metal and Miah did look like someone who worked metal. He had already sliced the top of his arm with small cuts in order to deal with the other cables. Had these been Fiction workers, they would have treated him with more suspicion. But Lyonnians were used to sanguinem, even down on the south coast.

Miah shoved his rust-spotted thumb in his mouth, worked it over his gums, then stepped back with a sigh. 'It's only surface rust. The core is intact.'

Miah's report sent audible murmurs of relief through the gathered workers. The complainer was right to have spoken, however. A broken cable could cut a man in half as cleanly as if he were butter.

Then Miah turned to Mr Lindsay, frowning. 'Where did you get this wire? Someone with *mandatum* has been around it.'

'There have been *sanguis mandatum* bloodworkers here in the past,' Mr Lindsay said. 'My family hired only the best craftsmen for their operations. Check the other wires, Mr Anguis, and then meet me at the dynamo-house.'

Dynamo-house, Arden repeated quietly to herself, committing it to memory. It sounded as if all this effort at a perpetual motion machine was in aid of a giant electrical system. She peered down the hillside and confirmed her suspicions. Berthed securely at the pier, *Sonder* showed no damage from her ambush of the day before. Now Mr Lindsay had the battery-powered ship that he had dearly wanted. Yet, puzzlingly, a pair of fast electric-powered cargo boats in good condition were tied nearby. And a third rested in a makeshift dry-dock. He was clearly not a man in need of electrical transport . . . so why did he need *Sonder*?

Further up the hill a team of men and women hacked a path through the forest using brush-cutting knives, axes and 'endless saws', which the locals called 'chain saws'. The stink of tree sap and distillate-fuel smoke poured down the slope to murk like a noxious mist at sea level. The shower Arden had gratefully taken that morning was all for naught as she walked through a cloud bank of sticky dieseline.

The workers' previous efforts at clearing the treeline had already revealed another curiosity apart from the giant pulleys. It was an object resembling a flat-bed carriage for a goods train, crookedly loaded with an uneven number of giant granite blocks of a size that would have been better off making an antediluvian god king's tomb.

'What is that?' she asked, too irritated by the stink to be prudent now.

'A counterweight sled,' Mr Lindsay replied proudly. 'You're standing on a track now, in fact.'

So this was the *counterweight* the foreman was speaking about earlier. Arden looked down and saw that under her boot the flat length of a steel rail protruded through the leaf litter. Some of the women had already dug the rail free of the detritus.

'Isn't it missing a couple of weights?'

'Ah, a good observation, Mrs Anguis. We think one of the slab weights fell off further up the slope. The workers have been requested to fetch it, though it appears . . . unfortunately . . . they've not made much progress . . .'

Mr Lindsay watched their exertions in silence for several minutes. The foreman came by again to report that the tray was in place, and once they found the remaining block in the regrowth, they could start winding.

'Once they *find* it? They've had all morning to look.'

'My apologies, but none of the men will go into the forest without the sled-road having been cleared first.'

'Offer them extra wages.'

'Sir, they won't do it. They're afraid of what is in there. We need to clear it first.'

'Then cut their rations. I shall not be messed with, Mr Locke.'

The foreman – Mr Locke – scratched his head under his cap and managed to look aggrieved and scared at once. But Mr Lindsay was a greater and more present threat, so he withdrew with forced obsequiousness and Mr Lindsay continued jauntily on down to the dynamo-house with Arden in tow.

The dynamo-house was easily the largest building Arden had seen so far, other than the plantation house and the distillery sheds. Decades of neglect had left the outer shell to rust paper-thin and sunlight lanced through pinholes in the dim, hot space. The great circular dynamo – the device that converted the movement of the cable to electrical power – could have fit three motor vehicles into its steel housing. The housing was in the shape of a fat torus, with a wheel about a central spindle. Arden could see that someone had prised a section of dynamo housing off to reveal the internal rotor, likely recently.

Inside the rotor, skeins of unusually bright copper wire wound about the armature like a giant wickerwork basket. It was perhaps the cleanest, most untarnished copper Arden had ever seen. It was so bright the colour was almost pink.

Now all the effort made sense. This was the device that could charge *Sonder*'s recalcitrant batteries to full power, not the tiny trickle Chalice had managed with Arden's help.

Mr Lindsay saw her investigations of the dynamo. 'Impressive, yes? This generator once powered my father's cargo boats. A full charge could last us from here to Clay and back again.'

'If you don't mind me asking, and since I'm a prisoner anyway . . . why would you even want *Sonder* or *Velleity* if you already have electric boats?'

He wagged his finger at her enigmatically. 'Curiosity killed the cat, my dear. I've answered enough questions.'

Her hands prickled even though the dynamo generated no electricity. The machine was in pristine condition when everything else had turned to rust. It was not natural.

And Mr Lindsay was looking at her as if he *knew* she felt something strange in his dynamo machine, something that wasn't quite right.

Evidently finding her too curious for his liking, Mr Lindsay took her elbow and steered her back outside. 'Why not sit in the shade with my cousin, Mr Sword? There is a lot of work to do, and I cannot play the chaperone to the extent it is required.'

'I would rather be indoors . . .' Arden started, then gave up and let him drag her back up the cleared slope to where a small gazebo was set up over a dainty, elegant desk. A man in a light blue suit sat on an inexplicably out-of-place wing-back chair, while a bored youth held a parasol over his head.

'We missed you at dinner, Horatio,' said Mr Lindsay on his approach. 'I'd have preferred to introduce our guest in more formal surroundings.'

Mr Sword was a thin Lyonnian fellow edging towards his sixtieth year. His face was pockmarked from a childhood disease, and two creases ran down his cheeks as if he spent most of his time folded up out of the sun. On one side of the wing-backed chair leaned a walking staff of unicorn ivory topped with gold, and on the other sat a crystal glass full of a purple port. The decanter was on the table, having already left half-moons of claret in several places across the silk.

'Ah, Claude, I do believe I've exhausted my welcome with your other guest. I thought it best to keep myself scarce.'

'This one is much nicer, I assure you.'

A canvas folding chair was already propped up next to

Mr Sword, and Mr Lindsay offered it to her. 'There you go, Mrs Anguis. Don't talk her ear off, Horatio.'

'I'm afraid that is your speciality, not mine.'

'Humph.'

Arden sat in the chair guardedly as Mr Lindsay walked off. Mr Sword smiled at her. 'Oh, don't mind that little prat, my dear. Living in the big city has given him airs and graces beyond his station.'

There were no marks of Lyonne Order about Mr Sword, not even a delicate brooch of a rose bound in iron thorns, and though she didn't trust him any more than Mr Lindsay, Horatio Sword did not radiate the same kind of ambitious malice that his cousin did. He was more like a redolent bull who'd had his fill of cows and battles, and was more interested in whiling away his remaining years in pasture.

'I am told,' he continued, 'that you are Mrs Arden Anguis, the wife of Miah Anguis, who will be assisting us in winding the counterweight up the hill. So, you are sanguis as well?'

She exhaled. 'Yes.'

'From Clay City.'

She nodded, and Mr Sword launched into a longer introduction. He was the steward of the Lindsay Estate, he said, because his and Mr Lindsay's mothers had been cousins. There had been a great raft of brothers back then – and Mr Lindsay was a hidden youngest, a half-brother conceived out of wedlock and born in Clay. They'd only known him through letters and business associates hired on his behalf. He had always been a mystery, even to his family.

'My estranged prat of a cousin was fortunate. He escaped into the embrace of the Lions, and they cared for him as a brother. Things were bad here, for a long time. The Lindsay paterfamilias was a despot, as cruel and controlling as a god king of antiquity.'

'The workers must be glad that he is gone,' Arden said.

'Indeed, and gone in such a strange way. The forest folk and indentured shorefolk suffered all kinds of indignities under the senior Lindsay's patronage. He was a nasty man.'

'The apple doesn't fall far from the tree then.'

Mr Sword hid a giggle behind his handkerchief. 'No, it doesn't. Anyway, even despots take missteps. See, Pater had forgotten that humans are a difficult animal to husband. They have long memories and take umbrage with slights. One day he orders the hand of a child cut off and its eye put out because it had burned the oudwood in a dry distiller. None of the soldiers would do it for him though, and he ended up doing the deed himself.'

Arden stood up straighter. An eye? A hand? 'Is the child still alive?'

'Who knows? That night the forest came alive and the wraith-things in the trees came down and carried Pater Lindsay away. Screaming. They made short work of the half-brothers after that. Young master Claude ended up an inheritor of an empty house and vast wealth, and I was called back here from my Morningvale accounts offices to manage the plantation.'

Down on the thin, miserly beach the first loads of creepers torn from around the winch's broad spindle smoked in a heap. The smoke rolled up the slope, driven by the cool sea breezes the morning showers had brought, and mixed with the heavy oily mist rolling down, creating quite a miasma.

The one-eyed man who'd found Jonah had to be that same boy, Arden thought. And he was definitely one of the workers. Where the hell could he be?

For the rest of the afternoon she sought out every face, and to her dismay, every one of them was unfamiliar. By the time the work had stopped for the evening and Mr Lindsay had given Arden her leave, she was torn between running back to her room to get the stink of tree sap and rockblood smoke off her, and staying to watch the last muster of the evening. More men were coming out of the forest . . . was he among them?

Still, there was nothing much she could do but return to the house, dump her dress in the laundry basket and take what passed as a bath in the stone-floored auxiliary attached to the guest wing. She kept the balcony doors open as long as she could, until the reports of the blunderbusses signalled that the time for forest security had come and one of the guards yelled at her from the next room over to close the shutters.

'It is night!' he shouted, as if that was all the warning he needed to give. 'It is night!'

15

In the hours

In the hours between sundown and bedtime, Arden fluttered about her gilded cage as if she wanted to throw herself against the bars. The guard Glaucon came in not long afterwards with two forest workers. Between them they carried a familiar steamer trunk.

'Yeh, it was on the black mangrove ship. Mr Anguis said the trunk belongs to you.'

He motioned to the workers that they should put the box down at the foot of the bed. Arden opened the lid of the trunk she had last seen on board *Saudade* a month ago. Inside, almost untouched since she'd last placed them there, were all her clothes and possessions. Once the deepwater clan had taken *Saudade* from the Burden Town docks, she had feared them lost forever.

'Oh, I imagined they'd have been thrown into the sea!'

Glaucon nodded. 'Mr Anguis ordered that you should have your property. Ah, and also this.'

Her old steamer trunk had so distracted her she had not noticed the bronze coat slung over Glaucon's arm. He laid it on the bed respectfully. The blue crust of the krakenskin glowed.

It was Jonah's coat, from *Sonder*. With a breathless despair she moved her hands over it, before finding the hole in the shoulder panel where a crossbow had shot him months ago. From then it was as if a spell of invulnerability had been broken, and it no longer seemed to protect him. Everything had gone wrong from there.

'Miah made you bring the coat?'

'Ah, no. Mr Anguis just delivered the trunk. My fellow found the coat in one of the rooms.'

'You must thank him.'

'Was not charitable. The forest folk are shore folk. They believe that anything reminding them of the deep sea brings them bad luck. This coat was similar to yours, Mrs Anguis, so perhaps you must have it.'

'Thank you,' she said, but could hardly bear to look at it. She wondered why Miah had not taken the krakenskin coat with him when he first came off *Sonder*.

'All right. Well. If you need anything, just call.'

Arden returned to the steamer trunk. It was a miracle to have the trunk brought back. Miah could have discarded all her possessions and would have been justified in doing so. She did not want to think charitable thoughts towards him.

Jonah's coat went in the wicker wardrobe under a pile of linen. She spent the rest of the evening going through her things. Close to a year had passed since she had last been at home. These letters and trinkets belonged to another Arden Beacon, one who had only yearned, never suffered.

Arden was distracted enough that she didn't notice the visitor slipping her way into the room.

'Miah is in fine spirits. I take it the reunion went well. Didn't throw in a couple of slaps for good measure, did he? Perhaps he wanted to preserve that high-born face, huh?'

'If you're come to gloat, take it elsewhere.'

'Oh, I'm not gloating at all. I'm just as fed up of this place as you, and I don't have the luxury of a man to keep happy. I find my entertainment where I can. Oh . . . there it is.'

She cocked her head, and Arden heard what she heard, the

music on the beach, the men making desperately merry with whatever time they had left. Arden knew exactly what *elsewhere* entertainment Bellis meant.

She grabbed the wing-backed corner chair and pushed it out from the wall.

'Devilment, sit here and speak to me if you must, just leave those people alone for tonight.'

Bellis sat in the chair and scratched one tatty strand of hair at her crown. When she found a louse there and bit it in half thoughtfully, Arden shivered.

'I hear you went to the Deepwater King's church when you were married to my dear sanguis-twin.'

Arden made a noise in the affirmative as she recalled the small island rock of her forced wedding night. It had previously served as a sanctuary for Bellis Harrow. For a brief year before Bellis' terrible transformation – from blood-talented Vigil girl to conquering Queen of the Sainted Islands – Stefan Beacon had kept Bellis safe, tried to guide her into goodness, stave off the madness that came with having such a terrible power.

'So, how goes my friend Stefan? Your priest-cousin?'

Arden put a folded scarf back in the trunk. 'He's dead. Or did Miah not tell you that?'

For the first time, Arden saw a genuine emotion ripple across the brittle porcelain of Bellis' face.

'In what manner was his death?'

There were many things Arden could say. The pain from Miah's beating. The despair of Bellis' tumble into evil. She could lay blame like a firecracker and watch it catch the tinder of Bellis' emotions alight. But to do that would risk the dozens of workers and their children. If not them, then Jonah, still alive in the forest.

She hid her anger and said quietly, 'You know he came back from Clay with a morphium addiction. When we met after the full moon, Stefan was already too far gone. And then he took more than was safe—' She snatched a summer dress out of the chest and folded it. 'Well, Pastor John Stefan – my cousin Stefan

Beacon – was already taking enough to bring down a man twice his size.'

By her previous actions Bellis should have not cared one whit about Stefan Beacon, but to Arden's surprise she looked properly dumfounded.

'It cannot be. Stef managed his condition.'

'The way you managed yours?'

Bellis squinted at Arden, and the familiar itch poked through her skull. 'Do not mistake the affection I had for that man for weakness. He loved me enough to try and save me.'

'But some things are greater than love to you, Bellis Harrow. You didn't *want* him to save you. You wanted to be the Queen of the Islands and enslave people like the Saint did. Now you want to be Queen of Lyonne, and that's why I'm stuck here.'

The itch subsided. 'I *will* be Queen of Lyonne, and right soon. Brother Lindsay knows how to meld my powers with Miah's. He has potions, medicines. And then . . . then we will be untouchable. I will say goodbye to dirty old grass huts and stinking volcanic islands. I'll be in the Towers, my dress made of silk, eating nightingale tongues for supper every night!'

'If you say so,' Arden said impatiently.

Even without the effort of *orientis* to read Arden's mind, Bellis was not oblivious to Arden's exasperation.

'You don't believe I will achieve such heights, adulterer?'

'If that's what Mr Lindsay says you will do, then who am I to say otherwise? You are his muse, it appears.'

'Yes, I'm his muse. He calls me his . . . his *amanuensis*.' She quivered with pride as she said it; evidently she did not know what the word meant, and how it was not as glorious as it sounded. 'Is being an amanuensis not a special thing? You tell me, Clay City whore.'

Arden thought it prudent not to tell Bellis that as Mr Lindsay's *amanuensis*, receiver of his creative urges, she was less a muse and more akin to a secretary or servant. Mr Lindsay was dictating Bellis' narrative, not the other way around.

Bellis turned as if to look through the walls and up the

mountainside to where the mysterious other weight was, the *plumb* and the *pit* that Foreman Locke had spoken of.

'You are right, adulterer, I'll give you that. I didn't want Stefan to save me from my greatness. I even told him to come with me when I left that stupid temple on his stupid rock. He could have been a prince. The consort of a Queen. How could he have chosen that life instead of me?'

'Because you were already married to Jonah for one—' Arden started, but stopped as she felt a pressure build up in the base of her lungs, a weight that made it hard for her to draw breath. Not from Bellis. Someone else.

Even though she should not have said anything to Bellis, the words came unbidden. 'Someone's using heavy blood—'

'What are you talking about?' Bellis snapped, before she too hitched a breath. Sanguinem were alike in the way they could feel the use of other endowments, and the power came in nauseating waves. From outside came shouts and blunderbuss cracks. Not random shots into the trees but concentrated fire, the noise reverberating about the denuded cliffside. Seconds afterwards there was the most unearthly sound, a rumbling, roaring noise that made the glassware rattle on the tables. The globe in the bedside lamp popped, raining sparks.

Bellis put her hand to her temple. 'Curse it, curse it!' she cried, and then was on her feet, staggering out of Arden's half-lit room as if injured. Arden watched Bellis leave . . . and not lock the door behind her.

The door yawned wide. Inviting. Whispering, *Escape, Arden. Escape.*

'Devilment,' she hissed to herself. She couldn't stay here in the near-dark, she had to know what was going on. The exploding electric bulbs had plunged the entire plantation house into darkness. The guards were running about desperately trying to light the spare rockblood lamps.

The lights spun to and fro, making shadows jump out from corners, sharp and fanged. Another low, grumbling trumpeting made itself known by the ornaments falling from the lodge wall.

She pushed her way past a gathering of servants crowding the front doorway and out into the yard. Down the counterweight slope, all the lights had converged upon a spot on the beach. The red waves rolled in like long slashes of afterimages, like a light shone too brightly into dark-seeing eyes.

'Sea monster!'

'No, a forest behemoth!' came a voice beside her. It was Mrs Valley. Then, realizing it was Arden she had spoken to, the housekeeper prepared to shout an alarm, but Arden was already running down the slope, sliding and slipping in the wet leaves, muddying her nightdress into a rag before she reached the sand.

At the moment she arrived at the water's fire-tinged edge one of the guards on the beach threw a canister of rockblood at the dark monster. A flood of blue, oily flame spread out across the creature's scrofulous back, igniting in the ride of bristles, and there at last was its outline.

A boar of gigantic, monstrous proportions, small red eyes aglow with rage, ivory tusks as sharp as scimitars.

No sooner had it started than the fire on its back went out, but the pain had riled the beast even more. The creature trumpeted again, a low, sonorous hoot of rage, and lunged at the men.

They jumped back. Each man carried a sharpened stake twice their length, moving in a complicated dance, keeping it away from the accommodation longhouses along the dunes. The monstrous behemoth-boar lunged at one of the men, and he shoved his spear into the pelt.

It went as far as the barb, but no further. He let out a yelp of concern before the monster shrugged the spear sideways, sending him flailing off into the night.

This happened in the space of seconds, but they were not seconds Arden could afford. She turned about and headed in the other direction – up the beach. Her goal was the pier and the boats, or maybe the trees, she didn't know. The sudden, flaring thrill of freedom made her too dizzy to think.

The workers' huts were there, too, and the one-eyed man who knew where Jonah was—

She reached the first hut – locked, but a brass key hung on a hook outside the door. Arden fumbled the key into the lock, pushed open the driftwood slab still bearing the name of the salvaged ship that had provided the wood.

A collection of startled cries greeted her.

In the cold glow of the rockblood lamp she could see there were easily thirty or forty women and children huddled inside the hut. She took a step forward, and her boot rocked on an uneven floor.

There may have been shadows aplenty, but she knew *chains* by the feel. They spread out in a tangle, like overgrown vines. Each ended at an ankle.

'Devilment,' she said in a whisper.

Once the shock was over, one of the women said, 'Is it still out there?'

The odd concern surprised her. Did the women not see their own condition? 'Y-yes,' she stammered. The boar was still trumpeting. She knew these captives, they were the women who helped with the clearing of the forest, who rolled the tobacco leaves, who made the food. She looked over them all and her eyes fell upon the girl Bellis had hypnotized, the one who had cut open her hand. Two of her fingers stood out straight like soldiers, while the others clenched the blouse of her mother.

'My God,' she said, 'why are you chained? I'll get you out—'

She had noticed that the plain tumbler-key for the door also fitted the padlocks, and knelt down in front of Bellis' victim, ready to free her.

Then the mother's hand fell on her own.

'It is night.'

'Everyone's busy! I can free you!'

The woman took Arden's hands in both her own, pushed Arden's gloved fists and the key in her numb fingers gently away.

'It is night and the Suitor of Tides will call us if we are not kept safe by our husbands.'

As she spoke, her daughter laid her head on her mother's chest, her eyes glassy with suspicion. Not two seconds later the door crashed open, and the housekeeper Mrs Valley stood there, panting hard, the hem of her dress a muddied wreck.

'Mrs Anguis,' she said, barely in control. 'You must come back to the house at once.'

'What is the meaning of this?' Arden cried, pointing at the strained, quiet faces of the Lyonnian women.

'You must come,' she said, and tugged at Arden's arm, and had there not been the contagious quiver of fear in Mrs Valley's voice, Arden might have stood her ground. The housekeeper was not trying to intimidate Arden, only to impress upon her a terrible truth. She could not stay.

Arden bent to tie her boot-buckle, and surreptitiously slid the key towards the mother's foot.

At first the mother ignored the offering. Then, as Arden stood, the cracked, dry hoof of a foot covered the bright brass.

Back on the beach the giant boar had reached the waterline while Miah stood in the waves, red flashes all about him like a vortex. The giant boar quivered in front of the *sanguis monstrum*, kneeling on its front legs. Its head was twisted at such an angle that the porcine ear was submerged in the wash of red tide. It let out short, sharp pants of rage.

'Quick, we haven't much time,' Mrs Valley urged, her hand slipping about Arden's waist. 'If the Master finds you missing—'

Broken by her own submission to Mrs Valley, Arden climbed back up the slope to the house, leaving sandy footprints across the floor.

But the chance to throw herself on the bed and howl melo-dramatically – her lungs had squeezed like two fists and only a scream would clear them – was spoiled when the third person in the room cut her crisis short.

The worker with one eye.

16

His hook-hand

His hook-hand sat on the knee of his rough linen strides. He had set the big cane knife on the floor beside him. His body, broad but hunched, belonged to a man used to fighting through the undergrowth of the forest.

Arden caught the shiver of sanguis feeling from him.

'I am Mr Green.'

'Was it you who called the forest behemoth?'

He nodded. ''Twas I.'

'I felt you, sir. And was it you who killed the Lindsays all those years ago?'

A sparkle and wink. He was not going to deny it. 'The reason I called my scrofulous friend down to the waterline was because I needed time to speak to you.' He exchanged a glance with Mrs Valley, who quietly retreated to the door, her ear out for unannounced visitors.

Arden fought the keep her face calm. She must not be impatient and demand things of this man until she understood better what his intentions were – until she knew what he would request in return.

'Speak then, sir.'

'Are you leaving soon?'

'What?'

'All of you. The witch. The man who commands metal. In front of the household staff they say that they are only here temporarily, but I would like to hear it from the unicorn's mouth, so to speak.'

'I . . . I think so,' Arden said. 'Bellis wants desperately to go to Clay City and ravage the place to the ground.'

'She will work the full extent of her bloodcraft and malfeasance there, I expect.'

'Yes. They are charging up *Sonder*'s battery pile to make that journey. Mr Lindsay wouldn't go to all this effort if he didn't intend to leave.'

'We already have a rockblood generator to power the boats and run the lights in this house,' said Mr Green, his brow leaning like a shelf over his one good eye. 'They could be gone by tomorrow if they wanted.'

'Yes, I have also noticed this.'

'Well, I am curious. Why dig out the old block and winch cables and restore the abandoned dynamo? The amount of power it generates is immense. You could not attach it to a motor. The battery would just leak out and ruin the pile completely.'

Arden shook her head. 'All I can think is that *Sonder* is old. She uses the power for stealth, to sneak up on monsters. Perhaps she could hold a greater charge.'

'How great?'

'I could not say. As a sanguinem I have some discomfort with electrical things.'

Mr Green rubbed his bristly chin. 'Sanguinem have issues with electricity. I too feel that kick when the house generator spins.'

'Now that I have told you all I know, tell me where Jonah is.'

'You might as well tell her, Hector,' Mrs Valley said from the doorway. 'The poor girl has suffered enough loss.'

The one-eyed man paused and hesitation showed on his face.

'We will take you to him tomorrow when the workers sleep during the hot hours. But I warn you – he is not well. He has the deepwater sickness. His mutinous spirit has taken hold of him.'

'Please. I just need to see him.'

'And you will. Until then, you must find out more about this intent of Master Lindsay's, this requirement to dig out what the forest has buried. It is important.'

A voice echoed from further back in the house. Mrs Valley cleared her throat. 'They come.'

He stood to leave. Arden stepped forward. 'Mr Green, one more thing.'

'Yes?'

'The women. Why are they chained in the lodge house at night?'

He exchanged a glance with Mrs Valley. Sighed. 'The Suitor of Tides may call them into the ocean otherwise. It keeps them safe.'

Arden swallowed. She had given the key to one of the women. Had she just condemned them to danger and death?

Wracked with second thoughts, Arden stood still as Mr Green slipped out onto the balcony. The shutters closed behind him just as the door's handle rattled.

And then Arden realized he'd left his cane knife behind.

Quick as a flash, Mrs Valley scooped up the knife, and what greeted Mr Lindsay as he entered was Arden on the seat, and Mrs Valley standing stern and cross-armed in front of her, cane knife threatening.

'Is everything all right, housekeeper?'

'Making sure she stays where she is supposed to,' Mrs Valley replied between clenched teeth. Her terseness made her seem furious, though Arden saw that it was only to stop her jaw from clattering in fear.

'Good work, Mrs Valley, though in future you can call one of the men to help. One need not wield such a hefty blade.'

'Yes, yes, you're right, Master Lindsay.'

She took her leave gratefully, only throwing the slightest glance of concern at Arden as soon as she was out of Mr Lindsay's sight.

Mr Lindsay had little to say to Arden, for the behemoth's arrival had rattled even him. He'd gruffed his displeasure at her dirty dress, and she explained her excursion outside by saying that she had been afraid, and the blood-sense had been so strong it had overwhelmed her, and she had fled out of panic.

It was truth enough, and thankfully Mr Lindsay's own duties distracted him enough that he did not interrogate any further.

After he left, Arden bathed and dressed quickly, rubbed more of the black salve into her hands and sighed at the stain left behind. The night was hot. She lay on top of the covers and waited in the dim room. For . . . something. For the next disaster that would confirm why she felt so on the edge of fleeing into the undergrowth and whatever waited in the primordial jungle. The faces of the chained women greeted her every time she closed her eyes. Was the Suitor of Tides a spirit so powerful it required this captivity?

Perhaps she slept after all, for the crunch of boots on the broken glass made her stir.

'Careful, the globe,' she murmured unthinkingly, imagining in some half-dream her step-sister Sirena back in Clay Portside, coming to pilfer a book from her bedside. Then she woke entirely and saw Miah there instead, staring down at her. He waited, abraded and strange in the dappled remains of illumination that came from the outside, and very much older. Exhaustion was on his brow, and he looked at her emotionlessly.

She knew now why his eyes seemed so bruised, for it was the black salve of Mr Lindsay's that did it, marking his treatment like a tattoo washed in rain.

'Are you all right?' she ventured carefully.

'I am fine.'

He sat on the edge of the bed and kicked off his boots. The fresh cuts on his flanks left stains on his shirt. The stains fluttered as he breathed, seemed to move. Jonah had sometimes cut himself so, when he'd needed to get the monstrosities of the Vigil waters to do his bidding. But he carried no shadow talent like his cousin Miah Anguis, had never been worked hard all day like this.

The silence grew long and she said, 'Has a medic seen to your cuts?'

He shook his head, his eyes looking at the wall as if he were seeing through it and into the forest outside.

'I am too tired,' he said. 'He wants so much of me.'

'Is this even worth it?'

He leaned over the bed to catch her face in his rough hand, and the kiss was somehow both filled with passion and impersonal at the same time. 'You are the exchange that makes this worthwhile, the gift he promised.'

Miah pulled off his clothes and did not wait for her to slip out of the plain shift of her nightdress, merely pushing the hem up and getting to work with all the enthusiasm of someone instructed. The weight of his body pressed Arden into the mattress as though something twice as heavy was residing in the architecture beneath his skin. It was not even like making love to a stranger, but a mechanical thing, a clockwork man.

And had she any choice in the matter she might have pushed him away and demanded to know what his problem was, but even if she did, she knew she would be afraid he would tell her, reveal a secret of this place and its ancient engineering in the forest, and tell her something she didn't want to know.

'Ah fuck it. I'm too tired.'

She didn't know if she were relieved or concerned. Apart from Mr Green and Mrs Valley, Miah was her only possible ally here. Was she losing his affection? For all that it was a burden and a disrespect, it was the thing she counted on to get her through this alive.

'It has been a day,' she said, a little too desperate.

He lay back, linked his fingers over his chest and closed his eyes.

At first she thought he might be sleeping. Unexpectedly he spoke. 'Something's wrong,' he said to the half-light. 'It's like something's here, crawling around in my head.'

'Bellis.'

'No. Something else. Older.'

She wanted to suggest that it was Mr Green he felt, until realizing that she too had experienced the disquiet of a former sanguis buried beneath the years. Only ghost wisps though, like the smell of a distant forest fire on a hot afternoon. As delicately as she could, as careful and casual as possible, Arden said, 'Today you told Mr Lindsay you sensed somebody else's presence in the wire, and Mr Lindsay said they'd once employed another *sanguis mandatum* who'd helped build the counterweight.'

He said nothing at first before giving a slow nod. 'I felt them.'

'But *sanguis mandatum* is an archival talent. Apart from you, and the Saint of the Islands, hardly anyone has ever had it. In Clay they document any *mandatum* talent so thoroughly the bloodworker might as well be kept in a zoo for all the freedom they'd have. Someone with that talent would not have been allowed to odd-job up and down the Firetide Coast. So how are you feeling something that shouldn't exist?'

She sounded anxious even to her own ears, and he opened one eye to look at her. 'Didn't I just say I was tired, Beacon?'

'Did you not start this conversation? Indulge me, Miah. All that machinery on the hill is the same age as the automata on Equus Island. It's all from the same era as the Unnamed Saint.'

He was silent, and Arden took it as encouragement to continue.

'You know what else is from that era?'

'What?'

'*Sonder.*'

Even with his eyes shut Miah frowned, annoyed at the constant questions. 'My great-great grandfather had her built, you know this.'

'With a ballast of copper and iron, to hide from the monsters? A ship that has lasted for centuries, the same as the lich ships do, and all the living metal of Equus? Oh Miah, haven't you even thought it through? The person you're feeling in the wires, the creator crawling in your head . . .' She had to take a breath, so utterly vertiginous did the answer make her feel. 'It must have been the Saint of the Islands who built her. And the Saint built the winch, and the counterweight.'

'We are a damn too many days' journey and in the wrong fucking country, in case you hadn't noticed.'

'The Saint was exiled to Equus. But we don't know what happened after that.'

'He or she got old and died. Damn it, Beacon. I'm supposed to be up at daylight.'

She had worked herself up now. She had to speak her suspicions, lest they fester inside her. Even if it was only to him.

'The Saint didn't die. I think they escaped and somehow came *here*, and Mr Lindsay's been desperate to get a boat of the same vintage for whatever reason is scampering around in that inexplicable Lion mind of his. *Velleity* was also a boat of that age. He has a plan, and I think it's bigger than just sneaking Bellis past the watchtowers and into Clay City.'

'Look, Beacon, if the Saint made a wasteland of Equus, they'd have done the same thing here. They didn't, which means it can't be the Saint I'm feeling. Now for the love of God stop talking and let me go to sleep.'

Miah huffed and rolled over and Arden mulled over what she'd said. The Saint of the Islands had reached the Firetide Coast, they must have done! He or she had disappeared from Equus so suddenly, and the Lions had never documented an investigation. Or even a death.

Miah was feeling the Saint's shadow and ghost, Arden was certain of it. But Miah was also right when it came to what had happened in Equus. If the Saint had come here, then by some miracle they'd not turned Lyonne into a mechanical wasteland like Equus on arrival. What had stopped them? Who – or what – had laid a hand upon the shoulder of this mysterious fugitive with godlike powers and said, *enough*?

And could the same thing stop Bellis Harrow if it came to that?

17

Mr Lindsay was no fool

Mr Lindsay was no fool, and he did not for one second suspect the behemoth's attack to be a natural occurrence. He had spent his formative years on the Coast and knew that the behemoths were naturally shy creatures, easily discouraged by loud noises. If it had come down to the waterline, it must have been *compelled* to do so.

When the men did not cough up the offending handler's name the next morning, Mr Lindsay had put the interrogation into the hands of Bellis Harrow. The geology of the Coast might have blunted her powers somewhat, but it did not remove them altogether. In the high work clearing, in full view of all of the forest workers, she had made two men draw their thicket knives and attack each other.

Arden came upon the work clearing at the same time as Miah, and saw the two figures slumped lifeless and bloody, still holding their thicket knives. Later, she would hear how they had wept and pleaded and shouted apologies, even as they slammed the blades into each other's limbs and chests. They had fought to the death.

One of them was Glaucon, the guard. A crowd of flies buzzed over his lifeless body. The other man Arden did not recognize but he had survived a minute or so more, enough to have crawled far enough from the fight to leave several yards of bloodied smear and gore behind.

Under the foreman's gazebo, Bellis sat with an odd, contented smile on her lips. Despite everyone's trauma at what they had witnessed, they all moved at double-pace. The chain-cutters' grey smoke coiled down the mountainside.

'What the fuck, Bellis?' Miah hollered when he came upon the slaughter. 'What the hell is this?'

'Mr Lindsay felt our workers weren't motivated enough,' she said slyly. 'And that little trick with the behemoth last night is an event that really can't be allowed to go unpunished.'

Bellis sounded very much like Mr Lindsay when she spoke and Arden could see that her teeth were black, the same metallic black as the stain upon her own palms and around Miah's eyes. What had Mr Berry said about the salve back on *Sonder*? The unholy medicine, he'd called it. *An immoral poison the Lions use for other things . . .*

And Mr Absalom had stopped Mr Berry from speaking further. With a gasp Arden looked at her hands. This was no ordinary cure.

Like a hog with a ring through its snout . . .

She could not rush off to wash, for Mr Lindsay was walking up the cable track to the day's new work clearing, still dabbing a towel on his freshly shaved face. Arden shoved her hands into the pockets of her floral-patterned dress, certain she could feel the prickling poison as if it were vinegar on a wound.

Upon his approach he cast a dismissive look at the dead men.

'Honestly,' he said with a kiss of his teeth. 'Queen Bellis – it's a bit much. We could have used their labour.'

'Motivation,' Bellis said again. 'The others will fill the gaps.'

'Don't overwork them, dear, we are past the shore now and need to get into the deep forest. Mr Locke' – Mr Lindsay waved to get the foreman's attention – 'can these bodies be removed, please?'

Arden tried to sit as far away from Bellis as she could, but it didn't help much, for the workers gave her the same termi-nally blank look as Bellis received every time they reluctantly passed by. She entertained the idea of leaping up and denouncing Bellis, but that would only get all of them in trouble.

If this was Bellis with her powers muted, the devil only knew what she'd be like unleashed.

Understandably, the drama had made Arden almost forget about the chained women in the lodge house from last night. It took a jug of cordial delivered by the domestic who had received Arden's key for her to remember and say, 'What is your name?'

She asked so suddenly that the woman recoiled, as if offended. Then the woman glanced around and replied, 'I am the wife of Mr Finch,' before beating a hasty retreat.

Once again the long, tedious hours of the day stretched out, made even more agonizing as Mr Green had promised Arden he would take her to see Jonah during the long daylight break.

But he had promised this before two men had brutally murdered each other in front of everybody for something that Mr Green had done. Perhaps there would not even be a midday break. Bellis seemed content to make them work through the day.

In the frowsy hours of the exhausting afternoon one of the workers came to the planning table dusted with splinters. He smelled of chain-oil and rockblood and stumbled with weariness.

Mercifully, Bellis was off taking a nap or enacting some bedevilment upon the house-servants, and wasn't around to snap at him to get back to work. Grunting from overheated discomfort, the man took off his protective jacket and thigh chaps – both sewn from layers of thick sea-cow leather in between wads of cellulose tree-fibres. If a chainsaw were to fall on a leg or a limb, the tree-fibre threads would immediately tangle up in the saw's driving mechanism, and stop the chain at once.

There had been, however, an ongoing argument between Mr Lindsay and Mr Sword as to which was more valuable. In Mr

Lindsay's view, a worker was *replaceable*, whereas a chain-driven saw was *delicate and expensive*. According to the interminably round-about arguments Arden had overheard from the previous day, they'd so far lost six men to the hospital-shed with terrible injuries. None of them had been wearing their traditional forest-worker's protection though.

The forest worker ladled out a scoop of water from a barrel, drank deeply, and – almost so offhandedly Arden would have missed it if she were not pondering his mysterious garment – said, 'When the tree over yonder falls, walk up the slope to the winch house.'

She wanted to know what he meant by *tree*, as there had been trees felled all day, but he picked up his chaps and slipped into the remains of the undergrowth, gone before she could even shout out to him. The chains buzzed and the thwack of axes echoed sharply on the rapidly denuding cliff face. There was even a steam shovel, pulling the debris off the winch slope so it might fall back down the cliffside. Mr Lindsay was wasting no time.

And then, like a gunshot, she heard the crack of a tree breaking, followed by a shout of alarm. The steam-shovel operator had only a bare second to swing his arm aside before the ragged trunk of a freshly cut grandfather gingko rolled past him and his machine.

It took Arden so much by surprise to see such an escape, from what would have been certain death had the trunk hit the precariously balanced steam shovel, that she didn't at first think of anything more than checking to see if the worker was unharmed. And then it struck her that this was what the forest worker had meant, for the log had created as much of a diversion as the behemoth had, and it would be her only chance to get out.

Arden pulled her skirt up around her knees and half-walked, half-climbed up the winch-cable track, past the huge standing block structure and towards a rusted shed in much the same condition as the dynamo-house. A swarm of griffin-flies sprang out of the cleared undergrowth, not the biggest Arden had ever seen, but as a dragonfly the size of a seagull, they were startling when they swooped, and they could inflict a painful bite. At least twenty were airborne, their double wings drumming in the thick air of the forest.

'Away with you!' She swung her sun-shawl about her head and wasted no time seeking the winch-house shelter. A griffin-fly slammed into the door as she pulled it shut, leaving a visible dent.

'Devilment,' she cursed, and then spun about, for she'd been too hasty and had not checked exactly what waited for her.

And what waited were two men, one of them the worker who had invited her into the winch house, and the second one Mr Green, broad and scarred in the low light.

'Arden Beacon.'

'I meant to ask, how did you know my name?' she inquired of Mr Green. 'Everyone called me Mrs Anguis back at the estate.'

'*He* said it when we tried to take the spirit out. When he came to the shore, he said your name.'

She could barely breathe. Jonah had said her name. He had spoken.

'Did you get it out? The thing that was inside him?'

Mr Green and the forest worker exchanged glances. Not a look that inspired confidence. Mr Green gestured for her to follow. 'This way.'

Having recovered some of her senses, she took note of her surroundings. The mechanism inside the rusted walls of the gear house was a strange cluster of giant gears on a spindle, as shiny and oily as the day the Saint of the Islands had called upon the iron to do their bidding. The automata of Equus had been constructed by a child trying to be helpful. This was built by an adult with their own mind. The gear teeth were all meshed chevrons, V-shaped interlocks.

Arden touched her deepwater marriage tattoo at the back of her neck as a shiver ran through her bones like a tide. That tattoo was also a chevron.

Mr Green lifted a trapdoor in the floor nearby, and they descended a staircase of latticed steel. A lamp hissed cold light. And in the centre . . . in the centre, bound and slumped in a chair . . .

'We brought him here because the *spirit* is less strong around the old mechanica,' Mr Green said when he saw Arden's horrified expression at this tomb-like cellar of a prison. 'The deepwater spirit quails in the presence of Them Who Made the Automata.'

The Unnamed Saint.

'What have you done to him?'

Jonah wore the same ragged leggings as he had when he'd gone into the water, but not the shirt. His tattoos were stark and black, chevrons, scales, squid-beaks and eyes. She pushed forward past the men, knelt at his side and tore the hood off Jonah's head.

For a second she'd have thought it a monster. His eyes were almost all black, as if she stared into a shark's eyes. He breathed heavy, as if drowning, and a veil of blank hate covered his face . . .

'Careful,' Mr Green said as she reached out to touch him, and she wanted to snap an angry word back at the forest man. She would have, were it not for Jonah attempting to sink his teeth into her arm.

She felt his teeth graze her skin, but the sleeve on the dress fouled his attack, and he came away with merely a shred of cotton.

Arden yelped and fell back onto the slimy floor. The Jonah-thing let the scrap of sleeve fall from his mouth, and continued to sit and pant, staring out into the nothingness beyond the wall of his prison.

'He needs air,' she said helplessly.

Mr Green came to her and helped Arden up. 'At least he is breathing here. Outside, the spirit takes over, and he begins to choke.'

'What can we do?'

'Nothing.' It was the other forest worker who spoke. 'We have tried our own ritual on him, our own potion. But on top of his possession he has been bitten by a sea dragon, and the venom has festered, making it worse.'

He pointed at a crusted gash on Jonah's thigh that showed little sign of treatment. To Arden's eyes it looked the same as the healing scar on Miah's leg, from when he'd caught the giant *Maris Anguis* last month, the deepwater clan beaching the massive sea dragon and slaughtering it upon the Equus shore. That catch had also led to Arden's first meeting of Jonah's cousin.

The worker told her their story. They had found Jonah on the beach, his body half submerged in the scarlet phosphorescence, the twilight after Arden had arrived with *Sonder*. At first, they'd mistaken him for a corpse wearing sailor's breeches and nothing else. The water had been cold, he should have been dead, and they would have left him there had the oldest among them not felt the superstitions of his ancestors gnaw his bones. They could not abandon him, for the man was marked, not only in the ink of the deepwater folk of the south but also in the harsh scarification of the Harbinger Bay survivors.

He wore other injuries too – the sea-monster teeth of *Maris Anguis*, and one ivory tooth, which was buried in his shoulder between collarbone and throat. Had it penetrated a finger-width left or right into either nerve or artery he'd have lost the use of his arm . . . or his life.

As it was, they dragged him up the hill to their forest redoubt and pulled the tooth out of him. Payment for the treatment they would receive, for the tooth of a sea dragon was a mighty treasure indeed.

But they could rouse him no further.

'I cannot believe it. Have you tried everything?'

'We can try putting him back in the water,' Mr Green said.

She glanced at Jonah, or what he was now. He'd always seemed so otherworldly to her, but this . . . it was less than a metamorphosis into a true self than a kidnapping and assault from within.

'You mean let him be taken over and die.'

They said nothing, for what could be said? At least they had tried to save him. It would have been easier for them to have let Jonah slip, wounded, back into the red-tinged water and allow him his final change . . . into a corpse.

She stepped closer to him and he bared his teeth. This was a stranger before her. Everything that was Jonah Riven, gone.

'I'd like to go now,' she said. Something was bubbling in her chest, a scream, a wail, a sound that, were it made, would seem inhuman in this stone room. Mr Green nodded, sympathetic.

She had climbed the stairs and was about to leave the gear house when Mr Green put his hook-hand upon her shoulder.

'Those two you call your queen and your husband – they must be gone from this place, and quickly. Glaucon was a good man. He did not deserve the death he received.'

18

Outside, the griffin-flies darted

Outside, the griffin-flies darted about the remains of the forest, and Arden stumbled back down the cable track, gasping for breath in the hot oily air. Only when she reached the administration clearing did she realize that she'd not even discussed with Mr Green the possibility of escape.

'Devils fuck it,' she said, sounding more like Miah than she thought she had a right to. She palmed some frustrated tears from her cheeks. 'Why couldn't you have *thought*, Arden?'

Footsteps sounded behind her and she quickly composed herself, but it was only Mrs Finch, salvaging the wild tobacco from the clear-felled debris. She had wound the big leaves into a bundle under her arm. She peered at Arden before looking back up the slope.

'Ah, you saw the man that came on the tide two days ago.'

Arden nodded. 'I saw him.'

'He was your friend.'

Arden nodded again, and a crawling in the back of her eyes made her take caution for Bellis had reappeared at the map table of Mr Sword.

Just as Arden was about to ask about the key, about the women, and about their odd requirement to stay locked up in the nighttime, Mrs Finch put her head down and moved off at a quick pace, not daring to attract Bellis' attention. It was not a moment too soon, for Mr Lindsay was back as well. His skin glowed youthfully from his bathing, and also from having taken the siesta he did not allow his men.

'Ah, Arden, there you are. For a moment there I thought I'd need to send a search party out.'

'I wanted to stretch my legs. I thought my husband might call for me.'

Mr Lindsay squinted. 'And why should he call? He is busy.'

Bellis gave a snort next to him, and climbed into the chair that had been obtained for her, a similar wing-backed tub-seat to Mr Sword's. It was upholstered in diamond-stitched green velvet, sun-faded on one side. 'Too busy. Too busy to be a man.' She winked at Arden.

'May I go inside?' Arden said. 'It is hot.'

'No, you may not,' Mr Lindsay said. 'Bellis, dear, go check on the workers at the cable track. They've been behaving oddly. I have a requirement for Mrs Anguis.'

When Bellis sauntered off, Mr Lindsay took the calf-leather case he'd been carrying under his arm, slid open the closure and opened it like a book. Inside were glass jars, a line of yellow rubber pipe, and a purse of steel syringes.

'Well, I suppose I do not have to explain to you what I need. *Sanguis evalescendi.*'

He did not. Arden knew he would ask for her blood at some point, although it was not so much a question as a sliding-scale test of her cooperation. She could either give a portion of her blood freely now or he'd have people hold her down so they might take it by force.

She would almost welcome the pain. Anything to take her mind off Jonah.

She must have hesitated long enough to make Mr Lindsay think she was preparing an argument, for he pulled another cylinder of black paste from his pocket and placed it on the map table. 'For your troubles.'

The gazebo gave little shade, and in the hot sun she sweated as she gave the portion. While her blood drained from her arm into the blood-jars, Mr Lindsay said amiably, 'We will have visitors tonight, business partners of mine from down the coast. It will make a change. It has been quite a dull few weeks for us, you see.'

'And will Bellis be in attendance? I'm sure a smashed plate or two might make for good entertainment.'

'You're tart today, dear.' He pulled out the needle, not bothering to be gentle. Blood pooled in the crook of her arm and she staunched it with her sleeve.

She heard a shout of alarm, further up the track. Bellis was evidently making more of her own mischief.

'Are you going to give her that?' She gestured at the blood-jar, now turned as black as a dark ruby.

'And it is your business, why?'

'She is no pet to do with as you will, Mr Lindsay. Your entire relationship with that woman has been leashes and control, and she'll take the first opportunity to be free of both.'

'Dear Mrs Anguis, when I let Bellis off the leash, it will be at a time of my choosing. In an hour you may go inside and have a bath. My guests will be here by sundown.'

Arden watched Mr Lindsay take the jar up the mountainside, and with Beacon-sharp eyes saw him chide Bellis for wasting yet another two workers, though this time she had not sported with them enough to kill them. They limped off towards the hospital lodge, clearly in conniptions of gratitude at being spared the same gruesome death that had taken their colleagues that morning.

The nearby cable-block shuddered.

Further up at the winder, she could see Miah had divested himself of his shirt and was winding the pulley with his own strength, the muscles of his tattooed back working like bridge cables beneath his tattooed skin. Even from so far away a fizzle of *sanguis mandatum* blood was in the air. The wound on her arm itched, and blood coursed to her fingers. The effect was almost like hypnosis.

The counterweight groaned and shuddered. Flakes of rust fell from the cables as they came taut. An engine kicked on somewhere higher up the slope, followed by the sound of a flywheel's humming, and Arden heard in her very bones that familiar rhythm shared by lich ships and Equus ghost-diggers alike. The Saint of the Island's mechanica was coming to life.

There were no cheers, as one would usually expect following all their efforts coming to success. Instead the disquieting silence persisted until Mr Locke the foreman managed to lead a begrudging hip-hooray, but it failed before the third shout.

'The counterweight block will ascend all night. It will reach the last winding post by tomorrow morning, well ahead of the clearing crew,' Mr Sword said to Arden as he arrived to pack up the silk maps and diagrams in the yellow afternoon. 'They'll have to dig it out of the forest.'

Arden realized she had been in a daze for nearly the entire hour. The temperature had fallen slightly with a rising afternoon condensation. With the sun obscured by the cliff and the shadow falling over the gazebo it was not so hot, and mist spilled over the top of the cliff face.

The steward Mr Sword closed the map box with its precious documents inside. 'It is splendid that they've achieved such success.'

'See what I told you,' Bellis squawked triumphantly, for she had come back down the cable slope with Mr Lindsay. 'Motivation.'

'Enough to bring our completion date ahead by nearly a full day,' Mr Lindsay said, pleased. He nodded at Arden, acknowledging her contribution. 'What a shame we cannot stay an extra hour to make the counterweight cover that distance. We could be completely finished by tomorrow night, ready to leave the morning after.'

'Oh goody!' Bellis cried, clapping her hands. 'I cannot wait!'

Arden held on to the gazebo rather than fall from the faintness that came over her. The day after tomorrow? Were they going to depart, and leave Jonah?

'Bring out the torches,' Mr Lindsay said. 'There should be enough light to see by. What say you, Mr Sword?'

The steward moved from foot to foot, his face a picture of discomfort. 'I would not try to chance the denizens of the forest, since we are past the cloud line here, and night comes.'

'Would be easier to burn them out.'

Mr Sword's face took on a gimlet stare. 'They tried to once, on the plantation south of here. The house is deserted now, nobody works those hills.'

Mr Lindsay affected a look of boredom. 'And here comes the warning.'

Mr Lindsay's mockery did not perturb Mr Sword. He only lit his pipe and swallowed the fragrant blue smoke. 'No warning, only the fact of an empty estate, home to the creepers, and the forest grown back twice as thick.'

That was that. Besides, neither Mr Lindsay nor Mr Sword could have compelled the shorefolk to work into the night. Bellis could have, but the people feared the cloud-layer creatures so utterly it would take a massacre to force them. They would need to let the counterweight move through the forest overnight on its own.

As if to underscore how different things were here, a segmented beetle the size of a bulldog waddled across the clearing not more than ten paces away. One of the workmen ran to catch it, hefting it up, its legs waving angrily.

'Ah,' Mr Lindsay said. 'No doubt we will see it on the dinner table later.'

The beetle clicked and chirred, rustling its glossy black elytra but to no avail. Its fate was already sealed.

19

In the back room

In the back room, the servants had already drawn a bath in the copper tub. Steam floated off the top. It smelled of oudwood, a scent of cedar and flowers. Candles guttered in their glasswear, yellow like a dozen pairs of eyes, watching.

It seemed too carefully arranged, like a trap. Arden undressed and submerged herself quickly. The heat soaked into her bones, dizzying her.

'I thought the bath was for me.'

She froze, indignant at Miah's arrival. 'Aren't there workers' showers?'

'Bellis has forbidden them use of the wash rooms. Her punishment for the behemoth, I suppose.'

'Punishing them, not you.'

'If they see me frolicking in hot water then I'll likely swallow a blade before morning. It's hard enough convincing them I don't give two shits about that woman.'

Miah had already stripped off his dirty clothes, gummed almost solid from sweat and tree resin, and discarded them. His arms and shoulders were ruddy from the sun. Streaked bruises bisected his thick abdomen where the cable had lashed into his body, refusing at first to move for this lesser *mandatum*, remembering the Saint who had forged each length and twist. He'd cut his upper arms amidst the ghosts of old summonings.

She wondered how he'd taken the *evalescendi*. Rubbed it in? Drunk it?

He was more animal than man, even in the way he slunk into the water, his eyes on her, not entirely tamed. Not entirely trusting.

'Almost too hot,' he said, though by then it had grown lukewarm, and his chest flushed as if he were radiating heat, for he was a coldwater man and this heat was not for him.

'It was hotter before.' His ankles slid on either side of her hips, his calves whiskering against her thighs. She tucked up her legs and debated getting out, before deciding against it. She'd damn well gotten in here first.

He flopped his arms over the sides of the tub, swung his head back. His bruised, blackened eyes became unfocused, and briefly she saw Jonah there. *Trapped in his stinking hole.*

'Mr Lindsay says we will be finished tomorrow night.'

'Did he? I can't really remember.' He rubbed his head.

'He said it down at the gazebo.'

'Oh.'

'Have you thought about what happens next? When you go to Clay City as part of Bellis' army?'

He raised his head and looked at her as if confused. 'I haven't thought about it.'

'You haven't?' Arden reached out to move a candle-dish before the wax overflowed into the bath. 'When Bellis gets past the sanguis sentries, when she overwhelms Clay with her *orientis* powers, I doubt Mr Lindsay will have much of a use for you. Clay already has people who can talk to metal, and they're pure-bred for it, too. They're not carrying monster-wrangling shadow-talents that get in the way.'

Her comments were measured but she intended them to land painfully. Miah made a sour face.

'Bellis has got shadow-talents too, Beacon. We're just piebald whirlwinds and I'm only along for the ride. I haven't thought about it because I don't care. Whether Bellis burns down the city or gets her lungs popped by a sentry before she gets within fifty miles of the place, it makes no difference. Afterwards, I'm going home.'

Miah clawed a cake of soap from the depression in the side of the tub and slid it over his torso. The water was too mineralised, the cake did not lather. A white ring of scummed soap floated on top.

She frowned at him. His speech sounded too *defeatist*, almost. The Miah Anguis she knew was so fiercely independent even the yoke of another benevolent leader was too much. He wasn't the type to follow any man around waiting to see what would happen.

'Are you all right, Miah?'

He glared at her. The real him returned. 'Of course I'm fucking all right.' He stood and clambered out of the bath, dripping the scummy water over the flagstones. 'There's no fucking problem except you stealing my sight.' He dived into the pockets of his discarded strides and pulled out a grimy stamped-metal pot, and without the slightest self-consciousness thumbed out the goop and heeled it into his eyes. Black tears of irritation ran down his cheeks.

She watched in silence as he dried himself and dressed in clothes that could only be called clean when held up to the dirty, blood-stained linens he had discarded. The wounds on his side puckered with a fresh scab.

Outside a blunderbuss coughed in the boundary.

'It is night soon,' he said, slipping his belt through the buckle and fastening it. 'Best not linger. Lindsay will be expecting you.'

Only after Miah had gone did she climb out and rummage through the bedside table for the second pot of Mr Lindsay's black salve. She had not applied any from the old container since the previous morning – Mr Lindsay had been too busy with his disinterring of the counterweight mechanism to check if Arden was being compliant. *The immoral poison.*

Now that she wasn't forced to think with Bellis and her

horrors nearby, she tentatively dismissed Mr Berry's assessment. Poison was too easy. And this strange substance *healed,* no doubt about it. But what if it healed a person of more than their ailments?

Unholy medicine.

If only Chalice were here, Arden thought with an unwelcome rush of grief. Madame Lion knew all manner of herbal potions.

A grumble outside interrupted her imaginings. She heard the chatter of an engine that was a great deal more modern than the winding mechanism thumping down the hillside.

A motor car. But of course, she was in Lyonne now, where such transport was not uncommon, and there were roads to accommodate vehicles. A motor car had been a rare thing in Fiction, only the Coastmaster – Mr Justinian – had owned one, and Bellis Harrow's father in his position as town magistrate. Bellis might have been a small-town girl, but her family had occupied a high place in the civic hierarchy.

'Mrs Anguis?' The voice came after the knocking on the door. 'The other plantation owners are here, you'd best get ready or Mr Lindsay will be looking for you.'

'In a minute,' she called back. 'I'm just drying off.'

The climate didn't require too many layers, and the mantel clock was ringing for supper as she stepped out in a somewhat decent pantsuit of tan, drill fabric and a wide belt of behemoth leather – a ridiculous sort of colonial get-up missing a safari hat, but there was not much else to choose from. A chaperone guard followed her as she made her way upstairs. Not Glaucon, who was now dead and buried without even the gift of a funeral. Someone else, a Lyonnian who barely met her eyes.

The bones of a plan knocked together in her head. Maybe Mr Lindsay's visitors could help her, somehow. Get a message to her father, to the Lyonne Order.

'. . . *all the years I thought you gone!*'

Arden stopped on the stair landing. There seemed to be some sort of commotion in the dining room, a sharp exchange of voices. She heard Bellis' shriek, but there did not come the usual wave of *orientis* with her anger. Bellis sounded genuinely upset. A man's voice followed, muffled.

'*Really, Bellis!*'

Of course it would be *now*, when she had no time to browse, that she would take notice of the many daguerreotypes and silver-prints framed on the walls. The one that most intrigued her showed the great winding block halfway constructed and half a dozen people staring at the camera. Could one of those people be the Saint?

Arden leaned in closer, wishing for more light.

'Get moving,' said the guard impatiently. 'They're waiting for you.'

'Goodness gracious,' she protested. 'I'm moving.'

Collecting her courage, she stepped up to the dining table, its long length set and populated. Seven faces turned to look at her. One of them was Bellis, who was inexplicably – and rather humanly, for once – in tears.

And another of them was Vernon Justinian.

20

You

'You!' Mr Justinian squawked. 'You, too, in this circus of mendacity?!'

'Vernon,' Arden said, and as much as she tried to compose herself, she knew the colour had drained from her face as if she'd seen a ghost. Almost a year ago she had come to the Fiction town of Vigil, and stayed in the Manse Justinian, the crumbling great house in the hill overlooking the village. The Justinian family had been clinging on to the rags of wealth.

Mr Lindsay smiled from the head of the table. 'Oh, you look surprised, Mrs Anguis. Did Mr Justinian not share this particular detail of his investment portfolio?' In the shocked silence that followed, Mr Lindsay gestured at an empty seat. 'Please sit, Mrs Anguis. And Vernon, if you would do the same, we can serve the entrée.'

A feather could have knocked her over. A pair of hands from one of the wait-staff gently guided Arden as if she were an invalid into the seat next to Miah. He barely acknowledged her.

Mr Justinian had grown a large moustache since she had last seen him, which added no improvement to his boringly hand-some face. He was dressed in a port-wine velvet suit that now matched the colour of his blushing neck.

'*Anguis?*' Vernon Justinian repeated. His face asked: *you wedded this brute?*

She tipped up her chin, a wretched pride returning, for she was remembering now who she had been back in that Fiction springtime.

'I am married. And you not, Vernon? I thought a bachelor such as yourself would have found a suitable bride by now.'

He darted a look at Bellis, sitting at the other end of the table. She had turned a strange shade of blue, like a child who has decided to hold their breath until they pass out from stubbornness.

'They keep turning out to be unsuitable.'

'Ah, the entrée comes,' said the woman next to Vernon, and Arden realized it was the Dowager Justinian, Vernon's mother. She was much the same as Arden remembered her, dressed in funereal black, her clothes several years out of date.

The entrée was the beetle from the afternoon, artfully placed on a silver platter, the shell-like elytra opened to expose the white meat of its abdomen. Around the centrepiece was a selection of vegetables, from sautéed pith from the blood-vine to snake beans and curry-tubers. A pile of roasted crickets made up the garnish.

Mr Sword had been coaxed out of his cups to join them. He sat on Arden's left. 'Try it,' he said as Arden hesitated over the beetle meat. 'It tastes like trilobite and nuts.'

Through the meal Arden took quick glances at the Dowager. Vernon was a lost cause, but wouldn't she be sympathetic to Arden's plight?

'You urged the workers along well today, Bellis,' Mr Lindsay said over their main meal, a tagine of stewed forest vegetables, peppery stone fruit, and another white meat with an oily taste that Arden suspected might be reptilian. 'Mr Anguis, you have also done magnificent work. We should reach the crest the day after tomorrow. According to the diagrams, there is a pit for the alternate weight. After that, it will take no more than an hour to give the boat all the power she can take.'

Mr Lindsay's praising words had no effect on Miah, who hovered over his plate and shovelled food into his mouth. Even after his bath and a change of clothes he didn't seem at all better, his hair still dirty and sap-stained, the replacement clothes having merely been rested, not washed.

'Why on earth are you uncovering this wretched mechanism after all this time?' Dowager Justinian asked of Mr Lindsay. 'Your grandfather declared it forbidden.'

'Ah, I'm glad you asked. I have decided to resume boat trade on the Firetide Coast,' Mr Lindsay said. 'My boats have been slow compared to the train route, and more power means they will reach the city quickly. So I am testing equipment I already own, rather than suffering the expense of something new.'

'And what does this test entail, that I should be called here?' Mr Justinian asked. 'And be subjected to such unwelcome surprises.' With that he looked at Bellis and Arden.

'My boats need to cover the proposed transport route on one charge. Obviously I require the seal of a Coastmaster to help me though the bureaucracy of entry, and a Coastmaster of Fiction holds much the same authority as a Coastmaster of South Lyonne. That is why I have called you.'

Arden had to bury her head in the meal so as not to make a face. He spoke with such a gloating air. She knew that what Mr Lindsay was saying was a complete lie. If only she knew what the exact untruth of it was.

'And of course,' Mr Lindsay continued, 'I would be happy to share cargo space with my fellow agricultural speculator.'

'Sounds acceptable,' Vernon said, his eyes lighting up. 'My greatest expense is transport. The rail barons have such a monopoly on haulage fees.'

'Then I'm sure we can come to an arrangement.'

The Dowager put down her cutlery. 'Why not ask the South Lyonne Coastmaster for your authorisation paperwork, Claude? It has taken us days to travel back to our plantation so we might have this meeting, and the Coastmaster Tanbark is only a few hours northwards.'

Mr Justinian stared at his mother, clearly horrified at her suggestion. The Dowager perhaps knew full well she had spoken out of turn, but she was not about to sit and listen to her son be led by the nose.

Mr Lindsay gave a sniff, and for the first time Arden saw him looking almost aggrieved. It was a notable expression of annoyance. The Lion was normally so judicious in what he showed the world.

'The man and I do not see eye to eye. Mr Tanbark is a jobsworth and a malingerer who does not understand the value of business. A fellow entreprencur, Mr Justinian, knows the value of haste.'

The subtle flattery worked its way into the crevices of Vernon's brittle ego. 'Yes, you did rescue the women and three of Grandfather's factory workers from the deepwater savages of Equus, for which we are grateful. My friend Mr Lindsay is very clever,' Vernon said, nudging his mother. Then his delight turned frosty. 'Though not so clever as to completely protect Guildswoman Arden Beacon from the ravages of that wild land. Sir, could you not have rescued your fellow Lyonnian *before* she was tied up in this bestial marriage?'

So that was the excuse Mr Lindsay used to explain her presence. A rescue. She looked to Miah to see how offended he was at being called bestial, but he seemed almost absent from the world. Had Miah and Vernon known one another in Vigil? The old Baron had kept many of the town's fisherfolk in indentured servitude and serfdom.

Vernon Justinian drank steadily, matching even Mr Sword. He became garrulous, inviting Mr Lindsay to this soirée and that, chortling over mutual trading partners who were in Vigil to do multi-page deals among simple folk who could not even read. Dowager Justinian, usually known to drink heartily, would not touch the served liqueur. Instead, she looked at her glass with a frown all evening.

With the serving of dessert, the last rays of sunlight kissed the sky, Arden sidled to the balcony window where she saw a row of women marching down to the waterline and the lodges. They carried with them torches and lanterns, a solemn procession.

'Why, they go to their beds so soon in the evening.'

Arden turned about at the Dowager's voice.

By then the dining room was empty save for the wait-staff clearing the last of the cutlery. Mr Sword, Mr Lindsay and Vernon had left for an adjoining room to sign the documents, and Miah was gone.

Bellis, too. How quiet she had been through the dinner, not daring to say a word.

The Dowager pointed out the window. 'Going so soon to bed? It's still light out.'

'Yes, it is rather soon,' Arden agreed. 'It's a tradition among them, I think.' She did not really wish to talk to Vernon's mother. Her vaulting hope she might get a message out had all but died now.

The Dowager looked at her for a long while before speaking. 'Was it tradition among the deepwater folk to marry their captives off so quickly? You have barely been gone a month, Arden.'

'I faced a difficult situation after I left Vigil,' Arden said. 'There was business to attend to before I went home. I made some wrong decisions. I needed to survive.'

'Surely you can leave him now you are safe among your fellow Lyonnians? That Mr Anguis looks such a brute.' She grasped Arden's numb hand and bent close. 'Oh Arden dear, say the word and we can take you back to our plantation by the coast. You could hide in the Manse in Fiction. Get an annulment paper from the magistrate. Marry my son and all will be well.'

Arden recoiled at the offer. It would be exchanging one prison for another. She extricated her hand and moved further out onto the balcony. 'I have responsibilities. My husband intends to make this run of his to Clay City the day after tomorrow and I must join him.'

The Dowager frowned. 'Clay City?'

'Yes, it's where we are going.'

'Dear, my son is signing an entry document for the forbidden estuary of Harbinger Bay, not Clay Portside. It's signed for tomorrow. Are you leaving so soon?'

'Harbinger Bay?' Arden repeated, not sure she had heard the Dowager correctly. 'Tomorrow?'

'Yes, it's about a day's sail north of here. There's a prison nearby, a hideous house of criminality, but at least they are all well secured, apparently.'

Arden shook her head, confused now. This was a day too early, and in an entirely different place. 'Dowager, you must be mistaken. Harbinger Bay is in the middle of nowhere. Nobody is allowed in that region, we've made no plans.'

'Nobody is allowed . . . except with the approval of the Coastmaster. There is a train line and terminus station. For the prisoners. I suppose one of those railway barons has struck a deal to use his line for more than hauling penitents, and branched out to perfumery instead.' She gestured towards a decorative brass distilling tank in the corner of the dining room, a minia-ture of the large oud-oil distiller in the basement level. 'Maybe I shouldn't be telling you this. My son doesn't even know I know about his business. But I *like* you, Arden, and I just can't stomach the thought of you and dear Bellis being dragged so close to the prison grounds, even if on a trading mission.'

We're going to the prison tomorrow? she thought to herself in a panic. What kind of diversion was Mr Lindsay planning? The infamous penitentiary country of Harbinger Bay was even more secure than the city. There was nothing there that would be of any use, just ten thousand criminals—

It was as if her body came to the realization before her mind did, a great electric spark jumping through her bones.

Ten thousand criminals. Ten thousand people all in one place, all vulnerable, because the security looked inwards to prevent people escaping, not outwards like they did at the Clay Capital watchtowers. They would not see Bellis coming.

She would get her army.

But to what end? Once Bellis was sated with a legion of workers, she was not likely to be distracted by other dangling carrots. *Orientis* would give her control over the prisoners, and that control would bring her a measure of drugged peace. She would not wish to do much more unless Mr Lindsay's offer was *very* special.

An indignant voice raised itself from the drawing room. Arden separated herself from the Dowager as Mr Lindsay and Vernon Justinian reappeared in the hallway outside, their business concluded.

'But, sir, you cannot take Bellis with you to Harbinger Bay, it is too dangerous,' Vernon was saying with a righteous quiver. 'It is a place where monsters are kept!'

They quickly moved downstairs, ignoring Arden completely as they passed.

Then Vernon's head reappeared in the stairwell. 'Mother,' he scolded. 'Grab your purse, we are going! This man clearly cannot see reason.'

The Dowager raised her purse. 'It's here, darling.'

Vernon Justinian's eyes turned to Arden and glittered with malice. 'A fine damn choice you have made.'

He slipped downstairs with his regretful mother following.

Arden felt herself tremble, such was the importance of what she had found out. Mr Lindsay was taking them to Harbinger Bay. A potential army of dangerous men, already captive, but clumsy and unwieldy to move. Add to that mysterious missing puzzle piece – the final part Mr Lindsay would play in his plans to destroy Clay Capital.

If only Mr Absalom were still alive, she thought in a whirl. But Mr Green, perhaps he would have connections, perhaps he should know what she had just found out, that Bellis wasn't really leaving the Coast—

Her left hand was yanked forward so suddenly it was as if someone had grabbed her and pulled her horizontally by several feet.

By her same hand she was flung into the air, levitating off the floor.

The pain jolted through the tendons of her wrist.

'Bellis!' she said breathlessly. 'Stop! I'm not fighting you!'

Miah stepped out of the shadow, sweating and clearly unwell. He was panting now, like something in pain.

She could feel the *mandatum* sizzling through her copper wedding ring. With the invisible force that allowed him to move metal, Miah lowered her, at first delicately, and then when his strength ran out he dropped her like a discarded thing.

His rheumy eyes met Arden's. 'You should never have come here.'

'Miah—' she started to say, before Bellis' shadow slid in behind him.

Even in the dim, yellow, electric light, Bellis' teeth shone black from Mr Lindsay's paste. Arden cradled her numb, throbbing hand. The copper wedding ring was tight on her purple finger. Had it not been for the metal of her sanguis coins taking some of her bodyweight, the wedding ring might have de-gloved her entire finger out of her skin, like the industrial accidents so common and terrible on the Portside docks.

Bellis pulled a small container out of her grimy lace sleeve, unscrewed the lid and sucked on the contents thoughtfully.

'Oh, it's not so bad that your slut is here. She has given us power and will give us more. You and I will enter the Bay and assure my victory. Then on to Clay Capital, and my coronation . . .'

'On to Clay Capital? You idiot, Bellis,' Arden croaked, hopeless and furious at once.

'What, I didn't hear you.'

'I said you're an *idiot*,' Arden repeated. 'Mr Lindsay hasn't signed any forwarding papers to Clay. Are you and a big noisy army going to walk all the way there?'

'Lies!'

'Not lies! The Dowager saw the documents! You go to the prisons and get ensnared by your army like a fly in honey – as for your ambitions . . . they'll end there. That's it! You won't go to Clay Capital! You won't march on your Parliament like a Queen! You'll be stuck in Harbinger Bay because Mr Lindsay has other plans that don't involve you!'

Arden had only been speaking from sheer desperation, trying to press every button, throw every lever against Bellis she could think of.

One of them must have hit the right nerve, for Bellis bared her teeth.

'Lying whore!' Bellis cried in a rage and raised her hand to strike Arden as Miah grabbed her from behind so she could not fight back.

The entry door opening interrupted them. Mr Lindsay stood there, shaking his head.

'Really, now? Arguing while my guests were just outside.'

'Was not an argument. Was a discussion.' Bellis glared at Arden as she spoke to Mr Lindsay. 'Can I urgently discuss with you the particulars of my grand entrance?'

He huffed. 'And what is that?'

There was a moment when Bellis seemed ready to blurt that she knew Mr Lindsay hadn't filled out official papers properly, that he'd applied for them to approach Harbinger Bay but to go no further. Arden winced as Bellis took a great, accusing breath . . .

But even a queen who could control everything knew the value of a little deceit. Bellis must have learned something under the guidance of Mr Absalom.

In a rush Bellis said, 'What dress shall I wear? Shall I dress as the Bride or the Conqueror when I enter Clay Capital? What will be the first image they see of me? What will be seared into their eyes and their memories?'

Well then. If Arden had been on Bellis' side, she would have awarded her a round of applause. Mr Lindsay rolled his eyes impatiently.

'We will have to discuss it later. You are tired, Bellis, I can see you are tired.'

Despite all her efforts otherwise, Bellis' eyes flickered and her head fell forward before she jerked back awake. She frowned, slightly confused, as if she'd forgotten what it was that was vexing her.

Ah, by all the gods, Mr Lindsay was the one in control.

'Miah, take your bride to bed, please.'

Miah nodded. 'Come.'

His hand steered Arden back into the guest wing. Surely he must have felt the rage quivering through her. By some miracle she held it in until they were ensconced in the guest lodge, and she could turn on him.

'Mr Lindsay intended to take Bellis to Harbinger Bay all along,' she hissed as quietly and vehemently as she could. 'What for? An army is only going to complicate things.'

'The Lion promised her an army,' Miah said with a weary shrug. 'And she'll get them there.'

'Look at Mr Lindsay, Miah! Does *he* look like a man who wants an army? He's distracting her with treats before she reaches Clay. Come on, you were never a fool.'

'Beacon, if he does or doesn't want an army it makes no difference. He is going to gift Bellis whatever she wants. Harbinger Bay or Clay Capital, it doesn't matter.'

'Miah, we need to—' she started to say, and then realized he had stretched out upon the bed and fallen asleep. If not for the rise and fall of his chest, she would have thought him a corpse.

Closed, his eye sockets looked empty, as if the undertaker had dug them out with a spoon. He looked in a word, awful, *decayed* almost.

The salve pot rolled about inside her pantsuit pocket as if the liquid sensed her hands nearby. So. This medicine was Mr Lindsay's control, the thing he used to tie both Miah and Bellis to him. He probably thought he owned Arden, too. However much she had put on her hands had not entirely been enough. Her mind still felt her own.

'Seems you don't know everything, Brother Lindsay,' she said to herself.

The mists hung down the mountainside, so heavy that they were close to rain, and the evening made her as jumpy as a bag of crickets. She could not bear the waiting and the keeping of secrets. If she did not escape, if she left this place with Mr Lindsay, she would never see Jonah again. He would die here, his mind wrecked and gone.

The moon rose above the mountain ridge, and through the clouds it was a sharp, waxing crescent. The last time she had viewed it with such purpose was on the full moon of last month . . . the Deepwater Night. Her fortunes had hinged on that night Miah and his clan had hauled the serpent from the waters. It had been the moment when everything changed for her.

She rolled the salve pot in her numb hands.

What do you expect it to do, Arden?

I don't know. Turn down the heat on what ails him, maybe.

In the darkness the night-hoods, the bioluminescent fungus so prevalent in Lyonnian greenery clotted in one corner of the yard, making the forest boundary appear splattered with delicate blue light, as if an artist had spilled his paints upon that black canvas. The weather remained undecided between rain and mist, so every source of light glowed with an aura.

Someone was in the wet garden. Not one of the guards, but clearly male from the expanse of his shoulders, the walk. He was dressed in a sleeveless coat of dark fabric, the simple rain cape worn by the local south Lyonnians. The figure moved stealthily in the night.

Arden knew at once that he was going somewhere she needed to be. She cast a glance at Miah, and had he not been raspily breathing, she would have thought him dead.

He was also lying on her coat.

'Ah, what rotten luck,' she said under her breath. 'I should have hung it up.'

Still, it was not her only one. Though she had no need to be quiet, she still opened up the wicker wardrobe with care and took Jonah's coat out. It was voluminous on her but would keep out the rain.

She left the room, closing the balcony shutters behind her. The balcony was on the lower floor, and the railing barely hip height. She climbed over it quietly and headed out across the front garden. The guards stood in plain sight under a covered lantern, smoking cheroots and talking in their soft language. With most of the undergrowth and heavy forest gone, there were no tree-things lurking in the boundary, and little to do. She kept to the shadows and they did not notice her pass.

Soon the clouds cleared, and in the delicate light of the moon the cable path girded by pale, broken branches was easy to navigate. The cables creaked as they moved through their guides. A hundred paces away the counterweight crunched through the undergrowth as it continued its journey to the start of the mountain.

As she ascended, the trees gave way to the clifftop coastline, and a view of the dark waters slashed by shoals of crimson below. Arden paused for a moment, as it was quite a sight, beautiful and deeply unfamiliar at once. Every once in a while she had seen things that reminded her keenly that she was far from home: the city of Burden Town, the Equus north shore and the sea dragon hunted in the shallows. She would add this ember bright ocean to the list.

Then onwards up the hillside. The perpetual motion gear house Arden found by feel more than sight; following that ever so subtle push upon her sinuses, she came upon it in the dark. The feeling had always lingered over Equus Island, an atmosphere both caustic and astringent at once. She had thought it was just the perpetual machines back then, but now she knew that it was the Unnamed Saint who tweaked her senses so.

Arden's first fear was finding the housing door locked, but need not have worried, for it swung open with the slightest pressure. A pair of rockblood lanterns spilled shadows across the gear house foundations.

'Hello?'

No reply, Nobody else lurked in these shadows. Surely someone should have stayed to care for him, though?

The giant bobbin of the gear spindle and its constant shifting plates groaned quiet and slow. Only a tiny wheel at the furthest end spun so quick it made the hum of an angry wasp, the other gears barely seemed to move at all.

Descending into the hole below the gear clusters gave Arden an odd, unpeaceable feeling. Now that there was a motion, no matter how minute, a dire panic crept upon her, waiting for something to fall, like this great toothed machine suspended over the maintenance pit.

'Jonah?'

How hot it was here. He lay in the gloom, still as death upon a mat of woven leaves, and she quickly ran to turn up the wick of the lantern, before sitting back with a gasp. His black eyes were unseeing. His lips were chapped. A fluttering, gasping breath escaped him.

If he'd been in the same condition as he was this afternoon, he'd have easily overpowered her, but now – his body weakened – they had not even found it necessary to bind him.

'Are you thirsty? Do you need water?' She spoke helplessly into the gloom. The last person here had left a bucket and ladle nearby, but the offered spoonfuls of water only dribbled over Jonah's unresponsive lips, across his sunken cheek and into the grass mat.

Arden bent her head over his chest and embraced him with all her might, his skin sticky and febrile, his body like a container that had seen the end of its days. 'Leave,' she wept to the spirit inside him. 'Leave.'

Maybe it would rise up and attack her. Maybe she was foolish coming so close to him. But he was as absent as a landed fish that has exhausted itself, and now turns its attention to its dying.

She had loved this man fiercely and briefly, but he was gone, and she had not the strength in her to continue. How much had she done? How much had she endured? Enough for the oldest gods to take notice. But it was over. She took out Mr Lindsay's black paste from her pocket and stared at it before daubing each cut and scar he'd received on his body in her absence, scars he had received due to her.

'You are cured of me, ghost. You may enter the deep, drowned halls of the King.'

The gears ground overhead, filling the air with a fine rock-blood mist, and a terrible compulsion came over her to place her hand over his mouth and nose and push him through to the other side of his agony, to save him from living this life.

It came and went. But so many things had been demanded of Jonah's body. She would not demand that he die so she would not have to worry about him any more.

And then the paste ran out. She discarded the jar, ran her stained fingers across her lips – not that there was much left.

The Jonah-thing panted.

She bent to kiss him.

The panting stopped.

She closed his eyelids with her hands, left black scorch marks there. For a long time she waited. For his passing, or for a sign of the spirit moving on. She took his coat off her shoulders and gently covered him, surrounded him in the krakenskin.

After a while her legs began to ache from kneeling. Her reservoir of grief had puddled out of her a long time ago, but she could not lose herself to numbness. She had lost one person she loved. There were still others.

Feeling as old as time, she climbed out of the maintenance pit and into the blessedly cool night. Gulped breaths, then blinked in surprise.

An old erosion scar had appeared in the treeline, the remnant of the afternoon's traumatic felling, exposing five great, high windows reflecting the crimson coast.

'Oh,' Arden exclaimed. 'There's a house.'

It wasn't a house. The windows belonged to an airship gondola, suspended in the V of a massive stand of tree-ferns. The craft was small, not so much bigger than a houseboat, the externals wrought and decorated in linear lines of a golden alloy with carved, floral-shaped finials. Why, it must be old, she thought. In the last century Lyonnian fashion tended to be severe and practical in all things, from clothes to engineering.

The rest of the airship's inflatable envelope had long gone save for some tatty lengths of metallic fabric caught in the upper branches. The remains of the inflatable frame laced through the trees. A sudden and traumatic descent had crushed the envelope, leaving only the gondola intact.

Relieved to be distracted from her tumultuous feelings, Arden climbed up an exposed belly of granite rock before reaching the entry ladder. It was at the ladder that the voice spoke behind Arden's shoulder.

'It's how she got here.'

Arden turned around, and saw Mr Green was on the rock, bathed in the puddle of light from his lantern.

'She?'

'The Saint.'

21

The Saint of the Islands

'The Saint of the Islands,' said Mr Green pleasantly, as if he were making polite conversation in a tea room, and not an ogre of a man come upon her in the night after she'd seen the love of her life pass away.

'When she escaped her exile on Equus she took shelter on this plantation, and in return for their silence she built the Lindsay family their perpetual motion machine.'

'So the Saint was a woman.' Arden climbed down from the ladder to Mr Green. 'Odd that nobody else knew except the Firetide forest folk.'

'Oh, a few others knew. There are photographs in the Lindsay house. On the walls. All over. The Lindsays did love new-fangled things.'

'Tell me, sir, how did *they* survive the Saint? Why did all of Lyonne not become a wasteland for two hundred years like Equus?' She stepped towards Mr Green. 'And if Lyonne survived her . . . then, how can they survive Bellis now?'

'The Saint left. As Bellis will leave. That's how they survived. That's how we will survive.' Mr Green peered at her. 'You came to see your man.'

The thought of Jonah derailed her, and Arden nodded. 'Yes.'

'Is he gone now too?'

Ah, this emotional chasm. So easy to fall into. She'd been lost in grief before. It provided arms in which to rest, but they were cold arms, and the world was cold within them.

'Yes, he is gone.'

Maybe she did fall into somewhat of a faint, for next she felt Mr Green's hand and hook grab her hard by the upper arms and shake her.

'I see it in you. We have walked that path,' Mr Green said gently. 'That road where everything is taken from us. This is not your first journey into this dark place.' He let her go. 'It's dangerous for you to be here, Arden Beacon. After what your witch did to the men yesterday, the others are afraid she'll kill us all before leaving for Clay.'

'That's what I came to tell you! They're not going to Clay. Mr Lindsay is using the counterweight to charge *Sonder* and take Bellis to the Harbinger Bay estuary. He signed the Coastmaster entry documents tonight. They intend to leave tomorrow.'

Mr Green frowned. 'Are you certain? The prison lands?'

'It will give Bellis the army she was always promised. But it will trap her on the Coast. If you wanted her *gone* gone, I'm afraid that will not be happening. I wish I could have brought better news. I only found out tonight.'

The forest man scratched his chin. 'It is not the worst of news. Harbinger Bay may still be the Firetide Coast, but there's a hundred miles between us.' He nodded. 'The witch is leaving this estate and going to a place that will bind up her powers, snarl them as if in a thicket of vines. Neither we nor Clay Capital will be endangered. I will thank you, Arden Beacon, for the aid you have given us. You may now flee this place.'

'Flee? Mr Green, I am a prisoner here, a guest of Mr Lindsay . . .'

'Nobody is a guest here. I will call on guildsmen that I know, they will be here tomorrow before the boat leaves, take you home.'

It was an unexpected resolution to all Arden's troubles, but it had come too suddenly, left too many loose ends. Mr Absalom had been so certain that Mr Lindsay was headed for Clay Capital. The diversion to the prison lands sounded more like a waypoint stop, not the end.

Mr Green saw Arden's hesitation. He stepped towards her. 'You ask what really saved Lyonne from the Saint? *Love*, they say in these forests, among us who hew and husband the oudwood. She fell in love.'

'Love? Mr Green, Bellis had all the love in the world – her father, Jonah, Stefan. It didn't stop her.'

Mr Green was practically on top of her by then, his unlovely face close to hers, his breath that smelled of the sharp turpentine and menthol of pinecones. He spoke in a near-whisper.

'The Saint did not stay here long under the patronage of the Lindsays. Our legends say it was love that sent her to Harbinger Bay. She built something there. Something terrible and magnificent at once. Harbinger Bay remains one of the few places that evades the Lyonne Order and they cannot enter at will, though the Order's own criminals are housed in the Bay. Even the most powerful sanguinem.

'Then you come tonight and say that the master of this plantation and his witch queen will go to the inescapable prison.' He exhaled. 'It is good tidings. In Harbinger Bay, the witch's progress ends. She will go no further.' He touched her shoulder. 'This nightmare is over.'

Arden heaved a breath. 'Of this rescue – you have a Guild contact? The Seamaster's Guild?'

'The shore is part of the sea. The Guild may not be the Lyonne Order, but it has its ways.'

'What about Jonah?'

'He will be buried in the shorefolk fashion. In the early morning the women will take his body to the sea.'

Miah's copper wedding ring was tight on her finger and the Saint's powers pressed all around her, almost unbearable. She slid off the rock.

'Let me be there when it happens. When he goes in.'

Mr Green's face took on a tenderness. 'Child, if I could grant such a final goodbye, you know I would. But there are so many eyes upon you now. The witch wants her powers magnified, and only your blood will do that. You need to leave quickly.'

She wanted to complain to him. Her heart having broken, it now cut her up inside like shards of broken glass. Yet what he said made horrible sense. Bellis would punish anyone who got in her way.

'Treat him with honour, Mr Green.'

'He will be sung into the ocean with great respect, Arden Beacon.'

She nodded then, the pain too much for words. Then, with all her strength gone and her body captured by the tide of Mr Lindsay's ambition, she pulled herself away from the gear house and the gondola, and headed back down the dark forest path.

22

Even though

Even though the return journey to the house amounted to little more than a short stroll, it gave Arden a long time to think. The grieving was something she needed to put aside. Jonah's death was too big for her, and she did not want to return to the instinct that had propelled her across Equus. Not yet. Not until she was safe and she knew her family was safe.

But despite Mr Green's optimistic pronouncements, something itched away at Arden. Whatever oral history the forest folk told each other about the Saint's connection with Harbinger Bay, Mr Lindsay would have known the tale as well. A cunning Lion would not blunder into a legendary trap so lightly.

No, if he meant to get into Harbinger Bay, then he was doing it from a place of certainty.

The guards were outside her window now, so she crept through the side door, wincing at the crackle of ornamental stones under her boots.

Inside, her attention went at once to the walls covered in photographs. There was enough light to see the same stamp of genetics all through the silver-print faces – handsome but sly and thinly boned. On the women it made them fey and beautiful, but in the men that family brittleness made them fragile, as if they were too delicate for the rigours of the forest and needed to supplant their missing physical strength with cruelty.

And then in one picture she saw a young man who could only be Mr Lindsay's direct ancestor, so similar were they in appearance. His dark hair was cut in far too juvenile a style, as if his family were trying to keep age away from him, keep him young forever. The unfinished bobbin of the cable winder lay in pieces behind him in the photograph.

'I see where you got your looks.' She took the picture away from the wall and found a tag on the back that read: *Claude.* 'And your name.'

But there were so many people in the pictures, how could Mr Green have identified one as the Unnamed Saint? The machine was clearly a source of great pride. Both family and in-laws posed before the finished mechanism, in gaggles of twenty to thirty.

The door handle rattled, and she put the picture back, reluctantly retreated to the guest room.

Miah lay where she had left him, a big, fleshy, mountain of a man. She lay alongside him, and wished for sleep.

Too much was going on in her head. Too many thoughts fighting to be front and centre.

'Where did you go?' he asked.

She froze, then realized he was half-asleep, and that the words had been mumbled in a dream, unaware of the passing of time.

'Outside, to the bathroom.'

'Don't let Mr Lindsay catch you.'

'I won't. Miah—'

'What?'

'If you had the chance to escape, would you do it? Go back home?'

He did not answer. Instead, she heard his breathing slow and lay for what seemed like hours, waiting for it to stop.

That time never came, even though it felt that the whole world should stop, for how could things come to an end like so, and the sky not burn down to its foundations? In the deep night she heard the remains of a song, the merfolk in the bright crimson waters singing to each other.

She dreamed of Jonah Riven among them.

Their previous day of hauling the counterweight up the hillside behind the forest-clearers and burning out a path for the winch cables had been a free pass from the malice of the forest spirits. Now those spirits would make their presence felt.

The winding mechanisms failed, and the counterweight slipped back down the length it had travelled the day before, skipping off the sled and grinding the concrete into the dirt. One of the cables broke and its kickback injured two men – had they been but a step closer both would have died.

And it rained; lashings of cold squalls upon the coast, the climate suddenly remembering that down south it was still winter, and perhaps it would be best following suit.

Arden sat under the miserly gazebo in her krakenskin coat, shivering. Her attention kept roaming to the gear house. Had they removed Jonah's body? Had they put him into the ocean? She sought out the faces of the men, but they ignored her, and she did not want to chance attention by leaving the administration site and walking up by herself. Besides, today Mr Green would affect his promised rescue. She need not concern herself with these people any more.

While the repairs were underway the forestfolk stood around in wet, miserable knots and spoke in low, surly voices. They'd heard the rumours of the witch's leaving, and this seemed altogether like a delay. The women became restless and watchful, for their lives operated on the fulcrum of the men, and where the mood of their husbands went, they would be bound to follow.

Miah paced about the machine house on the second stage. Black grease stained his hands, smeared one side of his face. He seemed even more feverish today, wearing only a light pair of linen fisherman's pants and a raw silk shirt despite the wet weather. Every once in a while a headache would pain him, and he would crouch, his hands over his eyes.

The remaining ropes creaked and sang as the winder dragged the counterweights up and up.

Then, at last, a cheer. The weight had been reconfigured, the cable fixed, and the sled at last reached the top of the incline.

In contrast to Miah's rapidly declining health, Bellis sat content beneath the gazebo all that morning, smoking sweet tobacco from a water pipe and drinking thimbles of tea that the servant girl with the ruined hand brought. Mrs Finch's daughter. Two fingers poked from the Finch girl's bandage, permanently stiff from where the broken porcelain plate had sliced her tendons.

For the most part Bellis ignored Arden. If she had worried about what would happen after their entry to Harbinger Bay, at some point she had made peace with it. She was going to get her army tomorrow, and her cruel joy was infectious. Already the children had begun to bring Bellis flowers from the forest, turning her chair into a throne, getting a pillow for her feet. The very air about her trembled with possibilities, and Arden watched from her own bare seat as small scarab beetles flew into Bellis' orbit, then fell to the ground like winged stones. Soon the Queen was surrounded by dead beetles the colour of steel and copper.

With the counterweight now operational, the team transferred long snakes of insulated current wire from the dynamo to *Sonder*. They had not been working long when a commotion became obvious further up the slope.

Arden, stuck between Bellis and Mr Lindsay in a mass of expectation, perked up. *The diversion. Her rescue.*

One of the counterweight team barrelled down the incline to the administration desk. Several more workers followed him in a hollering, terrified pack.

'What the devil is going on?' Mr Lindsay demanded, rising from his desk. 'Why have you stopped?'

'You need to see this, sir,' the man said between pants. 'As we cut into the forest, the last leg before the plumb-pit, people would sometimes go out of sight . . . for a minute, just a minute . . . and . . . he's . . . It's a mess, sir. We managed to kill it but . . .'

He turned ashen and staggered onto his backside. One of the women ran to him and patted the fellow's slack cheeks.

'Bellis,' Mr Lindsay was affable, but the command lay beneath. 'He was explaining to me why they have neglected their duties. Give him back his tongue.'

'I didn't do it,' Bellis whined in between puffs from the water pipe. 'Oh, look, they are all running downhill like rabbits chased by a fox!'

'For devil's sakes, we have not the time for this. The weather and the cable break have already set us back by hours.' Mr Lindsay left his seat and nudged his dozing steward. 'Up, Sword, we need to sort this out.'

'See,' Mr Sword grumbled. 'There was a reason we let the forest overgrow.'

They lurched through the ashes towards the treeline, Mr Lindsay and Mr Sword first, and Arden following, even though the men had not invited her.

But they had not told her to stay behind either.

The rain had put out most of the clearing-fires, and the remaining smoke crawled knee-deep across the ground. The wall of unburnt forest could have been a battlement, so impossible was it to find entry. The few remaining forest-clearing workers lingered about the edge, torn between fleeing and their moral obligation to their fellows to stay.

Given Mr Lindsay's short stride and Mr Sword's inebriation making him constantly stagger, it was Arden who reached the crest first, desperately trying to ignore her ankle, which after all these days of mild twanging had decided to hurt properly again.

Behind her, Mr Lindsay found the foreman Mr Locke among the group and seized his arm. 'Speak, guy! Why have we stopped?'

Mr Locke raised a shaking hand and pointed into the treelines. Although it was almost hidden in the undergrowth, Arden could see a disturbed track parting the black foliage. Deep in the forest, shouts. The plaintive calls of terrified men.

'Sir, they were working in the clearing when . . .'

His voice faded as Arden sidled into the undergrowth, following a lurching instinct to *move*. The feeling would have been a call, almost, a whisper too quiet to hear. Mr Locke's explanation and Mr Lindsay's criticisms became inaudible as Arden slipped through the curtain of the forest.

Nobody saw her leave.

Inside, one could imagine a light having gone out, so utterly did the sun fail to penetrate the upper storey. A living warmth surrounded her, as if she'd been wrapped in a too-tight embrace. The smell of the aloeswood resin was strong here – it offered a slimy welcome.

As her darksight came she moved through the space afforded by the overgrown trail, careful where to put her hands. The trees rustled and creaked. The insect song buzzed like a telegraph static. Warbles and hoots sounded from the high branches.

And then she was in a clearing, or at least some denuded open space populated by a few desultory crown trees. Something moved behind her.

She turned, thinking it was a man, and her entire vision filled with blood red veined with blue, like a giant, glistening wound, pulsing wetly.

And *hot*, hotter than blood, radiating heat like a corpse rotting in direct sun.

'Goodness—' she squeaked, and the wound-thing puffed a cloud of yellow dust. Arden was quite captivated by the colour, by the waves of musk-scent, by the hypnotic look of the fleshy protuberances, the grossly inviting depths from where the spadix upthrust like a male organ—

With a great shove the flower hurled her sideways, causing Arden to land hard on her shoulder. When she coughed a breath, a cloud of pollen came with it. Eyes streaming, Arden looked up to see a whirling, fleshy mouth descending upon her, before a hooded figure wielding a forestfolk's hacking blade jumped into its path. Dumbfounded, Arden watched the fighter take off one be-petaled jaw before swinging around and slicing a great chunk out of the other one.

A creeper would have taken them both off their feet if the new arrival hadn't backpedalled out of the way and quickly chopped the offending branch from its stem.

Bleeding gore, the flower-head raised back, hissing and shivering like a cobra about to strike, and for a great, vertiginous moment it appeared the man was done for, blade or not.

Then, with a crunching, sucking retreat, the plant pulled back into the undergrowth, leaving only the remains of its altercation. Arden spluttered and coughed, her vision almost entirely reduced to tears.

The hooded person knelt next to Arden and with a strong hand expediently tipped her head between her knees, slapped her back between her shoulder blades.

'Pollen out,' they said in a voice with a clipped Shinlock accent. 'Darling.'

23

Arden coughed pathetically

Arden coughed pathetically, and through a film of tears saw her rescuer.

No. It can't be.

The boat had overturned. Only Jonah had made it out, and hardly with his life. Arden decided she must be dead, of course, must be dead or in those dreaming-throes of trauma.

Arden wanted to lie down, but the Chalice-vision was having none of it, tipping her back up.

'Drink first.' A bottle spout slipped between her lips and bitter liquid followed, though most of it ran over her chin.

'Chalice? How did you—'

'Drink!'

'Ugh,' Arden said between splutters. 'Your medicinal teas are sometimes the worst, Chalice.'

Speaking her friend's name was not enough, and Arden had to touch the woman's face to be certain it was her.

'Please tell me how you are here, or I won't believe it.'

'One more sip and I will tell you.'

Chalice wouldn't stop fussing over the tea-drinking and Arden had to brush her aside and finish off the potion herself. The bottle spout belonged to a little iron kettle, warm and ashy from a pre-emptive brewing.

Whatever was in the tea, it had quite an effect, not only at alleviating her symptoms but also by creating such a halo of calm indifference Arden only looked at her resurrected friend with mild interest.

Chalice wore the drab waxed cowl and coat of forestfolk. Arden was certain she'd seen her somewhere earlier, skulking with the others. As Arden's head began to clear, she suspected that Madame Lion may have been around since they'd arrived, and Arden hadn't noticed.

'Did Mr Green send you?' Arden asked dreamily.

'Nobody sent me, I've been here all this time.'

'I thought so, but I dare not imagine such a miracle. How did you get here?'

Chalice patted Arden on the back and hauled her upright. 'Mx Greenwing's iron boat doesn't sink, not even with a dent punched in the hull by a sea serpent.'

Arden frowned and shook her head, for she'd seen it sink.

With an airy flip of her hand Chalice pretended to be a magician revealing a trick. 'It's a craft meant to sit *below* the waterline. That's why it had such a peculiar shape.'

'Goodness,' Arden said a little weakly. 'A submarine boat. How curious.'

'Fortunately it also collected us up before we became monster meals. Our lifeboat was overturned the same time as yours. Mrs Cordwain had *opinions* about that, let me tell you.'

'Oh! I almost forgot about them. Where are they now?'

'Gone back to Clay with Mr Absalom to raise the alarm about Bellis.'

Arden coughed in disbelief. 'The boat went on without us? Chalice! Now we're both stuck here.'

'Your capture necessitated a small change of plan, but only a very small one. Like Mr Absalom said, we needed you to find out all you could, and then we would effect a rescue. Well, this is me effecting a rescue.'

Even through the emotion-damping effects of the calming tea, happiness swallowed Arden like a great, dark blanket and she threw her arms about Chalice's neck. 'I was so worried. I thought I'd lost you, and you had lost me.'

'The Lyonne Order never loses anyone, darling.'

Arden could have stayed forever in this glow of love and relief, except the effects of the tea wore off quickly, and the anxiety returned. Chalice rocked back on her heels and with the butt of the long, spear-like blade, flicked a piece of carnivorous flower into the damp undergrowth. 'Can you walk? If we can make a way down to the road, I have transport out of here. Thank the gods and devils that Lyonne has actual *roads*.'

'I can walk.'

'Try not to make too much noise.'

Arden followed Chalice up the incline. Chalice might have been better at scrambling, but Arden was taller than her, and her longer stride helped her keep up. The trail was rough, but clearly marked, and when enough distance had been covered that their voices might not give them away, Chalice leaned towards Arden to speak in a voice that was hardly louder than the drone of insects in the forest. 'It looked like they were leaving for Clay earlier than expected.'

'They're not going to Clay Capital,' Arden replied in a low, careful murmur. 'They're going to Harbinger Bay first.'

Chalice glanced back at her with a blink of surprise. 'The bay or the penitentiary?'

'The prisons. Bellis is going to get the army she's always wanted.'

'Oh what glorious luck!'

Arden let out an annoyed breath. 'Doesn't it worry you that there could be more to Mr Lindsay's sudden change of plans? He never struck me as a man without focus.'

'What plan? Imagine the time it buys us. The Bay is a chasm, darling, there's no kindling for plans there. I've worked the lighthouse at the estuary entrance for years. If anyone sneaks in, friend or foe, they're not coming out. Not in any great condition, anyway.'

Arden recalled Mr Green's explanation at the gondola crash landing site. *Something terrible and magnificent at once.*

'But Chalice—'

Chalice dropped out of sight.

Not a second afterwards the ground slipped from beneath Arden's feet and she was propelled in a cascade of loamy debris and down the cliffside on a sliding carpet of moss. One moment she was standing on an incline, and the next she was sprawled across the vertical branch of a bent tree-root that stuck like a coat-rack out of the cliffside.

'Devilment,' she croaked, winded. The crown trees of the jungle were barely an arm-span beneath her dangling toes. 'Oh Chalice! Where are you?'

'Where are you?' came Chalice's disembodied voice from below. 'Can you get down?'

'I'll try . . .'

The cliff's angle was not so acute here, and the moss made it soft enough to consider a scramble. She edged out from her tree-root perch . . .

. . . Only to have it bend and slip through her fingers. With a cry she dropped into the dark green shade of the jungle, sliding and tumbling among the loose moss.

It turned out not to be a great fall; the mossy incline had given way in parts, offering her protection from the impact. Had she not been wearing her gloves she would have skinned her palms.

But their path had disappeared several feet overhead, crumbling into a shelf of tree-roots and bare rock. If there had been a road, it was now inaccessible to them.

Not wanting to stiffen up, Arden took weight on her

complaining ankle. Bits of lichen and crumbled granite had worked their way into her hair. She swayed groggily. The insects shrilled louder. It was so hot here.

'Shit,' Chalice cursed again from where she'd landed in a small stream. 'Shit and buggery, we'll need to take the long way – quickly.'

A voice behind them said, 'Let me help.'

Arden turned about. A man was standing behind her. 'Let me help,' he said.

Why, Arden thought, he looks so much like Jonah, and his eyes are so kind. He had the face of a marble church saint, except there were subtle overlaps and wrinkles in the skin, like tissue paper sculpted about a form it struggled to approximate, and for a second it was Jonah, and then for another second it was a completely different man, spinning all these visages at her to find the one she reacted to the most.

And he was completely naked, and no genitalia marked where his legs converged, only fronding petals—

'Ahh, devil's shit!' Chalice's rage was short-lived as a lashing, muscular tendril snaked around her torso and squeezed the breath out of her lungs. With a deflated squawk the Lion was lifted off her feet . . .

Arden instinctively dived for the bloodknife at her bodice and realized a shade too late her dress had neither, she balled her fist and punched desperately at the beautiful man's head, only to have it disintegrate in a cloud of pollen and orchid-scent as if she had struck a particularly frowsy rose-flower.

A tendril dropped heavy from the tree canopy, striking Arden's shoulder. She grabbed the tip as she fell, a terminal end as brittle and firm as an aloe-leaf. It snapped off in her hand, oozing juice and latex down her scratched forearms.

A cloud of images followed, a record of all the faces the monstrous plant had memorized in its mimetic urge to copy and lure. A hundred, a thousand men and women and children flicked through Arden's consciousness until it settled on one. This image was strong. A fair-haired woman of middle years and vague Fiction ancestry. From Arden's point of view she looked limpidly upon the creature and brushed off the imprisoning tendrils at her shoulders as if they were the unwanted embrace of a drunken suitor.

Creature, I'm not the one for you.

As if Arden were looking through a glass of water she watched the vision-woman turn about and walk away. Her salty-yellow braids about her head parted at her neck.

At the nubbin of bone above the vision-woman's spine a chevron tattoo of kraken-ink moved with her skin. The deepwater marriage tattoo, just like Arden's own.

'You were married, Saint—?' Arden asked across the centuries, and quite suddenly she was dropped into the harsh present, her arms and torso covered in vine-juice and, the blossom-man sliced to ribbons, bleeding white latex blood next to her.

The woman's back faded, replaced with Chalice still dangling on a tendril.

Except now the tendril was loose and only snarled her up. Cursing, Chalice untangled herself until she dropped out of the living net.

'For goodness' sake, what else will this damn shrubbery throw at us?'

If she wanted Arden to respond she would have to wait. The bolo knife that had cut up the blossom-lure now cut the stem at its head. As the false-body fell, another one stepped in to replace it.

'Oh.' Arden released the sticky vine in surrender. Of course her rescuer would be Miah Anguis.

24

She counted

She counted four of Mr Lindsay's guards before surrendering to the fate of the captive. The pursuit through the carnivorous jungle hadn't been easy on them either. The men were a mess, lashed practically to ribbons, and one had a large, weeping blister on his arm. Arden's arrival made them shout and one even stabbed the ground in front of her.

'It's a trick, cut her!'

'Enough, the orchid is dead. That's the real woman. Grab her. And *her*.' Miah Anguis appointed his large bolo knife in Chalice's direction.

They hauled Chalice up in a clatter of clearly purloined implements. 'Relax, it's only a teapot!' she exclaimed when one acid-splattered and clearly irritated guard searched her for weapons.

The remains of a fight littered the clearing. Twisting vines ended in sap-bleeding stumps. Chunks of fleshy blue and red flowers. Everything smelled of blood, a charnel house.

Miah had suffered only flecks of the carnivorous plant's venom, but the blisters appeared just as painful.

A rustle of trees brought Mr Lindsay and Mr Sword into the clearing, along with a half-dozen recalcitrant volunteers they'd bullied into providing protection duty.

Mr Sword kicked the remains of the monstrous flower. 'Ah, quite a fight with our legendary locals.'

'What the devil are you talking about, Sword?' Mr Lindsay said, quite irritated. 'What the hell is this mess? I've lost men!'

'I'm talking about the reason we let the forest overgrow. The chopping brings out the carnivorous orchids. They began to grow here about twenty years back, but since you've not spent enough time in the high reaches, I suppose you weren't aware.'

'Burn it then,' Mr Lindsay said. 'Bring the petralactose accelerant up here and burn it.'

'But the aloeswood, all our profits—'

'I said burn it, fool!' Mr Lindsay frothed. Arden had never seen him quite this angry. It was at this moment he noticed Arden and Chalice Quarry standing in the sloppy remains of the clearing.

'Oh, you sly trollop, Sister Quarry. I am mortally offended to see you here.'

Chalice shook off the fellow investigating her collection of cutlery and assumed a mutinous stance. 'And I you, Brother Lindsay, planning to take Harrow and Anguis to . . .' she paused so slightly Arden barely noticed, before saying, 'Clay.'

'What I intend is not the business of a junior Order agent. Why, the last we met I believe I'd given you orders to return to Head Office.' He moved upon her like a cat, circling but not daring to get too close.

'And the last we met you were a man who had vowed to serve Lyonne to his last heartbeat.'

He smiled benevolently. 'And I am, sister.' He turned to the guard. 'Take her to the house.'

Chalice shrugged against the men, then – once a knife was brandished – allowed them to lay hands upon her. She threw Arden an inscrutable glance as a pair of guards led her from the clearing. Arden could not tell if the unspoken communication was meant to tell her to hold fast, or to run, or to just give up.

Then she was out of sight and Arden felt her knees grow weak. It was an effort just to stand upright.

Mr Lindsay stood in front of Arden and looked her up and down. 'You have a knack for staying alive, Mrs Anguis. But this little escapade? I cannot have any more of it, do you understand?'

If she'd been brave, Arden would have spat back some pithy comment, but she had not the strength for bravery, not with her hopes dashed again and again.

But she need not have worried who would get the last comment. From the direction the guard had taken Chalice came a shout of protest and a scuffle, followed by a triplet of ringing notes as if a bell had been struck three times.

'What the devils?' Mr Lindsay exclaimed.

The guards emerged, staggering and sheepish, sans Chalice Quarry. One of them wore a rapidly swelling lump on his forehead, the other might have had more of the same under his hair, for he held Chalice's bloodied kettle in his hand.

Arden wanted to whoop out loud at their failure. What looked like a tea kettle clearly did double duty as a deadly mace of cast iron – Chalice could have killed them with it had she been less charitable. Arden imagined Madam Lion pretending to fumble at her tea-making implements as a feint, then walloping them both faster than a blink.

She bit her lips and hid her smile at the small victory.

'She got away,' said one who now held his hand up to his bleeding forehead. 'The men are after her.'

Mr Lindsay hardly seemed surprised. 'Have two men search, but don't waste any more time. They won't catch her.'

Of course they wouldn't, Arden thought. Mr Lindsay knew Chalice well enough. If a Lion didn't want capture, then they'd be impossible to pin down.

'My apologies, she was so quick.'

He waved the apology away. 'No matter. She's not important to us. Set the fires.'

The revenge fires burned all that afternoon, crowning in the trees, moving up the slope before extinguishing in the wetter growth of the high ground. By afternoon the sun had sunk below the ridge, casting the shore into that odd shadow where the sky burned red but the land cast black, and the mountainside glowed with embers.

Something in the fire made everyone nervous. Their livelihoods were in the forest, and to see it burn up so quickly brought a dire mood upon them. The oily smoke roiled and sank, almost too heavy to rise. With nobody to watch the cables, the dynamo had to be stilled. A stopped dynamo meant no power to fill *Sonder*'s ancient batteries.

The men's deaths had put their departure to Harbinger Bay back by at least twelve hours, Arden calculated. Tomorrow afternoon the charging would finish and Bellis would move on to the Bay with Mr Lindsay, Miah and Arden in tow, and these people would be free of them. It already felt as if they'd overstayed their welcome.

Even the key Arden had given to Mrs Finch had remained unused. Arden knew now she had been clumsy in her gift, they did not want her to be a saviour. They just wanted her gone.

Worst of all, Mr Lindsay took her down to the oudwood boilers, and had a chain affixed to Arden's ankle.

At first she thought a familiar lock might fasten her, like the women in the nighttime shelters, hiding from the Suitor of Tides and His whispers. She had a key for such a lock. But a purse of leather and sand was slipped between the iron shackle and her skin, and to her horror a small crucible of molten metal poured where the lock would have gone.

'Don't move dear. It is for your own good,' Mr Lindsay said as the sullen worker knelt at her foot, carefully filling the lock-gap. 'Your instincts will be rapping upon the door of your common sense, telling you to flee. But I cannot allow it.'

'Why are you going to Harbinger Bay?' she asked with barely concealed fury, torn between staying still and kicking out, causing the melt to go everywhere.

'The Queen needs an army,' he said blithely, and with a touch of irritation. 'It is inevitable now.'

He placed the end of the chain in a guard's hand. 'Make sure she stays within reach, Mr Nathan.'

Then she was bled again, Mr Lindsay's touch so intimate and horrendous it took all her strength to remain stoic. Lull him, she thought. Lull him. A pint taken, maybe more. He took his time, and afterwards she felt dizzy, and could not stand up without help.

'Mr Nathan will go wherever you wish, within reason. Why not fetch a bite to eat?' he said with malevolent kindness. 'It will be a busy day tomorrow.'

The flowers had killed three men. The women wrapped their remains in spare lengths of waxed canvas from *Saudade*, and the shorefolk among the plantation workers put their own markings upon the funeral cauls.

Mrs Valley appeared in the balcony doorway. 'Would you like to join us?'

Behind the housekeeper, Mr Nathan lurked. Mr Nathan was very much a loyal Lyonnian, pulled from a hundred bar-fights, his nose broken at least twice, and his grey hair pulled into an insipid little queue. He was not going to let Arden go far.

'I would, actually,' Arden said. 'I lost someone recently as well.'

The bodies were laid in one of the tender boats that lined the beach. Arden wished she had something of Jonah's to give as a tribute, to join his sacrifice to theirs. But she did not know who to ask, and besides, she was securely imprisoned now.

At eventide the shorefolk cast the funeral boats alight. As the last to see the men alive, Miah volunteered to push the boat, burning, past the small waves and the glowing red phosphorescence until it was certain to float, then returned to shore where he could watch it go out to sea.

Arden waited with the women, her emotions a mess. And she was worried about Chalice, on the mountainside. Was she still hiding, or was she making her way to a place she could get a message out?

A message to someone. Somewhere.

Arden caught sight of human-like heads on the silvering water, a dozen at least.

'Merfolk,' said Mrs Valley next to her.

'Will they come close?' Arden asked, remembering the grotto under Stefan's island, all the creatures that lived under the old ruins. She was aware of Mr Nathan nearby, listening in. It was too dangerous for them to speak, but the question had escaped her, unbidden.

'No,' Mrs Valley said. 'They have been warned off once. They will not try again.'

Another of the women came up to Mr Nathan and began speaking to him, and no sooner had she diverted the guard's attention than Mrs Valley murmured in Arden's ear: '*Tonight at the women's lodge. Look in the closet. We'll get you out.*'

All the hairs on her arms stood up. She tried to catch Mrs Valley's eye, but the woman only nodded, and slipped away.

Arden stood as still as a statue. Chalice was not the one Mr Green had sent. This was the real rescue. Oh, surely Mr Nathan would hear her heart thundering in her chest and be suspicious!

With the going down of the sun, the forest women and shorefolk left for their shackles and shelter. Only the men remained. Miah Anguis approached Mr Nathan, held out his hand.

'Give her to me.'

'Sir, I have been instructed by Mr Lindsay—'

'Then you can damn well stand in the bedroom and watch,' he growled. 'My wife is coming with me.'

Miah radiated brutality, and the guard was not willing to fight, so the end of Arden's chain went into Miah's hand. Truth to tell, he looked awful, drawn and sweating. He barely acknowledged her as they returned to the house.

Bellis' voice was loud in Mr Lindsay's adjoining study. 'The boat is ready. Why don't we go *now*?'

'She's not very happy,' Arden said.

'She has no patience.'

The seawater was still on him, along with the grieving of the men, and whatever Mr Lindsay had given Miah to be compliant had caused him to lose much of his vigour, but when she came to him in eagerness he did not stop to think what made her so generous with her affections.

She knew him now perhaps more than any other man, and knew that, even weary, he grew vital when she rode atop him, and he slipped within her body with a trembling exclamation.

'I will bring you home to Equus,' he said in joy before he spent himself within her, and she felt him as always, a few degrees colder than her own skin.

He did not notice that at the moment he reached his climax, she pushed her bloodied thumb against the metal shackle, and the brittle braze split into several pieces and fell out of the joint.

Arden had always known it, but her brazed shackle had told her most of all what her future entailed were she to stay even a day longer. Mr Lindsay was not going to let her live. Another pint of blood would render her unconscious. She still felt the weakness, the way her heart fluttered knowing that she was not carrying quite the amount of blood she should.

She lay on the bed as still as a stone, waiting for Miah to fall asleep. She could see by the clock it had been barely fifteen minutes, but the time crept by as slow as treacle. Finally, Arden slid herself off the bed and fumbled for her undergarments, reciting the excuses she would make if he woke. Inside the closet there was an unfamiliar dress, the kind of garment Mrs Valley wore to perform her household duties. It was a dark fabric shot through with gold and emerald threads in the back panel, and on each of the sleeves were three gold buttons.

She bundled her krakenskin coat under her arm and tested the door. Unlocked.

She was certain she would struggle to find her way down to the beach with the guards present, but somehow they were off on other sides of the house, investigating odd sounds and movements that hooted and yelped, and Arden stumbled across the tide wall and onto the sand.

The dynamo-house flashed shades of blue and green as the dynamo inside spun within its armature of steel and magnets. She could feel her numb hands wake up and itch. Her nerves jumped and sang.

Her boots made the wooden foundation of the lodge house creak. Inside, there came a rustling.

'Who goes there?'

'Me, Arden.'

'Come in and shut the door quickly.'

She moved inside and shut the door. The same ammoniac scent from last time – of sweat and too many people in too small a space – hit her. Her darksight made out the dim faces, but it was only when the lamps came on again that she saw one of them was Chalice Quarry.

And another, blinking in the half-light like a newborn, was Jonah Riven.

25

Arden threw herself at him

Arden threw herself at him and as she kissed his dear face, he complained, 'By the devil, enough! I'm sore and my head hurts.' Then he allowed her to kiss him some more.

He was beat-up and dirty and could have used a wash that was more than a dunking in seawater. His hair stuck up in odd spikes from blood and salt, and his beard was definitely long enough to go ginger, though at the chin came a few patches of white. The women had found him new clothes – a forest-worker's linen shirt, leather breeches, and boots that had seen better days.

'The salve worked!' she exclaimed, not daring to let him go. Half of it was from glee and half because, if she did, she feared she would crumble to the ground from the shock of it all. 'I wasn't certain it would work. Oh, Jonah, how do you feel, what do you remember?'

Jonah sought out her face, as if trying to place her in his mind.

'I remember Stefan's funeral . . . there was a boat on fire, and then things became blurry after that. Madame Lion has been telling me an odd story I'm not sure I can believe.'

'A better story than falling asleep in the Sainted Isles and waking up on the Lyonnian Firetide Coast like magic,' Chalice

188

said. 'According to Arden and these ladies, you were afflicted with an old case of deepwater possession, Mr Riven.'

'I've heard of it. But shouldn't a possession be over after a day?'

'Yours was the worst I've seen. How ironic that Lion Brother Lindsay is inarguably the best chemist and apothecary in both countries.'

Mrs Finch lit another of the lanterns and hung it on a hook. 'The Suitor of Tides called us last night,' she said, 'to go to the gear house and take the body of the man to the beach. Such a strange call, for normally he calls for us to go into the water and join Him as his brides.

'We did this and floated the man in the shallows, wrapped in the coat of his deepwater monster. He did not sink, but the water spun around him, brighter than we have ever seen.' She gave Jonah a shy look. 'And he woke.'

Chalice was the only one who seemed less than astonished. 'Surrounded by his little monsters. The plankton that glow in the water,' she added.

'Monster calling is strong in my family line,' Jonah said. 'As I believe it may be in yours, Mrs Finch.'

Mrs Finch squinted at Jonah. 'Those eyes can see more than they let on.'

Even though Arden was in the ecstasies of reunion, she had not become muddle-headed, and the part of her that was always brittle with clarity soon took its place.

'Chalice, Jonah, how do we get out of here? The road is guarded, and the forest is too dangerous. I'm done with going back to the house.' She showed them the scab at her elbow where he drew blood. 'Mr Lindsay will not chance me leaving a second time.'

A blunderbuss fired a shot nearby, startling them all. Mrs Finch ran to the door, peered out. 'Ah, all the lights are on. They know you've escaped.'

'I'm not going back,' Arden said again, forcefully. 'I cannot be responsible for Bellis. You need to deal with her yourselves.'

The women looked at each other. Mrs Finch nodded. 'We can deal with her. We have been thinking ourselves powerless, but we can.'

'And we will leave by the sea,' Chalice said.

Jonah shook his head. 'How? *Saudade* is almost out of fuel, and we don't have the starting handle for *Sonder* or any of the other boats.'

Chalice dived into her pocket. 'Mx Greenwing gave me a gift.' With a mad grin she pulled out a starting handle, the one with *Velleity* written down the side. 'This. I don't know why I hung on to the handle. I must be getting sentimental in my old age.'

A scratch started in Arden's throat. A tightness. Bellis was trying to find her. 'We have to go now.'

Mrs Finch tipped the door open. Jonah was the first out, before motioning the women to follow. From here they could see the searchers spanning out over the cliffs, the torchlights dancing like stars. The buzz in Arden's head grew stronger. Hard to tell if it was from the dynamo or Bellis, it rather felt the same.

Hidden by night, and guided by insulated wires as thick as Arden's wrists, they jogged down the length of the pier. *Sonder* bobbed and nuzzled the old iron pylons – the tide coming in had freed her of the sand. A green corona of light glowed from her forecastle, the place where the cables terminated at a pair of ratcheting handles.

The guards' lanterns swung along the shoreline. There would be precious little time before Mr Lindsay's security detail caught up. Jonah swung up into the wheelhouse. Imprinted and feeling the loom of terror, Arden began to follow. She watched Chalice do the groundwork, untying the boat, and dragging the gangplank in. But the cable terminal proved too risky for Chalice to approach. The electrical contacts at the forecastle sparked and arced at the touch of seawater when a sloppy wave cleared the transom, and Arden's whole body itched from the electrical field.

She startled when she saw Chalice preparing to go over the side. 'What are you doing?'

'I'll have to go back to the dynamo-house,' Chalice wailed. 'The master switch. We'll get electrocuted!'

'Don't you dare, Chalice Quarry! We'll put this tug in reverse.'

'But you might rip off the entire deck!'

She looked up at where Jonah was hunched over the dimly glowing instrument panel, frowning. 'What's wrong?'

'Just remembering, that's all. I was only a boy when I last saw this boat.'

'Remember later,' she said, and held up *Velleity*'s starting handle. 'Let's just go, even if we have to tear *Sonder* in two.'

He nodded and took the handle. Already a half-dozen men were running down the pier. One of them fired his long-arm, and the bullet struck with a *thunk* of breaking wood near *Sonder*'s nameplate.

Water surged up from below as the propeller spun and the cables, which had been lying gently on the pier, instantly sprung up as tight as harp-strings, flipping two of their pursuers into the air. Yet the power-lines were still firmly attached to the boat and going nowhere.

'More power!' Chalice cried.

Electricity arced like ribbons across the ratcheting contacts. Chalice retreated to stand near the cabin door as the yellow sparks showered the forecastle.

Then *Sonder* bucked once, twice, and the cables flew up like the heads of angry snakes.

Fortunately for the guards, the dynamo-house had suffered damage, for had the detached cables been live they would have killed them all. Chalice disappeared down below decks for the moments it took Jonah to turn the boat around, and then reappeared with her thumbs up as the motor churned them away from the pier.

'I've isolated the contacts. Battery is full, it's good!'

'Oh gods and devils,' Arden sighed and laid her head upon Jonah's arm. 'It's done, we're free.'

Jonah kissed the top of her head, but at once she could feel the worry in him. The coast was rapidly disappearing behind their backs, yet their freedom seemed conditional.

Chalice appeared in the wheelhouse. 'We *are* going fast. We'll outrun anything, and they'll be careful about putting in too many miles in the deep night.'

She said it as if she was merely commenting, but Arden heard the chiding beneath her words. Nighttime was a time to slow down, lest the monsters came.

'It's not me,' Jonah said between clenched teeth.

'I'm sorry?' Chalice asked.

He let the wheel go. It moved gently, as if an invisible hand were steering it.

'This boat is steering on her own.'

Whatever relief Arden had scraped together now drained out of her. She looked ahead in the sheer blackness of the ocean punctuated by the crimson Firetide plankton shoals. 'On her own? Like an Equus petralactose ship?'

'A lich ship,' Chalice said. 'Oh dear. This is not good. Maybe it's just stuck. Maybe I can have a look down below.'

'Nothing's stuck.' He tapped on the glass compass next to the wheel, their course arrow pointing resolutely northeast-wards. Any ordinary boat would have possessed various dead man's switches, and losing the skipper would make it veer into a permanent circle and remain in place.

Sonder was going somewhere.

'Whatever hand is on this wheel, it's not a random course.'

The Saint. Arden sat back and exhaled. The Saint had built this boat. She alone had set the perpetual motors in Equus running, breathed a command that would last for centuries.

'I think we should go where it wants us to go,' Arden said at last. 'We have food and water – *Sonder* was stocked for tomorrow's journey.'

'And what if it takes us so far out to sea we can never get back?' Chalice countered.

'Then let it be,' Arden said. 'We will be too far from Bellis or Miah or anyone to ever get to us.'

'I agree with Arden,' Jonah said. 'Sometimes the best thing is to wait out a current. Don't try to fight it when it is strong.'

None too happy about it, Chalice chose to take first watch in the wheelhouse.

Below decks Arden shuffled through the supplies, left out in crates, all the while hyper aware that Jonah was watching her. She pretended to check her hands for injuries – when one could not feel anything, it was too easy to get a cut or an infection and not know.

'It seems so strange,' he said at last.

'What.'

'Last time I saw you. How different you were then. Harder, I think.'

'I *was* harder. I'd survived a week in Equus.'

'Chalice Quarry says it's been only two weeks since then . . . but it's like I've been asleep for a year.'

'Yes. It's only two weeks, but it feels so much longer. And to think, it will be springtime soon. We have known each other for a year.'

'Arden.'

'Wait, I'm still trying to find some passionfruit, I'm sure there were some put in here . . .'

'Arden,' he said again and stood behind her. 'We will go around in circles if you cannot stop still for a moment and look at me.'

This she did, and it was so hard to meet his eyes.

'I have said it before, but what you have done you have done to survive. Don't push me away.'

'I'm not pushing,' she said, before throwing her arms about his neck and sobbing into the linen of his shirt. The tears came out of her as if from a deep, wracked and bottomless place, but the hurts and horrors she kept to herself.

'Shh,' he soothed. 'Shh.' He rubbed her back, which only

made it worse in a way, because she wanted someone to tell her to stand up straight, stop sniffling, be strong. The boat bucked against a wave and they tumbled onto the pile of hessian sacks, and her mouth met his, and she could not let him go. She was hungry for all that he had meant to her, the life she had wanted, the dreams forever pulled out of her reach.

Clumsy with joy she slipped the buttons from his shirt open and felt him vital and strong, marvelled at the way his heart beat so steady under her cheek when her hands could not feel it. He sat back and seemed almost generously amused at the way she wanted him. She took off her coat and let Jonah slip the dress and her underclothes from her.

The boat's rocking provided the rhythm, and she felt herself melt about Jonah, and when he moved in her it was hard to tell if it was him or the ocean urging her on. They were together now, they were together and not apart, and she waited for the architecture of her happiness to fail, but it did not. With each breath she took she was still holding the man she loved.

'Let's not move from this place, ever.'

'Not even to eat?' he said. His face was flushed pink, he radiated heat, and she wanted to hold him forever. Their reunion had been strange – they were like two broken things that fitted so perfectly coming back together again.

'Maybe not even then.'

It had been a good few hours since they had eaten last and Jonah was ravenous. After they slept for a little while, he extricated himself from their embrace and Arden watched him with a pang of love and concern as he shovelled his way through the breadfruit and the cooked forest-chicken like a man who was starving. Arden found bottles of a dark, almost black beer among the supplies and they drank in near silence, contemplating their escape, the miracle of it.

But despite their bubble of joy, Arden could not fully relax, and when something bumped into the hull she startled.

'What was that?'

'Easy now. Could have been a fish or glass buoy.'

Arden allowed herself the relief of agreeing with him, weary from all the waiting. 'It's just that I worry that Miah sent something after us. Like he did when I first came to the Coast.'

He shook his head. 'My cousin would have sent his monsters sooner, if he could do it at all.'

Jonah was right. She had left Miah in a poor condition. Arden finished her beer quicker than was polite, but intoxication lay itself like a calm veil over her mind, and a little of the stress slipped its moorings, sank away. Underneath it all the motor hummed. The ship bucked against the waves, a rhythmic rise and fall. Arden rubbed her finger over the divots in the glass bottle thoughtfully.

'Mr Lindsay intended to be on this ship when she took this course. I think he must have known *Sonder* was going to take him somewhere, even if it was out to sea.'

Jonah shrugged. 'Lion business. I won't dwell on it.'

'Still, if he was anticipating this journey, why would he have gone to so much trouble to get entry papers off a Coastmaster? I wonder if they might still go to Harbinger Bay after all.'

She stopped herself when she saw Jonah wince at the name. The prison had held him for fifteen years. He was not yet over the trauma, it still slid between the memory of his life as a child and his life as an adult. It informed everything about him, the way he was always closed off, careful.

'If they go there, then they go no further.'

'Everyone keeps saying that. It's been puzzling me even though I have no right to be puzzled. Did the Saint of the Islands really build something magnificent and terrible there, after she came home to Lyonne?'

'Who told you this?' Jonah asked, taken aback, and Arden knew that she had touched on a secret.

'Mr Green, the forest man back on the estate. There was a gondola wreckage high in the jungle. He said it was the airship the Saint of the Islands came on, when she fled Equus two hundred years ago. He also said she went to Harbinger Bay afterwards, and built something. Whatever will stop Mr Lindsay from moving on to Clay Capital . . . it will be there.'

'*She* . . .'

Arden laughed wryly. 'The Saint was a *she*.'

She waited for Jonah to exclaim some disbelief, but instead he accepted the revelation. 'I have always known in my heart that it was a woman's power on Equus. The island was once occupied by anchorite nuns. The Lions would not have sent a young man to a nunnery.'

'So, what is this construction that will stop Mr Lindsay? I'm curious now.'

'Does it even matter?' he gruffed, talk of Harbinger Bay making him surly. 'If luck holds, we will never see them again.'

Arden shrugged. Of course it didn't really matter. But they were now on a boat steered by the recognizance of a woman dead two hundred years, their future as uncertain as it had ever been.

He softened a little and said, 'I don't know of a construction, but I do know what lurks beneath the prisons. It's not such a secret.'

He opened his linen shirt and showed her one of his tattoos. Unlike the geometric shapes of the deepwater folk, this one had been inked in a looser style, more shorefolk in its artistry. A small eel, finned and sinuous. She had barely noticed it before amidst all the other decorations, as it sat somewhat out of the way along his flanks and under a black tower with a red light.

'This is the Wyrm of Harbinger Bay,' he said. 'It lives in the deep caverns and caves where the estuary river meets the prison, inland. The Brothers of the Wyrm, the priesthood of the prison, give it worship, and sometimes I could coax it out into the light. It is not so different to the sea dragons.'

He buttoned his shirt back up again as Arden pondered on what he had said. 'What is the importance of a giant eel in a prison?'

A footfall in the stairwell interrupted them. 'Well, isn't it obvious now, Arden?'

She turned about to see Chalice clinging to the open deck-door frame. Behind her the night was inky black. 'Sorry,' she continued. 'I gathered from your talking that you two were no longer occupied.'

'Please, come right in,' Arden replied wearily. She was well used now to Chalice barging in.

Madam Lion descended into the hull with careful steps, unsteady from the kick of the waves. 'It's what I never got a chance to say earlier, darling. When you asked why I was happy about Bellis going to the Bay. The Wyrm. It's invulnerable to any sanguis-blooded person.'

'Including Bellis?'

'Even her. Once she goes to the Bay, Queen Bellis will be mentally imprisoned by the Wyrm's presence. Her and her ten-thousand-strong army.'

Jonah nodded when Arden looked to him in confirmation. 'The highest walls would not work in a prison for blood workers. The wardens have long used a more elegant method of confinement.' He rubbed his side where the Wyrm tattoo now lay hidden. 'Unlike any animal I've known, the Wyrm seemed most human. There were times I could almost feel its thoughts. They terrified me . . .'

Arden saw him slipping away, and she grabbed his hand.

'Then this will be what Bellis finds out if she gets there. What happens after—' Arden shot Chalice a glance. 'That's Lion business. I have a coin of instruction to return to Mr Absalom. We're going home.'

26

Home

Home. Easier said than done when *Sonder* showed no sign of slowing down on her nor'easterly tack. She rode the waves as if she were a toy ship dragged by an invisible string. Chalice agreed with Arden's suspicions: the high charge in the batteries had enabled certain components in the boat's directional apparatus to become active after lying dormant for centuries. A singular destination. They wouldn't stop until the power ran out, or they reached wherever *Sonder* had been set to go.

'Eventually, when the charge drops to a more realistic level, we can pull her off this course of hers,' Chalice explained.

'Could Madame Lion make an educated guess as to when that will be?' Arden asked.

'We're halfway empty already. It shouldn't be long.'

They had lost a lot of time in the camphorous under decks, and when the electrical motor stopped, Arden felt the loss of power as keenly as if she had been in a motor car at speed, and someone had slammed on the brakes. Her stomach lurched eastwards.

'We're stopping.'

Jonah nodded. Their eyes met, and she knew he'd had a similar thought. Their lives had been a collision of slow proportions, but this was where their diversion ended. This place the fulcrum of their meeting, the centre and purpose of it all.

Chalice's footsteps clattered outside and she threw open the cabin door. 'Arden, Mr Riven, come up here quick!'

Outside it was cold, still almost morning, and the sun had yet to appear on the eastern horizon. Dawn was not far off. The sky had given way to the colour of dusky pearl, and the air hung as still as a held breath.

All around there was nothing but sea and dawning sky – no reason for the boat to have stopped so utterly.

'Did we hit something? Did the power run out?'

In response, *Sonder* jolted and recoiled with the solid contact of hull against pier, except there was nothing to see.

'Other side,' said Jonah.

Cautious of *Sonder*'s jerky movement, Arden switched to the port side to investigate. To her surprise she found that the boat had sidled alongside a small platform of dressed stone. The platform rose a foot above the calm water, five full paces wide. Had the weather been anything other than glass-still, it would be literally invisible, covered by the waves. A triplet of iron fixings rose barely a foot higher.

Chalice joined her. 'What in the devils is an orphaned pylon doing out here? It's a shipping hazard!'

'It's not a pylon,' Arden said, recognizing the architecture at once. 'It's a caisson, a foundation for a bridge or a harbour. There are the anchorage footings, those metal plates. And there's a porthole off centre, see?' She pointed at a raised manhole on the surface. 'To enter the chamber. It would have once been hollow inside, all the way to the bottom of the sea.'

'But it will be filled with water now, surely.'

Arden did not reply at once, not knowing the answer. Bridge foundations built by mortal men were pressurized during construction, the air keeping the water away so they could work at the base, anchoring the foundation into the riverbed or sea floor. A friend of her father's had died from caisson's disease when the cofferdam at Clay Portside had been constructed. The

Saint must have lived in Clay Portside, Arden thought. She'd have seen in her childhood the famous locks and bridges. Remembered them for later.

But if this was built by the Saint . . . Why would she have ever needed it to be hollow? There were no men to keep alive.

'If the Saint made the foundation hollow then she meant for it to be hollow now,' Arden said with a sense of certainty. 'It was built to last. Whoever built this boat knew all about that.' Arden rapped her knuckles on *Sonder*'s transom. 'How deep it goes is anyone's guess.'

'Twenty fathoms,' Jonah said, coming to stand alongside them. While they'd been debating the caisson's appearance, he had been taking stock of their surroundings and figuring out what to do next. 'The sea floor is sixteen fathoms, seventeen men tall. It's technically shallow water.' He hauled up the marked rope he had dropped over the side.

As they pondered their not-an-island, Jonah looped up the rope and threw it over one of the fixings. 'Are we going in or not?'

'What?' Arden asked.

'Through the manhole. There, in the centre. *Sonder* brought us here.' He shook his head. 'I'm feeling something, Arden, something I've only felt once, a long time ago.'

She put her hand to her chest as a ball of panic spun about her heart. Jonah was not alone in this yearning *pull* to go further, to go inside. This was what Mr Lindsay knew would happen if he fully charged *Sonder* with the Saint's machine. He had yearned after the secret of this place. He had been planning to come here all along.

Her courage reached its peak. 'Yes. We need to go in.'

'Madness,' Chalice hissed under her breath, but winched the vessel tight against its moorings. 'Madness.'

Jonah turned to Arden. 'It's not the first time I've seen foundations like these either.'

Arden frowned. 'Where?'

'In the shallows beyond Vigil. Like a strange harbour footing, built as if it were made by madmen in the course of a storm, then abandoned, badly corroded and never finished. The sea had destroyed most of it. The fisherfolk around Vigil thought it was a relic of the Saint.'

'I wonder what the Saint was trying to build,' Chalice said tartly. 'As if she didn't pester the locals with enough ghost-ship moorings and rockblood refineries all up and down the coast?'

Panic flared in Arden's chest again with the realization that she had literally stolen Mr Lindsay's great desire from under his nose and what that meant. Before, she had only been an irritation to him. This theft would make her a life-long enemy.

Chalice finished securing *Sonder*'s ropes to the mooring. 'Regardless, the Saint created a shipping hazard, that's what it is. One of us needs to stay on *Sonder* in case something happens.'

Arden realized that Chalice had just given her a grudging blessing to do what her blood yearned for. She hugged her stormbride. 'I won't be long. I have to see for myself.'

Chalice unhooked a simple one-handed watch from the collection of items on her belt. 'One hour, Arden Beacon. Then I'll come down and get you.'

Jonah helped her off *Sonder*'s side and onto the wide platform. The just-rising sun was a line of fire on the horizon, and the wind blew cold against even the protection of the kraken-skin coat. The entry door in the centre was hemispherical, the same design as those she'd seen the Clay Portside bridge builders use when they pressurized the foundations. Mx Greenwing's submarine boat had the same design.

That was where the similarity ended. Inscribed on the hatch surface were all manner of chevrons and scales. She touched the back of her neck, experiencing a sudden lurch of recognition. Jonah knelt down to turn the equally shiny handwheel. Arden held her breath as the dogs clunked against the frame and the seal broke.

'Brand new,' he said offhandedly.

'Just like everything else on Equus.'

'No honour in waiting,' he said, and hauled the hatch open.

Darkness below. Jonah had retrieved one of *Sonder*'s perpetual lanterns from off the bow and hung it over the open space. The floor was only six feet below.

It was not her first time inside a caisson base. A Guild Signalmaster's certification had required a visit to every part of the infrastructure of the working docks, from the wharves and the locks to the foundations, breakwaters and cofferdams.

'If it's a pressurized caisson, there will be an airlock room before we enter the main space.'

Arden looked at him, curious at his knowledge. 'You know what to expect?'

'They put us to work in the prisons. The estuary is all swamp and water. It's the only way they can build on it.'

Jonah went first. In the low chamber he had to stoop, and Arden was overwhelmed by the twin instincts of protection and the whirling, vertiginous need to keep going *down*.

He closed the top hatch, and Arden swallowed the sudden rise of pressure as they were sealed into a curiously dry space that smelled ever so faintly of salt and hot metal. This was either threshold or tomb. Another hatch marked the centre of the floor, once again domed and shiny, marked with silvery chevrons that shimmered in the glow of the perpetual lantern.

He tapped on the dome with a knuckle and it reverberated like a bell.

'No water past here. It's hollow.'

As Jonah reached for the handwheel, Arden blurted, 'Did they teach you how to enter pressurized caissons in the Bay?'

'Yes,' he said and did not elaborate, and she was somehow terrified for the life he had led, of ships and locks and structures ploughed into estuary soil and then used to incarcerate human beings.

'This is it,' he said as his fingers threaded through the handwheel. 'I'll understand if you don't want to go any further.'

'But I do want to go further. This is it, Jonah. This is everything that's ever brought us together and torn us apart.'

Jonah turned the wheel sideways, the dogs clunked, the seal

broke. Arden's ears popped. A slight metallic clinking followed. A delicate light emerged from the darkness.

At the same time the perpetual lantern at their side extinguished, as if an invisible breath had blown it out.

'We've activated a switch,' he said, pulling the hatch back. 'Take care now.'

Arden peered down into the caisson. They were at the top of a chimney-shaft of stone, a great oubliette twice as wide as the platform above the waves. The base was wider still, somewhere in the misty illumination below. It was not dark, for the murk glowed with gradients of blue and orange. One of the illuminating lights sizzled and browned out nearby from a small patch of condensation on the contacts. Arden could see the pineapple-sized vacuum tube, the glowing filaments wrapped around the ceramic block, and was awed by it.

Jonah took the smoked-out lantern case, suspended it over the hatch, and let it fall. They counted nearly three full seconds before hearing the rattle of impact.

'Eighteen, maybe nineteen fathoms,' he said.

The walls of the shaft were stepped in convoluted up-and-down chevrons, like the carved step-well castles of antiquity . . . and Equus. Arden could feel herself tremble at the enormity of what she was seeing. The physics of maintaining such a structure would have been impossible without infinitely strong sanguinity.

'Where's the blue light coming from?' Jonah asked offhandedly, for not all the light came from the electric bulbs.

'Portholes,' she said. Arched windows were set irregularly into the walls. Seaweed fronded across the panes. Something outside, glowing with such phosphorescence that the windows lit up the shaft almost brighter than the filament lights.

There was nowhere to go but down. Helped by Jonah, Arden slid through the hatch onto the first stepped platform. Their footfalls rang loud in the empty space. The view from the entrance had been deceptive. The stairs were wide enough to navigate without needing to press precariously into the wall, although Jonah favoured one knee and Arden's ankle throbbed inside her boot. Their descent was easy. In a matter of minutes, they were approaching the curiously smooth floor of the caisson. Her ears popped again, and her senses alerted her to the great press of water all around her.

Before Arden could prepare herself, a blaze of light flooded the caisson from below.

Arden yelped, for what had been a dark expanse of floor was now a great pane of smelted glass, eerily illuminated from the phosphorescence outside. Under her feet a giant horn-skinned ichthyosaur chased a quicksilver school of jawless fish. A skate shivered on the silted seafloor.

She grabbed Jonah, almost certain she would fall through the glass.

'If it's not broken in centuries, it's unlikely to do so now,' he said.

'Of course.' Arden let him go. The air was heavier at this level, slightly stale with the odour of *mandatum* and corrosion. The lights reflected off Jonah's skin, made him green, made the tattoos move.

'Still, I'm not going to trust this lasting forever.'

'Yes,' she said. 'The bloodworking is effortless up top, but I feel everything *straining* here. Like she had to work hard to make this part.'

'Let's not waste time.' He gestured about himself. The base of the foundations spread out to left and right adits, like the crossways transept of a cathedral. A smaller dark descent lay ahead. 'Which way?'

Arden was starting to acclimatize herself to the eerily trans-parent floor and the foreign undersea vista and to recognize what was so familiar.

'It *is* a cathedral,' she said in astonishment. 'Oh Jonah, I know this place, I've been to the one in Clay Capital a hundred times . . . it *is* a cathedral, standing on its end!' She pointed upwards. 'The entry vault is the narthex, the lobby. This descent is the nave, and we are standing on the transept. Of course!

They exiled the Saint in Equus when she was a girl, when there was only the Redeemer's church there, and the anchorite nuns. But there was a cathedral, older still. It must be her most vivid memory.'

Jonah was silent and ever so slightly absent as he pondered what Arden was saying. It worried her, having feared the silence of him when the deepwater spirit was inside him.

Then he spoke. 'I don't see it, Arden. There was never a sense of religion in Equus – her creation was all clockwork, all automata and forced work. In our history, by the time the automata began multiplying itself, the Saint was like Bellis . . . she'd taken over half the island and killed all the nuns.'

'Maybe she changed her mind once she escaped. Their old cathedral would have been the one thing she felt most strongly about when she looked back at what she had done. The nunnery would have been her prison, but also her sanctuary, like Stefan's island was to Bellis, for a while.'

Jonah rumbled a halfway acknowledgement, before saying, 'And likely the symbol of her greatest regret.'

Arden remembered what Mr Green had said about love saving the Saint from becoming like Bellis. She had loved, of course. Was married in the deepwater way. Her tattoo was not like Arden's, it had been received in joy. Then something had happened to make her flee Equus and attempt to go home.

She pointed to the dark keyhole-shaped pit in the far floor. 'That's the *altar*.'

Jonah sidled to the edge of the pit and looked in with the trepidation of a man who is certain something will leap out. 'There's no light.'

'It should have light. The altar is supposed to be the centre-piece of a cathedral.'

Arden knelt at the keyhole pit. With her darksight she had already glimpsed a familiar brass insert an arm-length down. A tube with serrated edges set into the wall of the altar.

It was exactly like the one in her uncle's lighthouse, which fed the sanguis flame.

'The altar should be the brightest part.'

She pulled the glove off her numb hand. Lay on her belly. Reached down.

'Ah, you must not,' Jonah murmured in concern, but did not try to stop her. Arden took a deep breath and slammed her hand so hard on the tube that the pain reverberated through her body like an electric shock.

She needn't have worried that the *sanguis ignis* lantern would require more than a drop of blood, for at the contact the blue coldfire light blazed through inside of the altar as if it were the vessels of a heart. Both *evalescendi* and *ignis* together.

And inside . . . a person kneeling in the centre, facing away.

'Devilment!' Arden cried, scrabbling back onto her knees. Jonah caught her before she lost her balance.

'Easy. They're not moving.'

'It's a statue? What is it?'

As they studied the centrepiece for a while, it became evident the altar's icon was only ostensibly human by design. Otherwise it had no life in it.

'Could be a statue. Or a corpse. Let me go down and check.'

Arden was loath to let Jonah go, but the curiosity had infected him too. The keyhole altar-pit was accessible by a simple trellis-ladder at the base, a tool wrought in curlicues of bright copper at its flat end.

As soon as Arden touched the protruding top-cap, she felt the pain in the metal. She felt the last gasping effort to call on sanguis talents, the desperate command in the metal to do the maker's bidding.

The Saint had been struggling when she made this ladder. But struggling with what? The ladder was uneven and most of the rungs sagged by the time she reached the ground. She lost a gold button off her dress-sleeve in her efforts. It skipped away and landed nearby, glittering upon the black floor.

As she bent to scoop the button up she had to pause, for the feeling was strongest here, oldest.

The curved walls of the pit were lined with wood – black

mangrove wood, like *Saudade*. There were even hull ribs placed at regular intervals. This was the remains of a vessel.

And a woman at the centre, facing away from them and kneeling in repose . . .

The corpse was as desiccated and salted as a mummy. The preservation was unusual, for decomposition should have turned its skin and muscles to slurry and dust. They wore a robe that might have been purple or crimson, with long fair, grey-salted hair parted at the centre to hang over their shoulders.

'It's the Saint,' Arden said. 'It's her.'

'A woman's corpse here doesn't mean anything. It doesn't mean it's the Saint of the Islands,' Jonah gruffed. 'It could be a trick, a centrepiece for this . . . whatever this is.'

'No, I saw her back in the forest, inside the memories of the carnivorous plant.' She sighed, for such a complexity could take hours to describe, and they perhaps did not have that long. Since entering the altar, the air in the vertical cathedral had sharpened and freshened.

She even looks a bit like Bellis from behind, Arden thought. Small build, yellow hair. A common trait in Vigil, and Fiction.

Arden drew closer. Confirmed what she knew she would see. A tattoo on the base of the woman's neck.

'She was married,' Arden said to Jonah. 'She was married in Equus, then came here.'

Jonah walked about the corpse centrepiece, and as he stood before the woman, he stopped, and his shoulders sagged.

Even in the blue coldfire what little colour he normally possessed drained from his face. 'Ah,' he said. 'That's not good.'

She joined him, puzzled and fearful. What was wrong? They had come across a dead body, a corpse kneeling in prayer. There could be nothing more confronting.

Until she joined Jonah standing in front of the Saint.

27

In the Manse Justinian

In the Manse Justinian, back in Vigil, the old Baron had kept a jar in his study. A glass container, and in it the pickled corpse of a monster born twinned with a live baby.

Jonah's brother, they said. It was a family curse, a known disfigurement. Sometimes the deepwater folk gestated the creatures they hunted. Birthed monsters. Whether it happened by inheritance or infection, nobody knew, but this was no woman in prayer.

In one mummified hand of sinew, a rusted knife.

Her belly, excised.

She'd been precise. The tangle of petrified coils before her were not organs or intestines, however she had clearly been in a panic and whatever she had seen had scared her enough to cut twice, and too deep, so she had lost so much blood . . .

Or at least that was what Arden imagined from what she saw laid out before her. Any instinct could have driven the Saint of the Islands here to her abyssal church, even something so grim as a purposeful ending of her life. Had the cathedral come first, or had it raised itself around her dying body and her black mangrove boat like the tomb of a god king?

The faded power left Arden with the remains of vertigo, but

it was extinguished power, an afterimage. There was nothing here but a memory.

The monster-child corpse glinted, its centuries-old flesh covered in a black shiny crust like a *memento mori.*

Arden swallowed. Were this scene fresh, she'd have been ill, but the years had made it no more challenging than seeing a particularly awful painting. 'Whatever Mr Lindsay was looking for, it's not here.'

Jonah had sidled away, but at Arden's words closed his eyes and pressed his head against the ladder. The same thing had happened at his birth, but his mother hadn't died. That would come later.

'I was not expecting such a sight.'

'Nor I. I thought she might have ended her days in glory, but this seems . . . why it seems so sad.'

A crawling feeling made Arden startle and she turned about. There had been a change in the quality of the light, as if a great shadow had passed over them.

'Jonah,' she said. 'We need to leave.'

He opened his eyes as the shadow passed again. No sooner had he done so than a great pounding shockwave echoed through the caisson, and salt dust rained upon them. It was as if a thousand raindrops of iron pelted the side of the shaft, a volley of strikes.

'Go,' Jonah shouted, and pushed Arden up the ladder. Her numb hands could barely grip the rungs, they kept slipping off.

'I can't—'

He lunged behind her, his thighs shoving her up the rise. When they both reached the top of the ladder, Arden sprawled across the transparent floor as a crack shot through the transept glass with the sound of a tree branch snapping.

Outside, a fever of dark, angular shapes flitted across the portholes. Somewhere deep down one of the transept cross arms she heard the spray of water. A skin of liquid now coated the glass, and Arden couldn't find the purchase to stand, her hands and feet flailing. Grimly silent, Jonah dragged her off the ground and held firm her hand as he took her to the stairs.

As they hit the first step, another rolling shudder groaned through the tall rise of the caisson, magnified by seawater. The sound of spraying water became stronger now and water lapped out of the flooded altar-pit. Arden's ears popped.

'A breach will crush us,' Jonah said. 'Move.'

Arden had run in panic and fear before, but this was different. She found herself stumbling as she half-followed, was half-dragged by Jonah up the staircase, her skirt now twisting and tangling on her legs. A porthole popped open with a gunshot above them, and the water boiled up from below, filling the space with a roar of sound that would have drowned out a steam train.

She saw Jonah telling her to duck not even a half-second before another porthole – this one no more than an arm's width from her head – failed, and suddenly she was swinging in empty space, her feet flailing with the rising tumult of sea beneath her. If Jonah had not had such a grip on her hand she would have fallen. He lay face down and wheezing with effort on the stone stairs, his expression blank with concentration as he mustered the strength he would need to pull her up. Arden wanted to wail at him both to save her and let her go, and the need for survival filled her with an almost inhuman strength. She hooked one swinging heel against the stair, and with the added leverage Jonah yanked her back onto the stairs.

'I'm still here,' she said, though her voice couldn't be heard over the unholy noise.

He nodded, and they began to climb again. Arden felt every pain and injury from the last few weeks reignite, from her long Equus walk to the return to the Firetide Coast. Almost mad with pain, she reached the narthex chamber. She could not work out why Jonah even bothered closing the door behind him, as if he were sealing up the door to Hell . . .

It wasn't sealing properly, the tremors had warped the metal.

'Get up top, I'll follow,' Jonah shouted.

She was first out, gasping in the sunlight, and nearly tripped over Chalice Quarry lying on the platform, her face gone grey with agony.

At once Arden saw that Chalice had not come here easy. Her head was bleeding and her leg was broken. The bone poked rudely out of her shin.

The sight of her indestructible friend clearly hurt was so astonishing she could think of nothing but collapsing at her side.

'Chalice, what happened?'

Her friend howled in pain as Arden touched her and screamed a warning – *'look out!'* – but Chalice might as well have stayed silent, for nothing could have prepared Arden for the exploding agony upside her head.

For a second, everything went black, and a high kettle-whistle rang through her ears. In her whirling trauma Arden glanced sideways and saw the cause of the caisson's failure, a great fever of giant rays leaping from the water, their white bellies yellow in the dawn. They circled both the caisson, *Sonder*, and another boat – one of Mr Lindsay's small electric skiffs.

Don't faint, she thought above the pounding of blood through her temples. *Don't faint . . .*

'Those slutty bitches!' Bellis shrieked. 'I knew she would make a break for it. She should have been tied up with the goats!'

By now the belly of seawater was heaving through the narthex door, but the caisson had equalized with the ocean and no more water followed. The surface tension of the rising water let out a burp that spilled out over the platform, then receded to the level of the seas around them.

Jonah had not come out.

The jewels of hope nestled into the expanse of her despair. There would still be air pockets. He could hold his breath. They don't know he's here. *All they can feel is the Saint.*

'Settle down, Bellis,' said the familiar, cool Lyonnian voice of Mr Lindsay. 'Let me speak to our miscreant.'

'She needs to be punished!'

Arden lay wretched in the puddle as a pair of elegant shoes and pinstripe pants which never seemed to get wet or dirty moved in front of her.

Before Mr Lindsay could open his mouth to say something clever, she lashed out with her foot, causing him to skip out of her way. Well, it was not a blow, but it prevented him getting the first word in, and he nearly stumbled. The bubbles of air rising from the structure and the equalizing pressure sent trembles through the platform.

'You're a scheming liar, Mr Lindsay,' Arden spat as she sat up. Or at least she tried to say it, but she'd not much left of her voice, so the delivery wasn't as defiant or forceful as she'd intended. The blow had taken her balance and she listed like a ship taking on too much water as she tried to rise. Her lungs might as well have been filled with sand for all the space she had to gasp her breaths.

However, in the second's grace righting herself afforded her, she took stock of her situation. As well as Bellis, three guards loitered menacingly. More would be on the skiff, no doubt. One stepped forward with the butt of his blunderbuss – useless if it was wet, for it used a loose powder – and Mr Lindsay held up his hand.

'Net yet.'

At the far end of the caisson Miah hauled himself out of the water, the wounds at his side reopened. Arden met his eyes, and he seemed as guiltily defiant as a boy made to change sides in a schoolyard fight, choosing the stronger opponent over a weaker one with whom he'd once been friends.

She had never seen Mr Lindsay perturbed. Not like this, chewing his lips as if trying to hold back a shout, trying to maintain his composure, his cultivated preternatural calm having deserted him.

And then it occurred to her how young he'd always seemed in his photographs after every one of his generation was old or dead. Though Mr Lindsay had affected modernity, he always had a mysterious, old-fashioned way about him, as if he had stepped from a former age into the present and found it despicable, as if everyone was a child and he the only adult.

In Arden's mind came the silver-print of Claude Lindsay in front of the winder.

It seemed impossible, but she'd seen sanguis surgeons stop a heart beating. Seen them freeze a person like they were suspended in time so they might operate. Freeze for an hour. Maybe two. Maybe longer. Years. Centuries.

'Did you know she was with child when her airship came to your plantation, Claude?' Arden asked.

Mr Lindsay glared at her, too enraged to speak.

It was a feint, pretence, but she had to barrel on. 'Maybe you fell in love with her, but I doubt you have it in you to fall in love. No, I think you saw her as a way to cement your own power, but she escaped you, didn't she, and all this time you have been searching and you never knew where she went.'

'Oh for fuck's sake, why don't you just kill her?' bleated Bellis, but Arden's words had landed true. She felt a hand on her ankle – Chalice, silently willing her to – what? Go on? Shut her mouth?

Mr Lindsay stalked around Arden like a shark about a stricken boat, forcing her to turn into the rising sunlight and squint. The shadow hid his face. He may have suspected she was only throwing out rumours and tales to see which one might make the mark, but the hits had been true.

'What makes you think she escaped?'

Arden met his gaze, that look in his eyes somewhere between ethereal and ancient. 'She was already married. The signs of it were everywhere – in all the machines, in the chevrons in the gears. She wasn't thinking of *you*, Claude, I don't suppose she ever thought of you. You were a means to an end as well.'

'Then you saw her,' he said, shaking with the effort of composure.

After briefly debating affecting cluelessness, she answered honestly. 'Yes.'

'Uncorrupted, untouched by the grave's breath?' These words, again, were almost strangled.

Chalice's fingers bit into Arden's ankle.

'No,' Arden said. 'She'd cut herself open to get out—' She huffed a breath. 'She didn't survive it. She'd been dead for ages.'

Was that regret in his stance? Hard to say, for shadow covered his face. But rage came shortly afterwards. He tilted his chin at his men. 'Get in the boat. You too, Bellis.'

'Are we going to Harbinger Bay *now*?' she asked petulantly.

'Yes, now. And we will obtain your army, and we will obtain our weapon, and we will need no entry pass to Clay City, and before winter ends you will be Queen.'

She sucked a breath of joy. 'Oh good, good. Enough waiting, I am tired of it.'

'Mr Anguis, you will—'

'Wait,' Miah grunted. 'Have you got the stuff?'

His shoulders were hunched, as if he were ashamed, and Mr Lindsay, still atremble with rage, clearly wanted to stretch out the addictive torment. 'The what?'

'The stuff for my *eyes*, guy! What do you think?'

For a moment it seemed he would refuse. Then the Lion shuffled around in his pockets before tossing over the pot. Miah snatched it from mid-air and thumbed the black greasy lumps into his eyes.

'Now, you will come in my boat, Bellis, and Mr Anguis will take his wife.'

Bellis shook her head. 'I don't trust that slut not to work her wiles upon him.'

'One of the men will go along to make sure that doesn't happen,' Mr Lindsay said, gesturing towards the largest of his fellows. 'Bellis my dear, I'm not risking the pair of you fighting.' He turned to Miah Anguis. 'Anchor thirty miles offshore of the estuary entrance and wait for my signal. In one day our Queen will have an army, and with you . . . with you, we will have the world.'

Miah seized Arden's arm. She dug her feet in. 'What about Chalice?'

Chalice waved her arm wearily in an, *oh, don't worry about me* manner. The shock of her broken leg had clearly made her delusional.

Mr Lindsay made a tutting noise. 'Leave her. The lung-sharks will make short work.'

'Murderer!' Arden cried. 'You're leaving her here to die!'

She tried to fight Miah off, but he had a hold on her now, cold and brutal, and if Chalice had the strength to move it was a strength corroded by pain, and her face was the colour of waxy marble.

'Go,' she wheezed. 'Go, darling.'

Miah seized Arden around her waist and hauled her up *Sonder*'s gangplank. She cried and fought, raging at the loss of Jonah and the abandonment of Chalice. She broke free long enough to grab one of the lifeboat supply sacks and haul it over *Sonder*'s transom, not knowing if it reached the caisson's surface or sank into the depths below.

'I'm sorry,' she screamed as Mr Nathan – Lindsay's man – took over and dragged her down into the hull. Miah let the motor spin and she hauled herself upon the pile of empty sacks and sobbed, not just for herself but the remnants of her life strewn across an artificial island in the middle of the ocean.

28

Sonder's hull

Sonder's hull smashed into the hard waves, surfaced and fell. She had never been afflicted with seasickness, but wanted to be so now, while the sea was fighting them, so she could release some of the poison that weighed her down. Instead, she lay in a daze all that day until Miah came down, both to dress his wounds and to swap watching positions with Mr Nathan.

The big guard was hesitant, having heard Bellis' dire announcements about Arden and her wily ways. But he was charier of an argument with the tattooed deepwater man – they were equally matched in size, and Arden was under no doubt Miah would fight to win.

So when Mr Nathan left she pretended to sleep, and through her lashes watched him look down at her with his bruised, stained eyes. Such intensity was in his gaze she imagined her flesh scorched everywhere his attention fell.

'Was it good, seeing him again?'

She sat up, all pretence of sleep cast away. 'Who?'

'Come off it. My cousin was here. I can still feel him in this boat, and he was somewhere on that brick island, hiding.'

A thrill of hope made goose bumps flare across her arms and

her back, as if she were about to grow feathers and fly away. Jonah was still alive and Chalice was not alone.

Cautious now, for this was help she had not expected, Arden ventured, 'If you were so certain Jonah was there, Miah, why did you say nothing to Mr Lindsay?'

Yes, why hadn't he? Miah Anguis sat next to her, and she felt the quiver in him, regret and rage together.

'I do not wish to go further from my home than I already am,' he said. 'You would not forgive me if *he* died. Nor would you love me.'

She took the leap, laid her hand on his arm.

'Then turn this boat around. We can go back and collect them, Miah, we will go home.'

'Home.' His head lunged forward, his rough, unshaven mouth sliding across her cheek to find her lips like a sightless creature might seek out food, then caught her in a bruising kiss. He pushed up her skirts, or at least made the query of it, going no further than her knee. Arden quailed at first, and knew that if she should tell him *no*, then he would stop. It would be proof to him that there was no future for them, and that he should throw in his lot with Claude Lindsay, whoever or whatever that man was.

And that *was* the truth of it.

There was a dreadful chaste finality in the way he gripped her shoulders and released her as if discarding a meal that no longer tasted as it should.

He sat on his haunches, his peculiar eyes watching her in the below-deck gloom. He shook his head. She reached for his face, a desperate clutching at the straws of his desire, but he only jerked back.

'Everything with you is like a duty.'

'I have no other way to convince you, Miah. I have nothing, only to say you must not do what Mr Lindsay says!'

'Well, I have a duty, too.'

'You have an *addiction*! That poison in your eyes. My friend Chalice can reverse what it has done.'

'And replace it with what? You? Beacon, I know which

addiction torments me less.' He stood up. 'I will do what Mr Lindsay and Bellis Harrow require.'

Arden was incredulous. 'You're siding with Bellis Harrow, after everything she did to the Sainted Isles?'

`Miah seemed to flinch, but then his expression hardened. 'There's a monster coiled up in the bottom of the Harbinger Bay estuary that Lindsay has his heart set upon. He doesn't give two shits what Bellis wants, and I'm under his thumb until I've done my part.'

A feeling lurched under her roiling emotions, an almost prophetic shadow. This was the first time anyone had confirmed that Mr Lindsay didn't care about Bellis, her army or her conquering queendom.

But the Harbinger Wyrm?

'What do you mean, Miah? I thought his heart was set on razing Clay Capital to the ground, what meaning does a prison Wyrm have for him?'

'Oh, don't worry, his heart's desire has not changed.'

'Then you mustn't help him!'

'It's already done. Look here, Beacon, neither you, me, nor bloody Harrow were ever going to be part of his little invasion. That idea our mutual bane has about sailing up the Clay River and being the fucking Queen of Lyonne? It's impossible. Army or no army, she would be remotely exsanguinated by the watchtower workers miles before she set eyes upon the city. I'm from Equus and even I know that.'

'Yes but—'

'All those bloodworkers in Clay can pop all the hearts and tie knots in all the guts they want, but neither they nor the city will see what is coming. That's the gift Lindsay intends to bring them.' He made a wretched *ta-da!* gesture. 'The monster that comes at the end.'

'I don't understand . . .'

'You will. But it's too late for us.'

He retreated from her and went back out onto Sonder's deck. He left the door unlocked.

Arden wondered if Miah trusted her enough not to do something foolish like jump over the side. The thought was tempered by the realization that Miah no longer cared. Mr Lindsay had consumed and integrated Miah Anguis into his desires. Everything else Miah might think or feel was drowned out now by that one piercing note of command.

She could not bear the entombment of the below decks any longer and followed him outside.

It was late afternoon now, time having slipped away into the closing hours of the day. The sky was an ominous, low, sulky yellow that smelled like cold rain. The gathering fog had a milky-cream appearance and a stink of dead things in stilled water.

Jonah, she thought. *Look after Chalice.*

Miah was not there. He might have been seeking sanctuary from drama by hiding in the wheelhouse with the guard, Mr Nathan, but there didn't seem much respite up there either, for Mr Nathan had his spyglass out, and had caught sight of something on the waters that was causing them both much concern.

Hope came upon her like a flood. Arden dashed through the hold and up to the starboard side of the boat. Her Beacon-sharp eyes caught the roil upon the water.

From the broken-glass window came Miah's curse of, '*Fucking finfolk!*'

A battalion of the sapient creatures rode the frothing waters holding coral tridents that were as hard as iron, and Arden had to gasp in amazement at a sight she had only seen in books, a veritable platoon of finfolk astride fast-swimming hippocampii – those marine-equine breeds that inhabited the uncharted waters. She'd had experience with both finfolk and hippocampii before, but never together, never in the way that had inspired tale-tellers to hold entire Portside taverns in awed silence as they regaled the gathered sailors of enemy contact and pitched battles at sea.

Sonder shuddered as the propellers began to churn faster

– *Sonder*'s motor was so quiet – but they could not match the speed of the approaching finfolk hunters.

'Why are they tracking us?' Mr Nathan's accusing voice from the wheelhouse cracked with panic. 'You better not have called them, Anguis.'

'It's not me.' He glared down at Arden, still clinging to the cabin door.

She stepped back, startled by the unfathomable meaning in his words. 'I don't know who—'

But the words were snatched from her as *Sonder* shrugged sideways so hard the boat almost turned itself about. Arden was thrown back down the stairs and into the cabin, a wave of water following her.

She tipped back onto the bare wet floor, the caged light spinning in ever-decreasing, vertigo-inducing circles above her head. Another big collision followed, and were it not for the hull ribs catching her, she'd have gone flying. Shouting from the men. An unknown object had struck *Sonder* from below.

Dizzy and hurting, she crawled out of the hold. She emerged to a sudden, inexplicable sight that was both grotesque and familiar. Something huge moved in the water, something that, when she righted herself, she saw break the waves. It had a head the size of a motor car, great fronded horns and a sinuous body as wide as a locomotive carriage and almost twice as long.

Maris Anguis, the great sea serpent.

'The fin-fuckers are controlling the serpent!' Mr Nathan howled, and Arden saw Miah drop onto the deck, tear open his shirt and discard it as the rain came in a deluge.

'Get the rifle, the things are coming with it!' Miah shouted.

Mr Nathan half-jumped, half-fell to the deck. Un-cured tree resin and poor maintenance had made *Sonder*'s rear deck soap-slippery and he might as well have been skating through wet ice in the rain. His feet were unable to find purchase and he pulled himself hand over hand towards the cabin.

Arden hung onto the door as best she could with her elbow

looped over the handle and held out her numb hand in desperate assistance.

'Mr Nathan! Grab my hand!'

But the fool had not secured *Sonder*'s wheel properly. Without the Saint's commands, it did what an unmanned boat was supposed to do and began to turn in ever-decreasing circles. The centrifugal force sent Mr Nathan careening across the slippery deck.

Not only him, but Miah, too. Trapped by his own weight, he collided with a pair of finfolk who had been swept onboard. Caught in a similar circumstance, the four of them floundered in a sea of gravity. Arden wrenched herself to her knees, crawled along the joists of *Sonder*'s balustrades. A *crack* echoed from below and the boat stopped its spin and kicked out her rear end, sending Arden sprawling along with the others.

Miah was on his feet in an instant, running down *Sonder*'s boards, clearly trying to catch sight of the serpent before it tried to attack again.

A finfolk male dropped in front of him, but Miah batted the merman aside as if he were smoke. A war of blood and will swirled about the air in a tempest as the monster thrashed in its enslavement, compelled by both humans and finfolk and its own instinct for freedom.

'*Hold*,' Miah screamed into the wind, rivulets of blood flying from his fingers.

Through the rain Arden could see land – a long stretch of beach – and a pang of yearning went through her. Land, and a chance to stop this.

Arden grabbed the trilobite cages and hauled them down in front of her, a tangle of glass and wire blocking Miah's path. It was temporary, for he could easily have tipped them over the side and kept going.

Instead, he stood, rain-washed, panting behind the wires, swaying from foot to foot as Arden reached for the ladder.

'What are you doing?'

'We can't go to Harbinger Bay! We can't. You talk of home

but if you go through with this, you'll never go home, never! You'll be done, Miah!'

'You are *evalescendi*, Beacon! *Evalescendi* only serve!'

'I *am* serving. I'm a Signal Keeper of Lyonne, and it's my decision what does or doesn't make it into port. And this ship isn't going anywhere!'

Miah shouted and tried to haul the nets aside, but they'd locked in place. And as he ran about the decks to try and get through, the serpent came back up again, looming out of the water, its mouth open wide enough to swallow half the ship, white spume waving silver across the iridescent enormity of its scales. There was no way even all the blood in Miah's body could stop it now.

And so, whether it was through self-preservation or a small kernel of understanding left in him, Miah Anguis picked up one end of the broken charging cable, held it aloft at the bow of the stricken ship, shoved his bare foot into the contact plate, and as the serpent dived to consume him, shoved the bare cable end into his chest, completing the circuit.

29

Once upon a time

Once upon a time the forefathers of Fiction and Lyonne – the same ones who had built the ancient ruins and learned so much about the ways and laws of nature – discovered the great potentials of matter and energy.

Discovered how to put them to use, how to benefit from their labour.

But in their wisdom, they also saw the end of their society, the guttering candle of their civilization. Knew that to keep their culture alive would require more than books that decayed, or memories that faded.

And so they wrote their discoveries in human blood.

Apportioned labour to a human conduit.

Made the sanguis kind and gave them traits woven into their genome, their inheritable line.

Impressed upon them a creed that had been in effect even when their civilization had been great and unassailable:

For every boon taken from in the ocean of the unseen universe, a price must be paid in return.

A little of that impression remained in Arden now, slumped over *Sonder's* control panel by the wallop of the serpent hitting the top of the bow and sinking into the waves, instantly electrocuted. Just as she raised her head, *Sonder*'s battery-banks short-circuited, catching fire.

There was only one option left. Head into the shore, haul the burning boat up onto the sand, and when she had flung herself free of the pyre of flames, watch as they consumed *Sonder*.

But, their catch stolen, the merfolk tried to attack once again as soon as she had run aground, and in the last gasp of twilight Harry Tanbark arrived to rescue her and carry her into the Coastmaster's Lodge.

Book Three: The Bay

30

And the shock killed him

'And the shock killed him?' the shoreman Cadmus asked. He had finished his chowder and mopped up the remains with potato-bread. Lise was not part of the conversation and stood with her back to the table, yet she seemed tense and only half-aware of the sink of hot grey dishwater in front of her.

'With my eyes I saw him take the electrical load and kill the serpent,' Arden said, 'but I did not see him die. And it worries me.'

Tanbark shrugged alongside her. 'There are a lot of sanguinem with a feel for electricity. You folks all can sense it. No great stretch to imagine you could control it, too.'

Arden nodded wearily. 'Yes, and he is a man gifted in a great many things. Including staying alive.'

Cadmus ventured, somewhat in disbelief, 'And according to you, he's making his way to the prison grounds to meet a semi-immortal man and a mind-enslaving witch.'

'Yes, if they are not there already with one goal in mind.'

Cadmus shook his head. 'Stealing the Harbinger Wyrm. I find it hard to believe it, even if you did come to us in a boat on fire with silver in your hands.'

Tanbark cleared his throat politely. 'Sometimes when penitents are sentenced to terms longer than their natural lives, their lives are extended to meet the punishment. This Mr Lindsay may indeed be a former resident of the Bay, somehow escaped his natural end.'

Arden nodded. 'You do not have to believe my story, Mr Cadmus. You only have to take me to my friends, and rescue them off the caisson. They were abandoned out there!'

Cadmus pushed the plate away. One of his fellows entered the dormitory, Cadmus clicked for his attention, and murmured something in his ear, something brief in a dialect Arden did not recognize.

'I cannot take you myself,' he said. 'But someone may volunteer tomorrow.'

'What are you talking about?' Arden cried, standing up. 'They've been there for days!'

'I won't make any of my men sail in darkness, not with the monstrosities about. You can head out at first light tomorrow.'

'But—' Arden wanted to yank her sleeve away from Tanbark, who was now tugging on it with no small amount of enthusiasm, silently begging her to sit down.

Mr Cadmus went on. 'You may sleep in the oversummer sheds tonight.'

Arden finally surrendered to Tanbark and sat down.

'Thank you for listening to us,' Tanbark said. 'Excuse my companion. As you can tell, she's had a difficult time of it.'

'Thank you,' Arden said grumpily, when Tanbark nudged her.

'Don't thank me yet. Someone still has to volunteer a boat.'

The oversummer sheds were weathered permanent lodges built on concrete stumps above the high-water mark. They still held the dankness of having been used for storage during the tempestuous summer season. When the shorefolk moved on to take advantage of the finfolk-free summer in the north, the tools of their Firetide Season professions – the shoreboats, fishing line, nets and pots – stayed locked up for the better part of the year.

Arden found some blankets of a tough horsehair folded on the wide shelves, along with thin pallets of dried wool and linen, enough to make the most rustic of beds. She sighed, expecting another uncomfortable night. At least she was better off than Musket. Forbidden entry, the dog was confined to a box outside. Tanbark sacrificed a blanket to keep him comfortable, and Arden gave Tanbark hers, much to his protests. But she insisted. She was young and had a krakenskin coat. He was an old man.

'I'm sorry I had to take you from your bed, Coastmaster,' she said as they huddled about the hissing lantern, trying to find the warmth to sleep.

'It is no problem,' Tanbark said. 'At least I get to do some Lyonnian rescue business.'

'Does it surprise you that the Saint might have come here to this coast?'

'I think if what you say is true and she was married . . . maybe she was no longer wedded by the time she made it back to Lyonne. Maybe she was a widow. Perhaps the call of home had a pull she could no longer deny. She was a girl from Clay City, much like you are.' He paused and then ventured, 'It may not have even been her first child.'

'How do you mean?'

Tanbark gestured towards the doors that faced the ocean. 'Your man Jonah said he'd seen a similar structure to the bridge caisson, out on the Fiction shallows. Every expecting woman will seek out for herself a bower of safety when the time comes. Home, hearth, or a magical tower out to sea.'

Arden was quiet as she thought of what it meant. She rubbed her numb hands together.

'And her skills, *orientis*, *mandatum*?' Tanbark continued. 'They did not appear by accident. Even you touched on it, Arden. Her blood runs through the deepwater people of Fiction. Bellis Harrow and Miah Anguis could be her descendants. Jonah, too.'

Arden rubbed her hands again. It felt cold in this room.

'There's more to deepwater blood than just the Saint's talents,' she said. 'They are cursed with a terrible affliction. Sometimes no child grows in – well, the Saint died cutting monsters out of her. It was very hard for Jonah to see that. They say he was twinned with a monster when he was born. Imagine being the one to see it. The terror of seeing such a thing.'

'How odd,' Tanbark mused. 'The local stories say that the Harbinger Wyrm was born from the belly of a woman, centuries ago. How surprising Cadmus never brought it up when you spoke of it.'

A twang of understanding made Arden dip into the bodice pocket of her dress and take out the button. The Lindsay family crest ringed the emerald centre. She counted the ones on her sleeves, and they were all still intact. *She* was not the one missing a button.

'This button was there in the altar from the start. I didn't drop it, and there was no clothing the Saint wore.'

'Then your immortal Mr Lindsay was there earlier?'

'No, he seemed confused – angry, even – when he arrived. He had no idea of the caisson's location.' She frowned. 'This is a button from a servant's garment. If the Saint sought help, then she sought it from the household staff,' Arden said. 'I mean, what a stretch of imagination, but say one of those creatures survived . . . was brought to Lyonne—'

It was almost too much to think of. It made the Harbinger Wyrm more awful, that it was both monster and human at once.

'The Wyrm in the prison,' Tanbark mused. 'The thing with all the malign intelligence of a man and the powers of a Saint. What a thing to control, if you could control it.'

'Miah Anguis can control it.' Arden drew her knees to her chest and hugged them. 'I hope we're not too late for my friends. I don't wish for us to be around to find out how much control Mr Lindsay has.'

Tanbark turned down the lantern and in the gloom pulled up his blanket and settled in to sleep.

Sleep did not come so easily to Arden. She had no doubt Jonah had survived, and he would care for Chalice, but it was difficult not to worry about them. They would now have spent two days upon the caisson. The lifeboat sack contained water and three days' supplies, but after they ran out . . .

Jonah and Chalice could die out there. Jonah could summon a monster, but Chalice was in no condition to cling to the back of a leviathan. Arden's breath steamed in the cold. The hours crept by too slowly.

I'm on my way, Chalice. I'm coming.

But was she? The shoreman Cadmus had yet to find her a boat.

In the middle of her ruminating, on the edge of sleep, the door creaked. She winced, annoyed, for she might have finally fallen off the slumbering precipice had there not been that sharp grate of the metal hinge.

She went to turn over, and a man's face appeared in her darksight, grimacing with murderous intent. A great shiny mallet raised in his fist—

'Eee-yah!' came the scream even before Arden could grab a breath. A great loop of chain was wrapped about the man's face by the force of the throw.

He fell back, knocking over the rockblood lantern, and in the yellow puddle of flame Arden was confronted by a room filled with six or seven people – women – all soaking wet. Their musky, marine smell filled the shed with hot fury as they jumped on the man and bound him with the chain, shoving a rag into his mouth so he could only hoot in resentful complaint.

Tanbark was awake and smothered the flame with his blanket before relighting the lantern with the remnants of unspilled fuel in the lantern fount.

'Goodness,' he said. 'If Musket were here, he would have alerted us!'

The whole experience of turning her from being half-asleep in an empty shed to cramped in this hot crowded space with all these women had taken less than half a minute. Breathing hard, Arden kicked her coat off and stood up. The man was the shore-friend Cadmus had instructed at the dinner table, but to her surprise the others were also familiar.

There was Lise, Mr Cadmus' wife, still chained, however the other end was now wrapped around the interloper's shoulders. And there was Mrs Finch, and her daughter, and the others from the Lindsay Estate.

Mrs Finch handed Mrs Cadmus the key, which she used to unlock the shackle at her ankle.

Freed, Lise nodded at Arden. 'The little man you speak of, Mr Lindsay, he came to us last year in the springtime, offered my husband fishing licences and signed dispensations for extra catches all up and down the coast. He warned that someone might come searching for him. He wanted to be notified if anyone did, especially if they were to mention the *Harbinger Wyrm*.'

As she spoke, Tanbark picked up the discarded mallet. It would have been nothing to smash Arden's skull in, then turn its attention to an old man. He stared at it for a long time before slipping it into his belt.

The other women moved close. 'Come with us,' Mrs Finch said.

Although the invitation was to Arden, Tanbark was not about to linger either. He grabbed the lantern and followed.

Outside the oversummer sheds, Tanbark ran in an alarmed, old-man lope to Musket's box. To his joy he found his dog muzzled but unharmed. 'Shh now, boy. We need to keep quiet.'

Daylight was yet to come, but with her darksight Arden noticed the women's sopping wet clothes were inappropriate for the weather. Their garments consisted of simple shifts, and none wore shoes. How had they made it to this part of the coast so wet and bedraggled?

Down by the beach the bright waters lapped and receded. A few seals lolled there in the darkness among the small tender boats. Curiously, the animals did not hump away at their approach but instead lifted their heads at the approach of the lantern.

Then one seal stood up, and divested herself of her coat. Bare skin was illuminated in the lamplight and the fur lay in a puddle at her feet. And underneath – Mrs Valley, the Lindsay Estate housekeeper.

31

Tanbark

Tanbark covered his eyes at once.

'Selkie,' Arden breathed. 'Seal women. I have heard of your kind but thought them only legend.'

Mrs Valley gave a grim smile and accepted a linen shift from one of her comrades. She was sociable enough not to continue the conversation naked. The other seal-folk had stood up and were half disrobed, heads and shoulders showing, a startling sight, as if a seal had opened its mouth wide and a person were popping out. One young seal had a flipper that stuck at a strange angle.

'Can I uncover my eyes now?' Tanbark asked. 'I don't wish to be impolite.'

'We are decent now, sir,' Mrs Valley said.

Collecting herself, Arden gave a quick bow, remembering that such folk of the waters were very concerned about etiquette. Selkies were not merfolk, they could move between water and land easily, and be at home in either one. They made good brides, if a man could hide the selkie's fur skins away. Clearly the Lindsay Estate had collected a veritable stash of skins.

'We cannot stay long,' Mrs Valley said. 'The Glasman will free himself soon.'

Behind her, the half-dressed selkie-women had tipped over one of the longboats and were dragging it into the water.

'If it pleases you,' Tanbark said, 'do you know what happened to Maud Tanbark? She went into the water six years ago. I suspect she was one of yours.'

Mrs Finch smiled kindly. 'She went home, Coastmaster. She had a family waiting for her.'

'Ah.'

He sounded downcast, and Arden hugged him in support. 'It sounds as if she is alive and living a good life, Tanbark,' Arden said. 'I'm sure she remembers you with fondness.'

A light flickered in a Glasfolk dormitory window. Someone up to check on the progress of their murderous man, no doubt. Arden wasted no time getting into the boat and helped Tanbark in after her. Musket bounded through the flashing crimson waves and jumped in before shaking himself vigorously.

'Where's the engine—' she started to say, before realizing that the longboat was scudding quickly over the breaking waves and into the calmer, deeper waters beyond. She wanted to ask where they were going, but all the women had gone back into their coats, and their heads bobbed in the darkness, focused on pushing the longboat out of the sheltering bay and northwards.

Arden hung on at some of the larger swells. Once again she was fleeing angry men, leaving behind some unknown upset in her wake.

'I wonder where they are taking us?' Arden asked Tanbark over the cold slop of the waves. The crimson had faded now. They had left behind the Firetide Coast.

'No idea. We certainly aren't going back to the lodge,' Tanbark said.

'I still have to rescue my friends. Oh, perhaps they could take this boat out to them?'

'Perhaps. Maybe once we reach Harbinger Bay they might stop long enough for us to ask.'

'Harbinger Bay? Where is it?'

He pointed and she turned about, saw the flashing spire of

the Harbinger Bay lighthouse coming out of the pre-morning gloom. A solemn memory laid its hand upon her shoulder.

'That's Chalice's old lighthouse. She was a stormbride there for Stephen Pharos before she was with me.'

'Would have thought the light brighter, for a sanguis house.'

'Yes,' she said uneasily. 'It should be brighter, but it's glowing about the same as a rockblood lantern.'

The entrance to the estuary was wide and shallow and braided by clear stones that caught the sunrise, transmuting the leaden water into a dull yellow-gold. Hints of forestry operations were visible in the mouldering tree-stumps across the hillside, the regrowth coming back short and stunted. A tide wall of old, layered stone ran along the long length of the inlet and ended in a small pier. The usual fishing boats of a coastal industry clustered around it.

The Harbinger Bay estuary entrance looked a little like a discarded shorefolk town, similar to the Glasfolk settlement down the coast. If there were ever more substantial buildings, they were merely ruins now, the bare ribs of house-frames black against the sky. Arden remembered Chalice telling her how she had seen the shorefolk rituals from the lighthouse tower in previous years. If only they were still here, they could have helped.

The entrance was, however, occupied. A frame of steel propped up near the tideline was alight with a row of turning fireworks, so one could imagine the rolling of a serpent's body through water.

Or an eel.

A knot of people gathered under the sparkling lights, conducting some kind of early morning mass, a holy office. The sounds of a chorus in harmony, an entreaty to the ocean in the tones of a hymn, echoed across the water.

The longboat shuddered as it hit the rock-strewn beach, but when Arden leaned over to thank the selkie-women, they had gone. Their leaving made her panic slightly – how was she supposed to rescue Chalice and Jonah now?

She could not wallow in her despair for long, as in the morning gloom five men peeled away from the group, mossy and shapeless in their waxed canvas. Two of them held long-arms, not quite pointed at the ground. Harry Tanbark instinctively reached for the rifle that wasn't there and sighed. His weapon was still with Mr Cadmus.

'Who goes there?' gruffed one. 'Who interferes with us during the rites of the Wyrm?'

Tanbark stood up as best he could, pushing Musket behind him, for the dog was trembling from the air of alarm and excitement. 'I am Harry Tanbark; I am the Coastmaster for South Lyonne.'

'We have no business with South Lyonne.'

Arden piped up, 'I am from Lyonne proper, sirs, Clay Portside. I am Arden Beacon, from the Signal—'

One hulking shadow moved forward, long-arm held crossways, not pointed at them.

'Little Ardie? You've come all this way?'

The moiré of light through the clouds did not reveal him completely, but when it did – ginger beard, port-keeper's braids – Arden could not stop the tears that came.

'Gerry!' she cried. 'Gerry . . . it is me!'

She fell out of the longboat and scrabbled to her feet before anyone could stop her, running into the barrel-chested embrace of her father's old friend, the Guildsman Gerry Harris.

'Enough, enough then,' he said, as she hugged him, bawling like a child at the return of a favourite uncle. 'I've had all the reunions I can have this day, and I'm just about worn out *of* welcomes.'

She stood back reluctantly and wiped the tears from her cheeks. The last time she had seen Gerry Harris was almost a year ago, when he'd handed over the keys to her uncle's lighthouse. So much had happened since then that she felt almost shy around him, as if she'd grown up while his back was turned.

It took a while before she realized what he had said. '*Worn out* of welcomes, Gerry?'

'This way.'

She paused only long enough to wait for Tanbark to leave the longboat. As they walked under the extinguished worship-trellis, Gerry Harris said, 'I came here after I delivered your uncle's lighthouse to you, and oversaw the ending of this light-house.'

'It's rockblood now, I saw.'

He nodded. 'Stephen Pharos had been poorly for a while. This is no place for sanguis kind.' He kissed his fingertips before pointing at a structure that was half icon, half accident of a thousand strands of copper and steel, coiled and sinuous. 'The Harbinger Wyrm.'

'Gerry,' she said urgently, 'I've come searching for a boat, Chalice Quarry, my friend—'

He didn't seem to be listening to her, more interested in a hump in the ground, a barrow with two wooden doors set flat upon it, like a publican's cellar with no tavern. With the help of his friends, he swung them open.

To her surprise the inside portion was lit and lined with either dressed stone or lime cement. Certainly nothing natural. It was a twisting stairwell into the hillside, the kind one might go in and then not come out for a hundred years. It made her think of Mr Lindsay, preternaturally young, and the association was not welcome. Gerry did not hesitate in going inside, however, and Arden, still freshly traumatized from her experience at the caisson, had to catch a breath.

Tanbark patted her back. 'Stay firm, Arden Beacon. You've experienced worse, I'll wager, and you're among friends here.'

Musket, sensing her worry, nuzzled her hand with his wet nose. She took a deep breath and descended.

The stairs did not go down far. The barrow was shallow, repurposed from some old tor or tomb that might have sunken into the ground millennia ago. Or maybe it was just a root cellar left over from when the original house rotted away. Still, her knees and back twanged in complaint at all the running and stair-climbing of the past few days. If she concentrated on those small discomforts, she wouldn't have to think about what might lie ahead, of the arguments she would have to make, of more time wasted . . .

The space was little bigger than the boatsheds of the Glasfolk, except it was warm, and had actual furnishings befitting a meeting place; however, the attention seemed to be at the far side of the room, where at least four robed folk were indulging in some laying on of hands.

'Come,' Gerry said, waving her onwards.

The hooded folk – priests – stood back. Their attention had been upon a high table and the highly opinionated person on top.

'Torturers!' the person cried. 'Have you no shame!'

And because it was her wont to appear when all hope seemed lost, even in the middle of some abject medical procedure with her nose sunburnt, Chalice Quarry still found the motivation to prop herself on her elbows and croak, 'Oh, hello, darling.'

32

They had not been doing

They had not been doing a laying on of hands after all. They had been trellising her broken leg in the oddest contraption of wires and copper piping, and had only just finished the last turn of the screw.

'Why, it looks like you are getting ready to slot into a machine yourself,' Arden said dryly, keeping her distance to avoid dissolving into tears. If she had a reservoir of strength left, it was rapidly running dry.

'Well come on, give me a hug then, I'm not made of glass.'

Though she might have changed her clothes, Chalice still smelled as ripe as a pile of kelp left on a hot beach, but Arden could not have cared less. With her wrist she pushed Chalice's sweaty hair off her forehead. 'I am glad you are all right, I only doubted a little bit . . .' She was silenced by the number of questions flooding through her, some important, some not so.

But one question was paramount.

'Where's Jonah?'

Was that Chalice's face falling? Was Arden about to be told something most awful? Arden stepped back from the slab, and Chalice grabbed her hand, which made Arden wince as a dart

Firetide Coast

of pain shot through the parts of her that could still feel. Chalice
let her go.

'Darling, he's gone on to the Bay. To confront his cousin and
rescue you.'

'Oh devilment! When?'

Another spoke: 'This morning, before sunrise.'

Arden turned about at the stranger's voice, for she had not
realized that one of the priests was a woman. It was a standard
monkish garb she wore, but underneath the costume of worship
was a pair of bib-and-brace stevedore overalls over a stout
chest, and her sharp face was as flaky and gale-bitten as any
Portside windwife.

'Sister Quarry and her companion came yesterday on the
afternoon high tide. Borne aloft by those selkie wives in payment
for their freedom, apparently. Brother Harris vouched for them
both.'

''Tis true,' Mr Harris interjected, although there was a look
in his face that suggested he'd taken quite the leap of faith.
He'd only known Jonah as an unpleasant neighbour with a bad
history.

'Then Mr Riven *felt* something. A wrinkle in the air, a passing
in the night, who knows? I asked him to wait,' she continued,
'but there was no waiting in him. He had to go on and rescue
his woman, whom I now assume is you?'

'*You*, Ardie?' came Mr Harris' squawk of disbelief.

'Sorry, Mr Harris,' Chalice said from her procedure table. 'I
neglected to share who Mr Riven was in such a fuss about.'

'Oh, whatever would your father say, Arden, a man like
that—'

'Enough!' said the woman, who appeared to have some kind
of authority about her. 'Time to get up and walk, Sister Quarry,
'tis only your small calf-bone broken, and you on enough poppy
juice to fell a horse. The best medicine now is soap and water.'

After Chalice moved off the table and into an upright position that took two assistants and many hair-curling words to
effect, she was whisked away to the priestly bath-house. The

woman placed their exotic wire-work tools inside a waxed canvas roll before looking at Arden with a grey, gimlet eye.

'Mr Harris tells me you are full cousin to Brother John Stefan, who once held office in the Clay City Church.'

It was direct, but not unkind. 'Yes, he was once called Stefan Beacon before his ordination, and his father, Jorgen Beacon, was my uncle.'

'You may call me Mother Blackwell. I knew Stefan when he came to Clay as a skinny little Fiction applicant to the priest-hood, closer to the gods of the ocean than the One True God of the Church. He always seemed caught in a state of suffering. I almost thought it cruel to keep him, but the pull of God was – for a while – stronger.'

'He . . . ah . . . he died a few weeks ago,' Arden said awkwardly.

'So I hear. I also hear of the manner in which he met his end, and the *disaster* he tried to stop.'

'That *disaster*, she is unstoppable, Mother Blackwell,' Arden said despairingly. 'This is why I must try and catch up with Jonah. He is heading into danger on my behalf.'

'I have heard about all you have gone through. Have you considered that you two are not meant to be, Arden Beacon, if by all these twists of fate you are continuously torn from one another?'

Beside Arden, Gerry Harris gave a grumble of concern and agreement.

'Fine,' she said, a bubble of indignant pride rising in her. 'I'm done asking for help. I'll go myself.'

She left the cellar-room with her umbrage giving her a jolt of energy, enough that she could storm up the stairwell without having to rest halfway.

But no sooner had she exited into the cold morning than her resentment at Mother Blackwell faded into a loom of misgivings, because she could not tell where she was. A slimy sea-fog had rolled in, and her only direction was the lap of the estuary mouth against the tide wall. There was nothing else, not even a path.

Too wound-up to stay still, she moved on down to the estuary wall, beating herself up at all the time that had gone to waste. She had missed Jonah by hours. Maybe not even an hour! At the wall all she could do was dig her fingers into the rock, overwhelmed by such a glancing defeat from what should have been a perfect reunion. And when she looked down, she had torn the flesh off her fingers and had smeared blood on the stone.

'Possibly not the best course of action, for a sanguinem to use their talents in the Bay.'

Mother Blackwell had followed her. Arden looked about for Gerry and Tanbark, and found that the priestess had come alone.

'What does it matter,' Arden said with a sigh. 'You have the Wyrm.'

'Yes, we do.'

'Well, not for much longer. It has become the desire of a man to use for awful purposes.'

She wondered what Jonah and Chalice had told Mother Blackwell. They knew as much of Mr Lindsay's plan to steal the Wyrm for use against Clay Capital as Arden did. As it turned out, Mother Blackwell didn't question Arden's announcement, and only shrugged. 'Our faith says the Wyrm will be invulnerable to attack. To think otherwise would mean we had no faith in its power, which puts us in a dogmatic bind.'

'So you'll do nothing?'

Mother Blackwell came up alongside Arden and without a by-your-leave took her hand. 'Ah, those coins are properly infected.'

She pulled her hands back.

'I knew him, you know,' Mother Blackwell continued. 'When he was a guest at the Bay. Little Jonah. He said he could talk to the Wyrm. I didn't believe it of course, but maybe enough of the inmates did that he wasn't dead in the first year. The Bay is no place for children.'

'He never told me much,' Arden admitted. 'I suppose we never had the time to discuss it.'

Through the milky slump of the fog Arden caught the sound of voices, men singing on a low drone, the clump and grunt of horses moving over uneven ground.

'Guard shift,' Mother Blackwell said. 'Best come back inside else they mistake you for a convict.'

'They won't see me in this fog.'

'They can see everything.'

Arden was not yet ready to concede, but was given no chance to say her part, for the drapes of fog folded back over a mounted figure, its horse stepping slowly through the gloom, sparks clanging where the steel of its broad hooves met the grey rock of the estuarine soil.

At first, she thought in confusion that there must be something wrong, the horse was dreadfully injured, for what else could cause it to look so flayed and mucked with dirt and blood?

Then she understood. It didn't just *look* flayed. Across the broad chest its muscles bunched and released, the yellow tendons strumming like wires on bone fretwork. The demonic head tossed, skeletal and grimacing, the steel bit in its mouth clunking against the exposed molars.

And that was not just the horse. The rider was very much the same, and a hat did not do much to obscure the naked skull dressed in layers of delicate red flesh. The black, skate-leather coat might have given the man somewhat of a less menacing appearance, but it flapped open at his raw-meat chest, exposed his ribs and – most terrible of all – the fact that he had no legs and grew instead out of the demon-horse's back.

Mother Blackwell stood in front of Arden and pushed her behind. 'Ah, Mr Tammas, I see you've brought the mist this morning.'

'Was not I,' returned his grating reply. Behind him more figures moved, each one of them like the hideous Mr Tammas, being both man and horse at once. Or woman and horse, though she could not tell for certain as they were all of a type – denuded of skin, their arms so long that they could have well reached the underside of their horse-bodies.

'There is a silence in the hulks today,' Mr Tammas continued. 'Perhaps you'd have some knowing of its cause, *Mither* Blackwell?'

'I have not,' the woman said, but Arden was in no mood for extended dances for the cause of courteousness.

'Her name is Bellis Harrow.' Arden stepped out from behind Mother Blackwell, much to her hiss of disapproval. 'She is *sanguis orientis*, like the Saint of the Islands, and she has in her mind to do the greatest of damage to you all.' She paused, for now the horse-man was glaring at her from under the brim of his hat, one socket filled with a searing red eye as if a coal burned inside his skull. 'But you know this,' she said. 'You are *nuckelavee*, waterfolk. Your people are from the Sainted Isles, Equus, it's how the island received its common name. *Nuckelavee* are not unfamiliar with the Saint.'

'The evil that turned the island against us,' a second, grinding voice came from behind Mr Tammas, and Arden was correct in assuming that there were females among the group.

Mother Blackwell gave a snort of impatience. 'I apologize for my companion. We have had quite a few visitors bearing warnings and—' She stopped and sighed. 'I think perhaps we should listen to what she says.'

'We are invulnerable to *sanguis orientis*, and all the mind-controlling talents of mesmerism and psychics.' Mr Tammas walked his horse around them. Or he walked himself – hard to say. 'Even the talents of the Saint would be nothing against the Wyrm. Nothing can kill it.'

Mother Blackwell made the sign of the serpent upon her generous chest and said, 'It appears someone wants to use it for this reason. It may involve a theft of some kind.'

The *nuckelavee* guards looked among themselves in alarm. The sudden way they believed Mother Blackwell sent Arden into high alert. They'd seen someone who had convinced them that controlling a monster was possible.

Jonah?

The one who had spoken before said, 'Yesterday our brother, Neckar, was found crushed under the weight of his own body.'

'We thought he might have slipped during patrol and rolled over,' Mr Tammas said. 'But the ground was flat and he was young and sure of foot.'

'Yesterday? Then it was Miah Anguis who your brother saw,' Arden said with a stab of both relief and horror. Jonah had left later. 'He is *sanguis monstrum*. Well may *nuckelavee* be immune to *orientis*, but I'll beg your pardon and say that *monstrum* will do just the same. Oh devilment, I thought Miah was dead, but he made it here—'

Mr Tammas glared down at her. 'One man against the Wyrm?'

Arden nodded. 'I have seen Mr Anguis call giant serpents from the water and encourage a behemoth to drown itself. He is the one who will help take the Wyrm from Harbinger Bay.'

Mother Blackwell had a great air of distress about her. She did not want to believe their beloved monster coiled in the bottom of the estuary was not the all-powerful god of her religion, but the evidence was mounting.

'What of your man who went after him?' Mother Blackwell asked Arden. 'Miss Quarry says he is *sanguis monstrum* as well.'

Goodness, what *hadn't* Chalice told this woman? Arden thought. A touch of poppy juice, and she'd sung an aria worthy of an entire theatre season.

'If they meet again – I don't know what will happen. There's bad blood between them, and one will kill the other.'

Mr Tammas' horse-head tossed and a grating bleat came out of his black, bleeding throat.

'Then your fellow will need assistance. Can you ride, god child?'

'Certainly not,' Chalice said.

As delicately as possible Arden put her coat back over her shoulders. Mother Blackwell had made Arden put cotton finger-cots and leather gloves on over her numb hands, and now everything felt both bulky and clumsy. She hoped her mount would not require much work on the reins. Taking an unfamiliar animal through possibly dangerous terrain after a troupe of *nuckelavee* prison guards sounded like a great deal of work. Her body was falling apart just fine without it.

'This is not up for discussion, Chalice. If these people are going to lose their Wyrm, it is *their* business. I absolutely will not have Jonah mixed up in it.'

'And what of Brother Absalom's coin? The promise you made?'

To be brutally honest would mean admitting she had quite forgotten him, which she had. Arden fished in her bodice and brought out the coin on instruction. It had left a coin-shaped dent on her skin.

She slapped it into Chalice's palm.

'I'm going to be the last of their problems. I think they'll be too tied up with Mr Lindsay's new pet to worry about me for a long time.'

Chalice would have run after her, but her broken calf bone had reduced her to a pained limp with a staff, and the brass pipe wired to her leg caught annoyingly upon her skirts when she moved.

Still, she followed Arden outside to where Mother Blackwell had secured a pair of horses.

Arden had expected to be riding double with a *nuckelavee* and had been dreading it, but her mount was a proper, full-skin animal. She touched the soft, creamy, velvet nose and rubbed the white star between the animal's eyes. Her fingers slid around the bony protrusion just below the forelock, a horn as long as her thumb. It was said that the best horses in Lyonne had unicorn ancestry bred into the bloodline, but Arden suspected it was more likely a mare had gotten loose among a wild unicorn herd and come back in foal.

'If you can't manage a horse, Mr Tammas could carry you.'

Arden suppressed a shudder. 'Every high-born girl in Clay is given equestrian lessons from her third birthday, whether they want them or not.' She frowned then, realizing there were two horses. 'You don't have to come along, Mother Blackwell,' Arden added wearily.

'Excuse me, it's my Wyrm.'

Of course it was. Mr Harris and Tanbark stood nearby like a pair of funeral directors waiting for a solemn moment to say their ritual goodbyes and there was an air of her riding off to her doom as they set out. Musket trotted along beside them for a quarter mile, until they entered the forest line, and the daylight receded.

Instead of the riotous fecundity of the Firetide Coast, this part of the estuary country had a solemn riparian monoculture, a great many crown-shy conifers, more scrubby camphor-bushes along the great wide river and not much else.

The *nuckelavee* walked along the ridgeline in single file. No sign of life disturbed the foliage, not even birds, the only movement being the smoke coiling from the smokestacks in the distance.

Arden quashed all thoughts about the unnatural silence. From what the others had said, it was over fifteen miles from the estuary entrance to the prison complex along the wide deep river. Fifteen forbidding miles along a narrow trail. She wondered if any escapees had tried to flee through the conifer forest. There was almost no undergrowth, it would have been easy to make good time.

Unless a nuckelavee guard was chasing you. Arden did not doubt the flayed horse-men could cover distance and speed greater than an ordinary animal.

Though unicorn hybrids didn't need the rest, they stopped at a creek and Mother Blackwell shared a loaf of sourdough bread with Arden, washed down with turpentine-tasting water.

'Was a long time ago that I was a guest of these shores; I was barely a child,' Mother Blackwell said when they resumed their journey. 'Afterwards, I was old and all my family had gone, and I had nowhere else to go.'

'What were you confined for—' Arden didn't stop herself

quickly enough and went to apologize. It was rude of her to ask.

Mother Blackwell did not take the question badly. She rolled up her sleeves and along her arms, from finger to elbow, was a ladder of precise white scars. 'Let's just say I exceeded the contract of my station and used my blood-talents for revenge on someone stronger than me.' Her face hardened. 'And I was glad of it. I might have regretted the years lost to the Bay, but I don't for one second regret what I did to *him*.'

The talk of revenge made Arden look down at her hands. 'I have been thinking about why Mr Lindsay would do such a thing as that he is doing now. What is driving him to set a monster upon a city? Anyone he wanted revenge on, well . . . even their children's children are likely gone now. Everything he does seems arbitrary and capricious. Not a game of tactics, just knucklebones thrown idly.'

'He has been cursed with long life, Chalice Quarry says.'

'Yes.'

'Then how awful a life with a straight course and no deviations. No finite moment ahead or behind, each year the same in and out. It is considered a terrible punishment. He cannot create a life's work if his life is long and without purpose.' Mother Blackwell tilted her chin towards the first of the broken ships washed up onto the estuary beach, more floating heavy in the water beyond. 'I, too, have been thinking what it means. Only one answer came to me. Taking the Harbinger Wyrm to Clay will be his opus, his great destructive symphony.'

As Mother Blackwell spoke, Arden looked over the broken ships listing in the fog-shrouded shallows. *The prison hulks*, Arden thought with a quiver. Every Clayman alive knew of these disreputable ships of death, and those that had survived them would tell of jailhouse fiefdoms self-contained in each decaying hull, with too many souls and not enough food. Some of the ships were so infamous that even on the streets of free Portside people knew their strange, slightly authoritative names. *Felicity Compliance, Wherewithal Grievance, Fragrant Concession.*

The smell of the ships came off in waves to match the stinking bodies, reeking and ammoniac. But there was so sign of life, no guards, no prison-messengers scudding between ships. It was a ghost-town of an armada, ragged with barnacles, borer-worm and rot. Ahead, it appeared as if a hundred thousand footprints had waded through the soft mud. Not all had made it. A dozen bodies were visible, half-buried in the mud, men recently deceased, not like the human remains decaying in the gibbets. *Bellis has been here.*

One of them lifted his head and groaned.

Arden couldn't help herself. This was where Jonah had lived, this was the place that had made him. His suffering was in these waters. She slid off her mount despite the bark of warning from Mother Blackwell and her feet disappeared as the ground swallowed them.

'Goodness gracious, woman, they won't wait for you.'

But the *nuckelavee* didn't have an air of impatience about them; they were just as guardedly fascinated about the goings-on. Somehow the exodus of prisoners had happened under their fleshless noses. If one of their number had seen how thousands of convicts had disappeared, then they had met the same fate of Brother Neckar, who appeared to have either stumbled or been compelled to stumble, to his death.

She waded through shin-deep mud at a pace so slow she struggled to put one foot before the other. The oily water gurgled and spat.

Ahead, the man could barely raise his scarred head from the ground. Arden was exhausted and cold by the time she reached him, battled to leverage his head out of the muck. Mr Tammas drew up alongside them and with one ridiculously long arm tipped the man over onto his back.

'His body is crushed,' Mr Tammas grated. 'We cannot help him.'

'What happened, sir?' Arden implored.

The man only huffed air as if he were breathing through a paper bag. He stared, unseeing, into the sky. At last he croaked out in a wheedling, sing-song voice, *'Can you hear the singing? Can you hear the singing of the Queen? Come away, come away my loves . . .'*

His eyes closed, and the ragged breathing stopped. Mr Tammas' foreleg pawed the mud agitatedly, echoing what Arden felt.

'Bellis. She's so much stronger than she was a few days ago,' Arden said. 'Stronger than she was back on the Sainted Islands, even.' She rubbed her elbow where Mr Lindsay had taken her blood. He must have found a way to purify it, to meld it with Bellis' own talents. She recalled Bellis' teeth gone black. Of course, he'd been feeding the salve to her.

'Family recipe my *arse*,' Arden added bitterly and stood up. Several bodies floated out on the water. A sombre silence blanketed the inlet. Anyone chained or caged would have beaten themselves to death trying to get out and follow Bellis, as if she were a piper leading them to—

To where?

'Where would they have gone?' Mother Blackwell echoed Arden's thoughts from her horse.

Arden's senses lurched. Everything was oriented westwards, towards the main prison with its giant panopticon tower overlooking the circular walls.

'The prison proper,' she said. 'That's where Bellis has taken them.'

The travelling distance felt longer than she rightly knew it to be, for the main route to the prison was a water-one, as prisoners were not meant to be escorted overland. In the fading afternoon another sour odour assailed her over the smell of pine trees and river-mud. It was as if an animal's kill had been only half-eaten and then allowed to rot nearby.

Mother Blackwell reached out her foot and tapped Arden's heel.

'Look away now,' she said, but there was nowhere to look, for the trees that had obscured the source of the growing stench parted, and now they were walking through a scaffold of brick-work five storeys high. Bodies in various states of decomposition dangled from each supporting gallows arch.

Arden had to clutch the saddle pommel, dizzy from the horror of it. The bodies swayed in the still air and Arden dared no look too close, lest she see Jonah in one of those faces.

Mother Blackwell pulled up alongside Arden. 'These are old punishments. Our enchanted army has gone onwards.'

'Army,' Arden repeated, and the words barely assuaged the panic bubbling in the pit of her stomach.

Once the grave arch was behind them, Mr Tammas looked back over his shoulder, his red eye bright under the brim of his hat. 'Step where we step, and do not deviate.'

The horses were well-used to this journey and fell into step behind their nixie brethren, and at last they were in a great wide plaza. Had the prison ever been anything else other than a penitentiary, then perhaps this space could have been a parade ground for a forgotten king of old Lyonne. The remains of statues and other objects of veneration littered the open expanse, and in parts, wildflowers grew through the flagstones. The damage done to the statues was old, not caused by Bellis. The prison crouched half a mile away on the other side of the plaza, upon an uplift of weathered rock of grey stone.

One fork of the estuary ran under the rock. The cavern where the Wyrm lived.

From her closer vantage point, Arden saw that the prison's panopticon tower was strange. It had no windows, no place for watchers to look out.

One of the *nuckelavee*, in a display of impishness perhaps, leaned over its horse-body and with its long arms scooped a solid stone statue-head off the ground, and tossed it across the plaza.

The very second the stone touched the ground, the flagstones pounced up and all Arden caught was a riot of articulated legs the colour of bone before they retreated in the blink of an eye, the stone head wrapped in a pair of giant pincers.

'Goodness!' she cried and stood upright in the saddle, only to sit back down again when it looked like her mount might go in the direction she was looking. Apart from a radius of scattered pebbles, there was no evidence of the flagstones having been disturbed.

'It's not eaten,' said the one who had thrown the head. 'Ten thousand of god's children running across this ground should have sated its hunger. There should have been signs of disturbed ground all over.'

Mr Tammas nodded. 'Whoever led them through here knew where to go.'

They crossed the plaza in a slow, meandering trail. The monstrous guards placed their feet with vigilance, Arden and Mother Blackwell were careful to follow them exactly. They arrived at the southern foot of the uplift as the day's shadows began to lengthen across the pale flagstones. A set of stairs wide enough only to walk three, maybe four abreast wended up the stone ramparts and over a dry moat to a greystone Sally Port, a small arched entrance on the southward side of the fortifying wall.

'We can go no further,' Mr Tammas said. His terrible head was upon an angle, as if he were in pain. 'Whatever lies beyond is not for us.'

Arden shared a despairing glance with Mother Blackwell. The *nuckelavee* were terrifying, yet one felt safe with them. The mossy battlements were almost black from shadow.

'I suppose this is it,' said the holy woman. She slid off her mount. Gestured that Arden should do the same. 'Take our mounts back to the barrow, Mr Tammas. From here we go on alone.'

33

The Sally Port

The Sally Port stairway had never been intended to accommodate a large crowd, certainly not one maddened by an Orientine blood-song. At three abreast, hundreds of men would have had to wait patiently, and whatever patient voice that had guided the crowd of entranced prisoners across the parade ground without incident had turned to a commanding scream as they reached the stairs. Not all of Bellis' army had made it through the Sally Port. At the bottleneck of the port easily half their number had fallen off the stairs and into the dry moat, or upon the rock itself.

Some of the dead had wedged into crevices, sprawled across the foot of the great rocky uplift. The survivors' beseeching moans increased into a chorus as Arden and Mother Blackwell passed overhead. Of those that could still speak, they spoke in tongues, their minds reduced to babble by torment and longing.

'We cannot help them,' Mother Blackwell said, as a nearby plea made Arden pause to seek out the bloodied face, the reaching hand . . .

'My friend might be among them,' Arden said desperately, even as she saw that the man who'd summoned her was not Jonah.

'Then he may already be dead. This insanity is not the work of a Queen who wants less than total worship. Listen to them, Arden. They do not want our help. They only want to go to *her*.'

Arden pressed the leather glove to her lips, could feel Miah's wedding ring dire upon her finger. A cold wind blew off the estuary, carrying the ammoniac, cadaverine stink of death and dying. Mother Blackwell was right. Any man she could reach to pull out, would only knock her down to keep running towards the prison.

She reluctantly tore her sight away, and stepped through the Sally Port with her breath held.

In the last red hour of daylight the rotunda portcullis gates that led to the panopticon and the prison cells showed wide. The grounds of the rotunda, which should have been as blank and featureless as the flagstone plaza, was strewn with bodies.

'Oh, blessed Redeemer and the serpent that lies beneath—' Mother Blackwell said as if she were gasping for air.

Arden stopped at the portcullis. How could her mind comprehend what she saw? Where was the experience that could make sense of this unimaginable sight, this bloodless slaughter?

The Sally Port had only been a taste, a reckless massacre of the men from the hulks. This charnel ground of death contained the entire population of the prison proper, a mass grave scattered carelessly over the annular ground. No matter where she looked she was confronted by a multitude of faces, upturned, eyes popped in their sockets, tongues swollen black through their bitten lips, their clothing torn from them. They'd all died in agony.

'*Bellis* . . .' Arden mouthed.

Bellis Harrow's powers turned malignant and deadly. Her ten thousand soldiers turned into an army of slaughtered cattle.

Mother Blackwell spoke the question. 'What is the reason for such death? Why would she kill all those that loved her?' Her voice was close to a sob.

If there was an answer it would come from walking the

narrow path where no corpse lay. When Arden had been able to unfreeze herself from the horror, she'd spotted the gauntlet of welcome offside the portcullis entrance. A clear space leading right to the panopticon's door. Even in their dying the penitents had not crossed that invisible boundary.

Arden navigated through the bodies and walked the gauntlet path. Another wave of corpses lay strewn against the panopticon base and sprawled around it, as if they'd been desperately trying to climb the tower, crushing and suffocating the ones beneath. A wave of death.

The last crazed few had succeeded in scaling the panopticon's brickwork to such a height they'd fallen down and died upon the spiked stones of the rotunda.

Death, everywhere. A copper stench of fresh wounds, the unbearable miasma of opened bowels and unwashed bodies. Lice and fleas swam in the puddles of blood.

Arden stepped in a ghastly fugue-dream through the innards and the blood towards that unbearable tower.

The top of the panopticon's viewing tower shone as the sunset glinted off the glass surface. It would have resembled a lighthouse, but the high lantern room was surrounded by glass panels tinted too dark to cast any appreciable light. Nor would it have made a proper viewing platform. How could any warden see through black glass, or observe the annular galleries that held the prisoners in their ever-watched cells?

The black glass windows made no sense to Arden. What past designer had found it important to include such impossible, confusing architecture? Had the air not been so still, she'd have thought herself in the centre of a storm, for what else could press down so awfully upon her, as if each breath required fighting for?

The gauntlet ended at the tower entrance, a yett-door of woven forged iron.

Like the portcullis it was unbarred, and swung half-open.

Mother Blackwell's elbow knocked into Arden's side. To Arden's surprise, the holy woman was untying the cincture of her habit, unwinding the yellow rope with a slow, almost ferocious concentration.

'Mother Blackwell?'

'Tie me up.'

'What?'

Mother Blackwell's voice pushed through her grimacing, clenched teeth. 'Tie me up. *She wants me to kill you.*'

Before Arden could react, Mother Blackwell let out a screech and lunged at Arden, and it was all Arden could do to skip out the way. Overbalanced, the priestess tripped headfirst into a stone plinth, dazing her, making her slip in the gore.

Terrified at the sudden change in Mother Blackwell's demeanour, it took Arden longer than she would have liked to snatch the dropped cincture out of the muck and clumsily wrap it about one flailing wrist. She'd wrestled with enough tossing boats or waterlogged drunks on Clay Portside in her former life and she was especially good with knots. Thankfully, a year away had not blunted her natural talents. By the time Mother Blackwell and the command in her head realigned with their deathly purpose, Arden had her tied up against the iron doorway.

The woman let out a keening wail.

'The noise! The noise!'

So much for a surprise entry, Arden thought. She looked around for something she could use as a weapon, not that she even had the human strength to wield anything with her now near-useless hands. What if there was another *nuckelavee* up there, mind-controlled?

There seemed to be no guards among the dead, but that was hard to tell, for they'd torn off most of their clothes in their desperate scrabble to get to the upper reaches of the tower.

Devilment, she thought to herself. The sky had turned to fire, but the setting sun let no light into this high, tall tower.

It's just a lighthouse, she thought to herself. But a *dark*house. No light comes out.

One of the victims had been lame and had possession of a staff. Whispering apologies, she took it out of his stiffening hands and into her own numb ones. The entrance was a maw, nothing but blackness. Though her hands were no longer her own, she rubbed the bony part of her wrist against the stone and willed foxfire into her hand. It crackled like a little marble of electric-blue flame. The last time she'd had cause to use it was fleeing Miah on the night of her wedding. Though the flame had no heat, the presence of it hurt, as if she were holding a ball of ice for too long.

She thrust her hand up, to illuminate a tall, echoing vertical tower, with a black brass staircase. The *sanguis* aura of the place was nothing like the deep beauty of the caisson cathedral; no, this energy was masculine and unpleasant, much like its maker probably had been. Arden seized her courage and began to climb.

And like a faraway memory that comes on a quiet night . . . came the song of Bellis Harrow. Bellis in her mind, singing her up the tower. Bellis calling.

These last days had been hard and Arden felt all the weeks of her trials tugging her upwards. The staff took on the dull, cold glow of her blood. Arden was so set on not tripping over any of the stairs she stumbled at the last platform, unprepared for the sudden floor, the round room.

A lighthouse, she thought at once.

No, not a lighthouse. A *darkhouse*. A signal house that gave off only darkness. It smelled of cold, and salt frost, and blood.

Before she could cross from one side to the other Arden stumbled upon a ridge of metal, and it was here her foxlight illuminated a dozen radiating stellations upon the floor, all converging into a mercy-seat, a throne where Bellis sat in her dirty wedding gown, slumped and murmuring.

Arden quickly realized that what she initially took to be a black bib on the lace of her dress was actually a bloodstain, most of it having come from Bellis' mouth.

Horrified and curious at once, Arden shuffled towards the throne. It was a plain wooden chair of the kind recalcitrant prisoners might be tied into. Leather straps and buckles the size of her palms held the small woman fast to her seat. 'Bellis?'

But it was a different voice that answered.

'It's strange. Even when I cut out her tongue, they all kept coming.'

Arden whipped around, staff raised in defiance, for she would not suffer Bellis' fate. Mr Lindsay had been sitting in the gloom behind her, sweating and exultant. He didn't move, or try to stand up. There was something of an air of sickness about him. Normally he held himself neatly, but now he was slumped against the glass wall of the panopticon's dome, his arms wrapped protectively about his stomach.

'What are you doing? Where's Jonah Riven?'

By the quirk of his eyebrow she could tell that he was briefly confused. If Jonah was dead, he'd have known. Her cheer that Jonah had not met his end was swiftly replaced by the awful understanding that in her dogged pursuit of Jonah she had walked into this immortal Lion's den. Mr Lindsay was sitting right next to the stairwell, and the trapdoor that sealed it shut.

'Still fixated on the man, I see.'

Arden looked about her and could barely keep the disgust out of her voice. 'I might better ask *you* about the particulars of *fixation*, Brother Lindsay.'

'A cutting remark, but in fairness – you are correct. I am fixated. I have been fixated for a long time. But that changes tonight.'

The foxfire in her hands went out, but a different light filled the room, a raw, pulsing red, as if they were in a heart's chamber. And instead of being black, the triangular panels of the panopticon's walls were transparent from floor to ceiling as if they had been carved from red obsidian.

With a start Arden realized she could see an inconceivable distance, a distance that should be impossible even with the most powerful telescope, right to the spires of Clay Capital herself. A wave of homesickness and concern overwhelmed her.

'Yes,' Mr Lindsay said in a lazy drawl. 'Firetide glass, as red as the little monsters whose skeletons form the magic. You are a Beacon, a Lightkeeper's child. I have no doubt those eyes of yours catch great sights. I have wondered for years what would happen were a signal-sighted person to enter this far-seeing tower.'

She gripped the staff hard. 'You wondered? Or planned?'

'Both, perhaps. Oh, I tried to keep you safe, child. Dropped you in and out of this drama delicately, tried to keep you in the wings. But no, you wished to run into the limelight! At least my dear Bellis was steadfast and unchanging in her nature, not like yourself, going from obedient worker to incorrigible slut in a few short months.'

'I would strike you for that rudeness, but it appears someone has already struck you.' Arden put the staff end to rest on the ground, and leaned on it. Did not bother to pretend sympathy when she asked, 'Are you injured, Claude?'

While they'd been talking a black puddle had appeared beneath him, and it didn't seem to be stopping. He let his hands fall. A field dressing of a man's shirt had done nothing to staunch the flow of blood from his belly.

'I had to give a part of me to the Wyrm, to win its obedience. It is how they've always achieved it in Fiction, among the monster hunters of the Sainted Isles. I needed my heart for a little while longer, but a piece of my spleen seemed adequate in the meantime. A symbol of my disappointment in the whole fucking city, you might say.'

Arden shook her head. The wanton deaths had been wicked enough, but this was pure insanity. All this scheming . . . for no purpose. For this miserable end. To die in a prison tower.

'All this time you planned the fall of Clay I thought you'd want to be there to see it. Well, Clay still stands, Claude. Bellis and her army are no more—' She gestured at the Vigil woman, tiny and helpless. One could even believe she'd never be a danger to anyone at all. 'And in an hour you will be dead. What an utter ignominious end. What a waste.'

Mr Lindsay laughed, and it turned to a bloodied cough. 'I

do not need to be *in* Clay. You can tell me from here of the smoke you see on the horizon, the spires falling, of your city's destruction.'

She gave a haughty sniff. He was speaking like an old man of faded glories, of a vile act of destruction that had never eventuated. She needed to hear no more. He was already nodding off into a daze.

'A pity I don't have a coin of instruction to let fall in your lap. Enjoy your delusions, I'm going to get Jonah and then you can rot up here for all I care—' She took a step towards the stairwell, only to have Mr Lindsay, with the greatest effort, wake up and kick the trapdoor shut.

'Devilment, no!' Arden fell to her knees and felt for a handle. The door was a featureless square, no handle, not even hinges.

'This panopticon locks from the outside. Even this dome and the far-seeing glass is a prison-cell, my dear.'

She wouldn't give up. She ran at the glass with the staff, and struck one panel with all her strength. It would have shattered if it were plain glass, but instead the staff bounced out of her hands. She collected the staff and struck again and again until the soft, hollow metal bent sideways.

She bent over double, panted. The air was hot and stifling. Mr Lindsay's breathing came in a soft gurgle, and Bellis was next to useless now.

'Could you not call even one of those lovestruck fools to come up here and open the door?' Arden chastised her.

Bellis only rocked and murmured in her own autochthonic existence, the trauma of her queendom having reached its last evolution. Bellis had nowhere to *grow* now. The one thing left was to return to the sod.

Arden's hands burned from her efforts at smashing the windows. She pulled off the donated gloves, looked hopelessly at her discoloured, torn fingers.

At least she wasn't going to starve to death. Her hands would kill her first.

'Look northwards, my dear,' Mr Lindsay wheedled. 'Can you see my loyal, obedient Wyrm? Can you see it on its journey?'

Though she didn't want to look, Arden's hope and horror forced her to press against the glass to where she could see the deep estuary inlet below. She knew the centre channel to be nearly fifty fathoms deep in parts, and she hoped that there would be no seeing—

The water exploded.

Arden was flung back across the tower – it quite took the breath out of her – as a black mass slammed against the dome, buckling the frame with a screeching rend of metal and glass. The unbreakable panels did not shatter. Instead, they popped out with a dull thud and fell across the floor in a hundred killing blades.

The garish violet twilight flooded in, chaotic with displaced air. Bronze fins lashed the purple sky; whipping, crazed. The creature had literally flung itself over the annular walls of the round prison and wrapped itself around the tower like a giant serpent about the staff of a god. The rasp of its golden cartilage against the stone walls built up such a charge of static electricity that the air crisped and sizzled. Blinding white arcs of electrical discharge leapt across its flanks.

The Harbinger Wyrm's gills – snapping open and shut – loomed bigger than the drawbridge gate in Lyonne's Parliament. A crest of tentacles flared gold about its head. One great golden, faceted eye stared in through the empty frames. The tower swayed from the inertia of the creature's weight. There was no purpose to its throes; it was a beast in competition with itself, torn between leaving the estuary for Clay, or tearing down the panopticon which sang such a violent command.

The Wyrm was fighting to *stay*. It was fighting and winning, and now it had come for the one who'd issued that instruction, and unlike a human it could not be swayed by a mere coin.

When he realized what was happening, Mr Lindsay let out a howl of rage, an animal bellow from the pit of his eviscerated soul. '*No!*' he shouted at the lightning shattered sky. '*No!*' he shouted at the Wyrm as it lashed its barbed, bloodied tail across the remaining prison cells.

'*No!*' he screamed again, but it was all for naught, as the tower tilted over at such a degree Mr Lindsay tumbled across the floor and bounced into the remains of the window along with a million shards of glass. At first the frames cradled his torn, bleeding body, shoulder and hip, and a fleeting hope lit up his eyes.

'I cannot die!' he shouted in triumph.

Then the frame buckled, dropping him into the seething water and Wyrm-flesh below.

Arden would have followed him had her krakenskin coat not hooked on Bellis' throne, sending her swinging in a cloud of red glass dust.

Bellis remained oblivious to her position in the centre of the great psychic battle. She did not even leave her seat at first, so secure were the buckles holding her. But the Wyrm's fierce undulations had at last set the tower leaning close to horizontal past the cells and over the estuary waters, and Bellis began to slip out.

Maybe because it was the end. Maybe because there was at last a glimpse of the girl behind the monster that Bellis had become. Either way, Bellis suddenly looked at Arden as if seeing her clearly for the first time.

The bloodied mouth formed the words *help me*.

Arden held out her legs, tried to hook Bellis onto her shins. The krakenskin made a tearing noise and Bellis lunged for Arden's skirt.

For a moment she held . . . and then she fell.

34

Arden dangled in the twilight

Arden dangled in the twilight as below her the roiling storm of mind-wracked Wyrm twisted in the water. Electricity flashed in the maelstrom below her, a whirling chaos glimpsed only in parts – inky tentacle, fin, tooth . . .

By sheer will she managed to lever herself onto the back of the chair and huddled there. But however it had found its way into the tower, the chair had never been part of the original structure and it began to slip out of its supports, and Arden knew she was going to go the same way Mr Lindsay had gone.

She did not wait until she fell. Arden closed her eyes. In the dark she experienced the moment when the chair no longer held, and with agonizing slowness peeled from the steel floor . . .

And then there was nothing but air.

The fall would have killed her if not for the boil of disturbed water. Had she hit a calm surface, she'd have died in an instant. Instead it was a feeling of descending into cold foam, as slow as a celluloid film cranked at a frame a second, as the moment before a stevedore's load tips off the crane and kills everyone below. Slow cold crept into her bones, airless and dark, and she could find no purchase before a flailing fin batted her sideways with such purpose she broke free of the wash and tumbled across the surface as if she were caught in a sea-wave.

The krakenskin coat saved her. Immediately its preternatural buoyancy popped her out of the water and into the near-night. She wallowed and gasped air, her head whirling. 'Jonah,' she cried uselessly. Her body flopped inside the coat. Not even the strength to swim. Had she not been wearing it, she would have drowned.

A hundred yards away the rending of tower-metal had caused a spark somewhere in the rotunda. The prison, constructed from the resin-heavy pinewood of Harbinger Bay, went up like dried tinder, and Arden watched the ignition as she floated backwards with the estuary tide. She was too exhausted to even feel concern any more. What would be, would be. The Wyrm encircled the horizontal tower once more.

Is that your child, Saint? Arden thought. *Is that what your servant brought to the prison?*

The flames from the burning penitentiary licked the velvet of the sky. Outlined in yellow fire, Arden at last saw that the Wyrm was not merely on its own. A figure stood proud between the tentacle-crested head as if they were riding the Wyrm, suspended as if about to command it forward—

A flash of understanding bolted through Arden's mind. A brief, painful sense of inquiry. A plea, perhaps, through the background scream of pain.

Home.

And then the Wyrm was gone in a giant wave of displaced water that propelled Arden to the bank of the inlet. She hauled herself on top of the muddy, silted ground, rolled on her back and watched the flames destroy all that was left of the tower, and the prison of Harbinger Bay.

A pair of mud-encrusted boots stopped beside where she lay, and she was almost too tired and too without care to look at who they belonged to until a voice gruffed, 'You lie with your feet in water all night you'll have the death-chills by morning.'

Painfully she turned her head to see Jonah Riven stood above her, shirtless and dripping water, his tattoos almost alive in this strange hour, kissed as they were by flame. His breeches had been cut open above the knee in several places where he'd called on all his blood, all his strength.

'If this is a dream vision, Jonah, I will not forgive you . . .'

He held out his hand and dragged her to her feet. Almost fainting with elation, she held on to him as if he was a mast in a storm, unbroken and true, the centre of her world.

'Is it done? Is it done?' she repeated, wanting to hear it from him.

'It is over. Miah took it down.'

Something was in the water, lapping against the bank, and for a brief, terrifying second Arden thought it might be Miah Anguis, but it was not him; rather, it was Jonah's coat, which he had been wearing when she saw him last.

'Hmm, good to see that again.' Jonah released Arden to fetch the coat, and although he made a good show of it, it was clear he was suffering even worse than she was, not just physically, but in his mind, too. Coming back here could not have been easy. Watching his cousin die would not have been easy either.

This time she would not let him go and so led the way up to the conifer stands. He spread his rescued coat on a layer of pine needles, and she put her own over him and together they huddled in exhausted wakefulness, not really sleeping until the fire died down and the estuary became dark, and silent.

35

She'd have stayed asleep forever

She'd have stayed asleep forever if the snuffle of a horse's nostrils on her cheek hadn't disturbed her. Arden pushed the velveteen nose away. 'Go on back with Mr Tammas,' she said. 'Go now,' she mumbled again when the nose refused to quit pushing, 'I'm too sore to ride.'

She opened her eyes into the smoky sunlight, finding she was curled up alone in the two coats, and the horse was in fact not the horse she'd ridden here on, but instead a moonstone-coloured creature the size of a donkey with a twist of gold horn almost as long as her arm at the centre of its forehead.

'Devilment,' she said, startling, and the unicorn jumped back in agitation, before ambling back into the forest.

'Shame we aren't hunters,' Jonah said, stepping up from the riverbank. 'Alicorn gets more in the wet-markets than even leviathan ambergris.'

She turned to look at Jonah worriedly, having half expected that he would have reverted to his illness of two weeks ago.

He paused. 'You look like you've seen a ghost.'

Arden shook her head. 'I was preparing myself for losing you again.'

He let out an impatient breath of air that she should doubt

him so, and it pained her to realize how much of Miah Anguis was in him. Would she ever be able to bear it?

His wounds had scabbed over, but until she could inspect him, there was no knowing if they would heal quickly, or whether they would need stitches.

Over by the treeline, the unicorn had not quite gone back to join its blessing. It wended in and out of the smoke-softened pine-trunks, shy and curious at once. Jonah plucked his coat out from under Arden and shook the needles out. His perfunctory manner made her feel somewhat hurt. In a fug of nostalgia she murmured, 'Did you know I always wished for a unicorn to ride when I was a girl? Didn't realize it wasn't much bigger than a goat.'

'It's a yearling. They're more wary of humans when they get older – you'll never see them full size.'

'Funny how it came so close, I heard unicorns only ever get tamed by maidens. The books say it's the innocence that attracts them.'

He slipped the coat on. 'And women with child.'

She looked up at him suddenly, a thorn of guilt in her heart, one she had placed herself. The one she'd carried when she had first given herself to Miah Anguis.

Jonah answered her unspoken question of how he had known. 'You are no longer wearing my cousin's ring, and I know he did not take it off you himself.'

She looked at her hand, and was surprised herself to see it was gone. It must have slipped off during the ride to the prison, or the tumult of the Wyrm. She certainly did not remember losing it.

Arden stood up, ready to defend herself and any accusations of impropriety, knowing how much he'd been vexed last time they had spoken, but before she could open her mouth he grabbed her waist and kissed her thoroughly. Had her heart beat any more joyfully she'd have needed to let out a shout.

He let go, but his fingers still lingered on her hips. 'We'd have all of us drowned if you'd not added your voice to our argument last night.'

'Did Miah make it out . . . ?'

'I don't know. I went down to the river to check, but there's no sign of anyone getting out but ourselves.'

She didn't want to entertain the worrying thought of his survival. If Miah had survived, then it was nowhere near over. She did not have the chance to broach the concern with Jonah though as their conversation was interrupted by a, 'Hoy there, hoy,' from the direction of the burnt-out prison.

To Arden's amazement, a singed-looking Mother Blackwell strode out from the wreckage ahead of a gaggle of equally wretched-looking men.

'Onwards, boys, there's no rest for the wicked. If we get beyond the gibbets we can say grace and eat the meal the good Lord has provided us.'

The meal turned out to be one of the monsters that had lived under the flagstones, an *Arthropelura* centipede the length of three men, crisped inside its shell by the heat of the blaze. It was still hot inside when Mother Blackwell allowed them to put the cryptid animal down and break open its shell.

'Leave the front section,' she cautioned when they crowded around and dragged out handfuls of flaky white meat. 'The venom is not terribly tasty.'

To Arden's despair, Jonah went to push through the backs of the hungry men to tear out a meaty slab from one section before returning to her.

'Oh dear,' she said, looking at the meat wobbling in his hands.

'It's cryptid, not insect. Tastes like sea dragon.'

She nibbled a small amount just to get Jonah to stop looking at her as if she might break, and to be fair, it tasted more like shark than anything else, and she was hungry. There would be a long walk back to the barrow-mounds of the sorrowfolk.

The smell of food brought more survivors out, but not all, and Arden supposed that many would have run into the forests to try and chance the *nuckelavee*, or whatever else lived in the forests of the Firetide Coast. When they had eaten as much as they could stand, they discarded the carcass for the forest to finish off, and Mother Blackwell led them home.

'My God, look what the otters dragged in,' Chalice said. She stood outside the barrow in a sorrowfolk habit with a lantern in her hand, looking for the entire world like some odd, watchful saint.

They were a small group now. Half their number had peeled off by noon, for they knew there was only a small respite from their imprisonment. The officials from Lyonne would come, and the prison would be rebuilt.

Arden hugged Chalice with all the emotion she could muster. 'Don't let a mirror near me, I would break it.'

'Break it by the smell, I would think. Look at you, darling. More of a mess than ever – and I have seen you a right mess in the past!' She looked at Jonah and smiled. 'You went to your dragon's den and brought back your prize.'

'I could not have done it without you.'

'I take it our business with Brother Lindsay has been put to rest? We waited for the *bucca* to leave the harbour, were ready to use the cannons, but after seeing the fire . . . well, we weren't quite certain what was going to happen.'

Chalice was as friendly as always, but Arden knew too well when there was something wrong. Arden looked about and saw there were more boats in the harbour than there should have been, and they weren't all fishing boats either.

The milling survivors were busy going through the motions of greeting the sorrowfolk, many of whom appeared to be former prisoners themselves, and Mother Blackwell had already pounced upon Jonah to take him into her healer's barrow. With a small window of opportunity to inspect the new arrivals that had come in, Arden walked down to the harbour. There was something about the ships that worried her. They were fast Lyonnian cruisers, but their decks did not hold space for cargo, the accoutrements of fishing, or rich men of leisure.

Cannon emplacements, she thought. They were warships, ready to kill whatever came out of the estuary. Another boat on the other side of the estuary mouth had set up a military centre, and soldiers made patrols along the embankments.

'Arden Beacon.'

Her name was spoken by an unfamiliar male voice. One with a strong Clay Capital accent.

Devilment.

Two men in dark coats stood at the sea wall. Both of them wore the badges of Parliament. She did not have to look close to see the other notables of their station cast in gold lapel pins – the rose and the thorny briars of the Lyonne Order and Nomenclatures. One held a ledger under his arm.

She had to fight the involuntary reflex to turn completely submissive. She could see Mr Harris nearby, his own big hands clenching nervously. He'd been speaking with them moments before, and was clearly not keen to leave Arden to her fate.

'So, to what do I owe the pleasure of your company?' Arden said sourly, already searching them for both weapons . . . and *sanguinities*. One of them was definitely sanguis. Strong, too. He wore leather gloves, but there was no hiding the power that radiated off him. Why, he could have given Bellis pause.

The commonblood Lion had a lump in his coat pocket, and quite unexpectedly she felt *metal*. A gun, she thought. A pistol, and enough bullets to solve a great many problems.

'I am Mr Prentiss,' said the commonblood Lion, evidently the more senior of the two. He pointed at the young sanguine agent whose eyes had the cold sheen of anthracite, his face as still as a stone idol. 'And this is my offsider, Mr Crouch.'

Mr Crouch hardly acknowledged her, merely tightened the grip on a leather-bound ledger he had tucked under his arm.

'You will excuse me if I sit,' Arden said, finding a seat upon the wall. 'And you will also excuse me if I tell you to get to the point. It has been *quite* the few days; I am tired and most probably injured.'

'I apologize that we could not reach you sooner and give

assistance,' Mr Prentiss said. 'We are assigned to the Firetide Coast district, and only arrived with the Lyonne Naval deployment yesterday. To our disappointment, you had already made your way into the prison. We thought it best to take up position here in case you failed . . . or succeeded . . . or both.'

Arden let the shadow of the setting sun behind her obscure her squint of suspicion. Knowing the Lions, they'd have made their decision as to whose side they were on at the very last possible minute. She surreptitiously sat further back on the sea wall. If they intended to snatch her up, she would tip back and into the water. They didn't seem like the best of swimmers, not in their too-warm woollen coats.

Mr Prentiss sat neatly next to her, and his neck craned as he went to glimpse the back of her neck.

'Married?'

He looked at her so strangely Arden became flustered and pulled up her collar.

Mr Prentiss clicked his tongue. 'I'm not sure the Eugenics Society has a record of a sanguis marriage, do they Mr Crouch?'

The sanguis Lion opened his ledger to consult the paperwork inside, then shook his head.

'There's been no request made or dispensation granted. Mx Beacon was never qualified for such a union, due to never completing her posting at the Vigil navigation marker.'

Arden let out an indignant noise. 'May I remind you, your Brother Lindsay—'

Crouch shut the book with a loud snap. 'You were recorded as AWOL, which is a Dereliction of Duty, less than a month ago.'

'I completed my post,' Arden protested, then squared her shoulders. 'I had unfinished business. I could not come back until it was finished and, like you said, it has barely been a month since I last checked in. The Lyonne Order allows twenty-eight days to settle affairs related to off-site postings. I've read your silly little manual given to all us puppets. I am not AWOL until then.'

'Regardless of that, there are those in our office who might tie the waywardness of our excommunicated colleague Mr Lindsay to your absence, and hold you responsible for his crimes.'

'The Devils they will!' she exclaimed. 'Sirs, I had nothing to do with Mr Lindsay. He stole my boat, kidnapped me and tried to kill other Order agents, all to get Bellis Harrow out to this godforsaken prison! Then he tried to set the Saint of the Island's bloody monster-child on Lyonne – all the while, might I add, making me watch.'

The Lions looked at each other, their communication silent. She had spoken the name of the Saint.

Mr Prentiss gave a great sigh. 'Your violations are unfortunate delinquencies. And yet, you acted obediently in assisting the Order when we required your service. We received the communiqué from our agents, Ozymandias Absalom and Juliet Greenwing. They said you would help, and we trusted them.'

'It has been noted,' Mr Crouch said, patting the ledger.

'It also must be said that our syndicate has been going through some . . . restructuring of late. Jockeying for power. You understand.'

'Jockeying?' Arden repeated the word. It was little more than a whisper, but she could have shouted it indignantly. Was that what Mr Lindsay's crime had been reduced to? Office politics?

Arden sucked in a breath. 'Is this jockeying *finished*?'

'It is done for now. But there is cleaning up to do.' Mr Prentiss shook his head. 'The Vigil Orientine Sanguis known as Bellis Harrow has been reported dead, Brother Lindsay is missing and quite a mess remains. We're not just talking the prison. For example, whatever are we to do with you?'

Arden launched into her excuse that had served her well in a previous life. 'Sirs, I am *sanguis malorum*, dim—'

'We are talking of the *evalescendi*.'

The *evalescendi*. Of course. Her shadow talent. The thing that caged her, made her a servant of the Parliament and the Order.

Mr Crouch reopened the ledger. 'It's a complication. A great many sanguinem have been found offering their talents like mercenaries to whoever can pay the highest price, which has created quite an overheated bubble already. Economies of scale must be controlled in Clay or we could have an entire financial collapse in a matter of months. This mess must be dealt with.'

Arden would not have been surprised had he brought out a poison pill for her to swallow. They sometimes offered that first. She looked Mr Prentiss in the eye.

'Are you going to kill me, sir?'

The two men looked at her, then laughed. Not in humour but knowingly, the joke obviously being the answer was *yes*.

Mr Prentiss said, 'I never underestimate people's urge for self-preservation, given the chance.'

She saw him reach for the lump of metal in his pocket. She prepared to leap. Would have done so, if it hadn't made a loose, clinking sound.

'Take it. It's yours.'

In his hand was a coin pouch of stingray leather – a common wallet among upper-class Lyonnians. She frowned. Mr Prentiss held it out further.

'Go on. I've included your severance pay from the Lightmistress posting in Vigil, since you never came to our offices to collect.'

Severance pay? She took the pouch and found it was heavy, small, flat objects moving within. She twitched open the flap.

At least a hundred Lyonne Djennes were in the pouch, the common currency in two countries.

'This is . . .' she began.

'. . . Enough to start a new life,' Mr Prentiss finished for her. 'But there are conditions.'

'Such as?'

'You cannot come back to Clay,' he continued over the roaring of blood in Arden's ears. 'Or Lyonne, actually. It is rather encouraged that you return to Fiction instead. As far as anyone is concerned, you have been excommunicated.'

'What . . . what about my family? Is this a disappearance?

I won't go if you intend to erase my existence off the face of Lyonne completely.'

'Your father has been informed you're alive, and that you have been secretly relocated. Give it time and you may be able to correspond.'

Arden didn't know what to say, and hyperventilated quietly. It was more than she had hoped for. The Lion stood.

'Anyhow, it has been a pleasure dealing with you. If there are no more questions, Mx Beacon, we will bid you good day. On Hewsday I shall have a boat sent. It will take you wherever you wish to go.'

She sat there, numb, as if a storm had blown through the estuary and turned the world inside out. Not even the goings-on at the tower had caused her such a crisis.

'Oh,' Mr Prentiss said as he was about to walk off. 'My forgetfulness will be the end of me one day . . .' He pulled a leather cord out from around his neck. At the end was a plain brass cylinder, slightly smaller than the tip of her little finger.

'What is this?'

'It's a key,' he said, gesturing towards her hands. 'For taking out those old bloodletting coins of yours. Consider it payment for the extra trouble you had to go through. You know, in settling accounts.'

36

The sorrowfolk

The sorrowfolk bathing area was rudimentary, but enough to scrub off the blood and grime. Mother Blackwell used Mr Prentiss' key to remove Arden's bloodletting discs with a flourish that belied how utterly impossible it would have been to remove them otherwise. The holy woman packed Arden's wounds with spider-web so as to aid in their healing, then bandaged her hands with a poultice of charcoal and blue clay.

Then it was done, and Arden was finally completely free.

She and Jonah stole a few snatched hours of sleep in one of the disused barrows, away from the others. Oftentimes she would wake in the night and find him looking at her in the lamplight, and she would be disquieted. Her feelings for him had always been more of a year-long dream than a real experience. This man was a mosaic of parts, the Jonah of her mission, of Miah Anguis and the spirit that had come from her cousin's funeral waters.

'We made it,' he said.

'Yes.'

'But now we must decide what to do.'

'Shall we stay together, when the Lions take me South?'

Jonah was quiet. He did not say yes. Unlike Arden, he could

not slip into the polite societies of Garfish Point or Morningvale. He was little more removed from the prison than the refugees were, a wild thing brought out of cold waters. Mr Absalom had been correct – Jonah Riven would not have survived Clay. Wordlessly, she thought of a future that could very well have happened, of a hopeless few months trying to keep up appearances, followed by a fading away of vigour, of affection. She would then, perhaps, have woken one day to find Jonah gone.

The tragedy that would have been their lives made Arden clutch him close, already grieving their imaginary separation.

Or their real one.

Their barrow-shelter did not have a door but Jonah had earlier strung a blanket at the entrance, and as the daylight came, Arden saw the blanket twitch, and Mr Harris stood apologetically on the other side.

'Would have let you sleep longer, Ardie, but there's a boat in the harbour for you,' said the whiskered face.

'A boat?'

'Come see, it's hard to explain.'

Half-asleep, Jonah clutched Arden close and then let her go. She readjusted her clothes and pulled on her boots, following Mr Harris out into the grey morning. She spotted the boat in the harbour at once. Seeing Arden through the morning mist, its skipper climbed onto the rotting pier, something familiar in their heavy frame, their swaying walk, the intent at which they stomped towards the harbourside.

Arden met them on land, ready to introduce herself.

Instead the captain tore off the scrap of cloth by which she had been keeping the smoke from her face.

'I only have one question for you, Lightmistress,' Mx Modhi of Vigil snapped. 'Where's my devil-cursed, disobedient son?'

The boat kicked a little at the harbour, for the spring gusts were not long coming in this part of the world. The floating houseboat of the former Harbourmistress of Vigil had never been made for anything more challenging than coastal waters, and yet Mx Modhi had sailed her all the way to Clay Portside, and she had not the slightest hesitation in returning to the nearby Sainted Isles to reunite with her son.

Arden hoped David Modhi would not think of her too badly, directing the thunderous love of his overbearing mother back to his adopted home. Even after the half-day it took to say her goodbyes and have Mother Blackwell check her hands one last time, Arden remained a little shaken. It had been quite the reunion with Mx Modhi, a long accusing rant followed by a great bosomy hug and a few tears, along with exhortations that she had been looking for them both for weeks. Mx Modhi had taken her disagreement to the highest offices of the Order.

'They've had a restructuring, as you are aware,' Mx Modhi had explained. 'Jockeying for power, apparently.'

'Yes, I've heard.'

'Otherwise they would never have told me a devil-damned thing. So. You aren't going to stay here, are you, Lightmistress? It's full of criminals.'

'Well, I'm not really supposed to remain in Lyonne. The Lions are going to send a boat for me on Hewsday. They were going to take me to Morningvale, then on to Fiction.'

'And if, by chance, the *restructuring* doesn't fall in your favour? Like they won't change their minds in a week? *Pshaw.* Come with me, Arden Beacon. Forget about the Lions – make your own way to Fiction. What have you got to lose?'

What *did* she have to lose? Arden's belongings consisted only of the clothes on her back, the coins in her pocket and the krakenskin coat.

And Jonah Riven.

A small, superstitious part of her, the one which had read the old stories of fleeing wives turned to salt, did not want to look back at the prison remains as they left the harbour, but Jonah stood at the rear, clutching the rigging for support as he watched Harbinger Bay recede from view. Harry Tanbark, Chalice Quarry and Mr Harris waved from the sea wall. Arden waved back, a pang of mixed emotions in her heart. If she were to meet any of them again, it would only be due to a disaster.

Mx Modhi had been the one to encourage Jonah to leave with them.

'Mr Riven, you absolutely cannot consider staying here,' she had scolded him when first he'd voiced his intention to stay and help Mother Blackwell. 'Lyonne is no place for a Fiction man, and this is Lyonnian business.'

He had made a genuine protest, until Chief – Jonah's old terrier – had wandered out of the cabin door on his unsteady legs. Jonah had swept him up and Arden saw the tears on his cheeks, for that dog had seen him through two imprisonments. She went to him and laid her head upon his back when he turned about so she would not see him cry.

'Blackwell was right,' she'd murmured into one linen shoulder. 'It's time for you to leave.'

'And go where?' he'd asked hoarsely. 'I've nowhere.'

Miah's last word came back to her. A word spoken into her mind, magnified by the Harbinger Wyrm.

Home.

'Your people, remember? Your home is with the deepwater folk on Equus.'

He'd made a choking noise that was probably a mocking laugh until she added, 'I wear their marks, Jonah. The ring was Miah's, and now it has gone, but the wedding tattoos were for the clan. I belong to them.'

He was silent for a long time, before saying, 'They will not allow me. Not after what I did to my family.'

'You were Deepwater King for a night, Jonah. Remember? When you married Bellis to save her, you were given godhood long enough for it to matter. They will not forget.'

It was not until evening time, when the Firetide waters flashed crimson and Harbinger Bay was a half-day behind them, that Jonah relaxed. Without her bidding he took her hand and drew her close. His body seemed hewn from the precious wood of *Saudade*, laden with the scent of salt and fire, and the deep resinous memory of their first true encounter in her dark, intimate hold.

Ah, *Saudade*, Arden thought. Why am I thinking of her? She's probably firewood by now.

As if Jonah had been furiously casting his deepest desires along with his blood, they rounded the small spar that shielded the Lindsay Estate to find *Saudade* floating untethered on the crimson waters. She was seemingly undamaged, her precious mangrove wood as black as the abyssal waters against the setting sun.

'Goodness, we'd best collect her,' Arden said, trying not to sound too startled. 'Otherwise, that craft will lead someone else on an impossible adventure.'

'Yes, a southern boat doesn't belong in the north. Nothing but trouble.' Jonah nodded with a crooked grin. He could barely hide his happiness. 'I've kept a spare store of fuel hidden in her hold. *Saudade* can drag this floating nuisance to Equus in three days.'

Jonah went to speak with the Harbourmistress and Arden was left to her own devices on the houseboat deck. A gull landed upon the sign that still read *VIGIL HARBOUR*, then went to join the wheeling others that followed the boat's wash.

The plankton, little monsters all but no less aligned with Jonah's blood, made a bright river along the long line of the coast, while beneath them she imagined leviathans sporting in shades of green and blue. Arden pulled the krakenskin coat about herself, feeling the mysterious, perpetual warmth enfold her like an embrace, before leaving the deck to join Jonah Riven.

Acknowledgements

At last, the end.

Many thanks to my agent Sam Morgan and my editor Vicky Leech Mateos for sticking with me through my little "pandemic trilogy". All love and gratitude to my friends and family for their support during a time beset with many challenges, and especially Eric and Xavier, forever rock-steady in the wings.

So with one journey finished and others yet to begin: 'Onwards and Upwards to Narnia and the North!'